PRAISE FOR THE NOVELS
OF LAUREN JAMESON

LINGER

"Steamy and daring with a sexy alpha hero to swoon over and a heroine you can cheer for, readers will want to linger over *Linger!*"   —*New York Times* bestselling author Roni Loren

"Lauren Jameson's *Linger* teases and sizzles, bringing you to a steamy simmer. A thoroughly wicked and deeply satisfying read!"   —*New York Times* bestselling author Eden Bradley

BREATHE

"Tantalizingly sexy and shockingly intense. . . . Jameson does an excellent job making this story feel original and daring."
—*Romantic Times*

BLUSH

"The kind of erotica I really love . . . This is a pair who want more than either will admit and more than they think they deserve. . . . The journey that Lauren Jameson takes you on in this book is fantastic. The writing is wonderful, and the story is solidly romantic and erotic."   —Bookish Temptations

"Jameson's writing is free-flowing, which makes for an easy read."   —Under the Covers

continued...

"Sultry and alluring, Lauren Jameson's first full-length novel, *Blush*, is a sinful thrill of a read . . . a better-written and actually classy variation of the *Fifty Shades of Grey* madness."
—Books á la Mode

"The romance and fire between Alex and Maddy are scorching . . . both intensely emotional and insanely erotic."
—Once Upon a Twilight

"Well written. . . . The rich-and-famous lifestyle of a sexy man is always an exciting read!" —Fresh Fiction

SURRENDER TO TEMPTATION

"A quick, very sexy story." —Smexy Books

"Dramatic ups and downs. . . . Readers who enjoyed Beth Kery's *Because You Are Mine* will likely find this an even stronger serial." —*Library Journal*

"A well-written story that will open your mind to a whole new level of control and submission." —SinfulReads

ALSO BY LAUREN JAMESON

Blush

Breathe

Surrender to Temptation

LINGER

Lauren Jameson

A SIGNET ECLIPSE BOOK

SIGNET ECLIPSE
Published by the Penguin Group
Penguin Group (USA) LLC, 375 Hudson Street,
New York, New York 10014

USA | Canada | UK | Ireland | Australia | New Zealand | India | South Africa | China
A Penguin Random House Company

First published by Signet Eclipse, an imprint of New American Library,
a division of Penguin Group (USA) LLC

First Printing, September 2014

Copyright © Lauren Hawkeye, 2014
Excerpt from *Breathe* copyright © Lauren Hawkeye, 2013

SIGNET ECLIPSE and logo are trademarks of Penguin Group (USA) LLC.

LIBRARY OF CONGRESS CATALOGING-IN-PUBLICATION DATA:
Jameson, Lauren.
Linger/Lauren Jameson.
p. cm.
ISBN 978-0-451-47080-5 (paperback)
1. Man-woman relationships—Fiction. I. Title.
PS3610.A464L57 2014
813'.6—dc23   2014012815

Printed in the United States of America
10 9 8 7 6 5 4 3 2 1

Set in Arno Pro
Designed by Sabrina Bowers

For Kerry Donovan, who will always be the cutest little pushy editor in the world.

ACKNOWLEDGMENTS

This is quite probably my favorite out of all the stories I've ever written. But if my editor had accepted what I first sent her for a proposal for *Linger*, it never would have been written. So I have a huge thank-you to her for pushing me further. And an equally huge thanks to Deidre Knight, who held my hand while I struggled to get it right. I hope you enjoy your namesake in this book. Snort. For the fabulous Suzanne Rock, who had the brilliance to say "Maybe having the hero tied to the fence post in the first scene is . . . a little too weird." Well played, Sue. Well played. Thank you to the magical art department at New American Library for a cover that I am in love with. To Eden Bradley, Roni Loren, Erika Wilde, Cathryn Fox and Suzanne Rock for endorsing it. For Erica Haglund, aka the BookCellarX, for offering her thoughts and knowledge of all things bunny. And as always, to my husband, Rob, and my mom, Penny, for entertaining Mr. I Am Three so that I could spit this book out.

LINGER

CHAPTER ONE

Coming here always felt like home.

Scarlett Malone sucked in a deep breath, savoring the humidity that lingered even after the sun had set in Vegas. It was not yet fully dark; when she arched her neck and looked up, she found a blueberry-tinged twilight surrounding the old Victorian mansion that was her second home.

She was going to miss this, she realized, a lot more than she'd thought she would. The fantasies and desires that were explored here at In Vino Veritas, a wine bar and kink club, had started merely as sexual curiosity for her and instead had wound up fulfilling a deeply seated need.

There were no kink clubs in rural Montana, where she was soon headed, at least not that she'd been able to find. And even if there had been, nothing could ever be the same as Veritas.

Better make the most of your last night, then, Scar. Grinning to herself, Scarlett ran a hand over her sleek brown hair, which she'd pulled back in a tight knot for the occasion. She was sad to be leaving Vegas—her home—for an entire year, sure. But nothing could keep her down for long when a night of kinky playtime stretched out before her.

She would find someone good tonight; she could feel it in her gut. She hadn't been playing for long enough to have defined exactly what "good" constituted, but not being able to put it into words didn't mean she wouldn't recognize it.

Shifting her weight from one spike heel to the other—she loved how the leather boots looked but not necessarily how they felt, even on feet that had once spent hours in pointe shoes—Scarlett joined the line of people waiting in front of the massive wooden door that led to the secrets inside Veritas.

Julien Knight, the club's manager, waved and winked. Even as he checked the credentials of the woman dressed in a vinyl catsuit who was doing her best to catch his eye, he made an exaggerated show of looking Scarlett up and down, then whistling.

"Looking good tonight, Mistress Scarlett!" he called as he gestured her forward. His perusal of her body—and blatant appreciation—gave Scarlett a flurry of pleasant tingles in her belly. Tall and lean, with dreadlocks pulled back loosely from his face and a swarthy complexion, he was exactly the kind of man Scarlett was usually drawn to.

Except she knew she could never make it work with him. Julien liked to be in control. So did she.

But that didn't mean she couldn't look.

As Scarlett made her way to the front of the crowd, a woman laughed in the middle of the story she was telling, stepped back, and accidentally jostled Scarlett. Losing the precarious balance that she had on her spike heels—so much for those years of ballet training—Scarlett stumbled and braced herself to slam into the unyielding stone of the walkway.

As she threw her hands out . . . they connected with a firm wall of muscle.

"Are you all right?" The voice was warm, with a hint of a Western drawl. Strong arms squeezed her waist gently, making her shiver. Scarlett closed her eyes for a second, enjoying the sensation, before trying to step back, to straighten her skirt.

But those hands didn't let go. A spark lit inside Scarlett as she slowly looked up at the man who had saved her from a tumble that would have likely scraped her knees, her hands, her legs, effectively putting a damper on her evening.

His face was largely shadowed by the wide brim of a cowboy hat, but the piercing stare of his blue eyes caught her attention. She also quickly took in his tall form and wide chest, stretching the confines of a black T-shirt.

"I said, are you all right, miss?" The man's voice told her he expected her to answer, which started Scarlett's blood fizzing.

Arching an eyebrow, she looked up. When those blue eyes again caught her stare and held, she felt her heart skip a beat with excitement.

"I'm fine, thank you." A smile started to curve her lips—oh, there was no way in hell that this man was a submissive, but still, she couldn't deny the interest that was sparking throughout her body. Reaching out, she placed a hand flirtatiously on his biceps.

Beneath her fingers, the hard muscle tensed. The man tilted his head to the side, looking at her as though she were an exotic bird. Those flutters of initial attraction made Scarlett feel as though she'd swallowed a flute of champagne too fast.

She parted her lips—to say what, she wasn't entirely sure. Then the man nodded, released her, stepped back.

His touch remained like a ghostly imprint on her skin.

And then he was gone, waved through the doors to Veritas, leaving Scarlett to catch her breath and wonder what, exactly, had just happened.

That simple helping touch from one man—from a stranger—had excited her more than some of the most complex scenes she'd done.

She wanted more. And she wasn't the kind of woman who liked to take no for an answer.

*   *   *

Dr. Logan Brody barely looked around as he strode down the long front hall of Veritas. His pulse had accelerated—he could feel the steady beat pounding beneath the skin at the base of his jaw—and he knew exactly why.

That gorgeous little brunette out front—she'd gotten to him. He'd meant only to stop her from falling, a courtesy from one decent human being to another, though he wasn't sure he always counted as decent, at least not anymore. But something about her warm flesh beneath his fingers, about the way her spine had stiffened when he'd pushed her to answer his question, had snared him.

She was that perfect combination of softness and steel. When she'd laid a hand on his biceps, he had felt interest stirring. Had wanted to flirt in return, to see where their encounter would go.

That she was a Mistress, he had no doubt. Even if she hadn't been dressed like one, that calm confidence that every Dominant he'd ever known possessed had been like a halo around her.

The forceful presence, combined with her killer curves, the gorgeous face, the scent of vanilla that emanated from her skin when she moved . . . had left him wanting.

Yet something about her told him that she wouldn't be an easy Mistress, and he wasn't looking for anyone to dig past his shell. Still, he'd considered throwing all caution to the wind for one night—and then he had remembered where he was. His surroundings—the city, the traffic, the *people*—had slammed against him like a freight train.

It had thrown him off balance, had let the panic that he worked so hard to keep at bay gain control.

So he'd left, like a jackass. At least he'd remembered to nod a farewell.

Forget about her. Pushing through the door to the men's change room, Logan found an empty locker and opened it with more force than was strictly necessary. The sound of metal on metal clanged loudly even in the busy room.

As he slid off his jacket, his hat, his T-shirt, he tried to pull those mental shutters back down in place.

He came to Veritas for only one night, maybe two, every year—whenever the need got too bad to take care of himself. One of the owners of this particular establishment was an old friend, which made it a safer place in his mind.

If he had to get away, he could always go sit in Luca's office or his apartment. He wouldn't feel completely calm again until he was back on his ranch, the wide-open skies arching above him, but knowing he had a bit of a safety net helped, allowed him to get what he needed.

Unbidden, the brunette's face flashed through his mind again. Man, he was tempted by her. But she had trouble written all over her—he'd been in the BDSM scene for more than ten years, and that woman didn't look like the type you played with once and never saw again.

A gentleman would leave her alone—if she was even still available by the time he got into the massive playroom of Veritas. A Mistress who looked like she did, commanded attention like that, she wouldn't be short of potential partners.

"Pull it together, Brody." Giving himself a mental shake, Logan's hands strayed to the waistband of his jeans, then stopped. A Mistress might make him pay for it later, but he didn't think he'd strip down completely. Not yet.

Sliding his hand into his right pocket, Logan withdrew two strips of buttery yellow leather adorned with silver hooks. As soon as he snapped the cuffs in place on his wrists, he felt his anxiety ramp down, like it was sinking just beneath the surface of the serene lake on his property.

This was why he came here—because he needed to let someone take control, just for a little bit. He'd never be able to give over the reins forever . . . but for a little while . . .

He needed it. Craved that exchange of power.

And still, as he made his way into the playroom, as the angry, sexy sound of heavy metal and the slap of flesh against flesh began to reverberate through his veins, he found himself looking around the room, the various stations, the different pieces of equipment, seeking something out.

Looking for *her*.

CHAPTER TWO

Scarlett perched on a barstool inside In Vino Veritas, sipping at the glass of buttery Chardonnay that Luca had gifted her.

After the encounter outside, she had been unable to stop herself from searching for the handsome stranger once she was inside. A few male submissives had tried to catch her eye, but she found herself strangely uninterested.

"Look at me," Scarlett whispered. She'd been watching the man for a good five minutes, but he hadn't yet looked her way. He hadn't looked anyone's way, actually, seeming focused on his drink.

As if he'd heard her speak, though, he turned and met her stare. Scarlett's fingers clenched on her wineglass briefly before relaxing. Butterflies began to do a wild dance of excitement in her belly.

He reminded her of a tethered animal, restrained but only just. A heavy rock settled on top of the butterflies in her gut when she realized that the chances of this man being her type—being sexually submissive—were slim indeed.

At least eight inches taller than her own five foot six, he wore his raw masculinity like he wore the faded denim that molded to thick, muscular thighs and a tight ass that made her want to sink her teeth into it. His hair shone gold in the low crimson lights of the club, glinting as he lifted a bottle of domestic beer to his lips and reminding Scarlett of nothing so much as an ancient Viking heading to battle.

When he lowered that amber bottle of beer—no fancy wine for him—and continued to stare at her with those piercing cobalt blue eyes, Scarlett felt the desire like a punch in the chest. She couldn't explain it and certainly hadn't been looking for it—she was looking for a playmate for only this one night, a willing submissive on which to test her newly minted skills as a Mistress.

Scarlett held his gaze, her heart pounding in her throat. She might have been fairly new to the games of dominance and submission, but it was still far from her first time in this club. And yet she'd never felt attraction like this before. Never. Especially not to a man who looked like he would eat her alive if she let him.

When the man finally broke the stare, casting his eyes to the ground, Scarlett frowned, feeling a bit perplexed. Had he lost interest? Because surely she hadn't imagined the indefinable connection between them, the one that had sparked outside and now only pulled tighter with each passing moment.

She knew it wasn't all one-sided. It couldn't be.

She let her stare drop as well, following his line of sight. Her eyes stroked over the biceps, the forearms that were tightly corded with muscle—the arms of a man who used them for a living. When she came to his wrists, she stopped short.

Wrapped around the narrowest part of the man's arms were yellow cuffs—golden yellow leather, with metal rings meant for attaching to restraints on the various pieces of equipment around the club.

These were the yellow cuffs that the club had their seasoned submissives wear—the cuffs that signaled that the man or woman who wore them was looking for a Master or Mistress to play with.

Inhaling shakily as adrenaline burst through her veins,

Scarlett forced the fingers that had unconsciously clenched once more around the stem of her wineglass to relax.

As she'd watched him, she had hoped he could maybe, possibly be a submissive. From the way he was dressed, she couldn't tell.

And he hadn't lowered his gaze when she'd first caught his eye, either outside or here in the playroom, which told her that while he might have marked himself as a submissive, he wasn't going to be taken down easily.

Subs like that could eat an unwary Mistress alive. But still, arousal made her flush. Could she really be lucky enough to have found what she desired so deeply—a man strong enough to dominate but who chose to walk the submissive side?

She might have been green, but she had no intention of screwing this up. Everything about the man attracted her— the way his size made her feel small, the intensity in his eyes, the feral energy that surrounded him.

Topping him would be like taming a lion, and she couldn't wait to get in the ring.

"He's an ambitious choice. You haven't been flying solo for very long." A hand reached across the polished wood of the bar, catching the wineglass that she carelessly shoved away before she cracked the delicate stem. Scarlett turned to find her friend Luca leaning on the bar, the corners of his lips curled up in a dangerous smile, but concern in his eyes.

She fought the urge to roll her eyes. She'd known Luca for only a couple of years—since the first time she'd come to the club—but the big Dom was ridiculously overprotective of her. She knew it came from a good place, but still.

"I've never wanted easy. You know that." Scarlett spared Luca only the briefest of glances before turning back to the object of her affection, who was now leaning against the back of a chair. The posture forced his pelvis forward, giving Scarlett a glimpse of flat stomach and the sexiest hip bones that she'd ever seen.

Her mouth watered. She wanted a taste of him *now*, but she owed Luca the chance to say what he was clearly going to say regardless. They were both Dominants and therefore equal, at least here in the club, but he was a friend as well as her mentor in the BDSM lifestyle.

"No, you certainly don't do things the easy way," Luca agreed, and Scarlett flicked one more glance toward the massive sadist who had taught her everything she knew about being a Mistress. He was as large as the man whose presence kept calling to Scarlett, but though his wicked good looks attracted more submissives than he knew what to do with, Scarlett had never felt anything more than a mild buzz of attraction around him, even when they'd played during her training.

"Is this where you tell me to choose my subs carefully?" Scarlett forced herself to give Luca her full attention this time. Her mind was made up—she had to at least try—but she owed it to Luca to listen.

"I would never presume to direct a Mistress's choice of slave," Luca said with a twinkle in his eye, and Scarlett huffed out a breath of exasperation.

"Like hell." She fought the urge to turn around, to see if her mystery man was still watching her. "You're the bossiest Dom I know. You'd put *me* in a cage if you thought you could get away with it."

"And you'd deserve it, brat." Luca affectionately tugged at the tight coil of Scarlett's long hair. "You were the worst sub I've ever had."

Settling his not inconsiderable weight onto his elbows, Luca's expression turned thoughtful.

"I know him." He nodded toward Scarlett's target, and she fought the urge to twist in her seat and look again herself.

"He's not an easy sub. Not an easy person. An alpha who chooses to be beta in the bedroom, for the Mistress who can control him."

Scarlett knew he wasn't necessarily trying to deter her. Luca knew as well as she did that control was a heady aphrodisiac for Scarlett, a way of adding discipline to a life that had been chaotic until adulthood. Still, his tone annoyed her a bit.

"And you don't think I can?" Scarlett raised an eyebrow at her mentor, mildly insulted.

Luca shook his head, a grin playing over his lips.

"If anyone has a shot at taming that beast, Scarlett, it's you." He nodded toward where the man stood, gesturing with his hand at the same time. Something—was that guilt?—flickered over his face. He parted his lips as if about to say something, then closed them again and shook his head.

"What—" she began to ask, but was distracted by his next comment.

"I'd hurry up and make your move, little one. Looks like Mistress Avery has her eye on your tasty cowboy, too."

If anyone else had called her an endearment that sounded so much like he was talking down to her, Scarlett would have found herself grinding her teeth with irritation. But Luca had topped her while she was undergoing the vigorous training that the club required of their neophytes, and the term had stuck.

"Catch you later." Scarlett was off her barstool before the words had even finished leaving her lips. Mistress Avery was one of the club's most notorious Dommes, an androgynous-looking blonde around whom subs were never quite sure whether to beg for mercy or to ask for more.

She also had a reputation for convincing the most reluctant of submissives, male or female, that they wanted to play with her, although *coerced* might have been closer to the truth.

When Scarlett saw that the other woman was indeed making her way toward the delicious specimen of man, she hurried her stride, though she made sure to still keep her stiletto-heeled saunter deliberate.

BDSM was a game of control . . . even if something inside of her said that this connection, this man, was more important than most.

She sized him up anew as she made her way across the crowded club floor, trying to get some kind of handle on him before she reached him. Her intense attraction to him puzzled her a bit, because he wasn't entirely her type. He had that dominating presence that she had craved, yes, but Scarlett was typically drawn to Latin-lover types, men who groomed themselves impeccably and had suave charm to spare.

This man, who looked to be in his midthirties to her twenty-four years, looked like a rough-and-tumble Norse god. His pale hair was weeks past needing a haircut, and matching stubble covered the strong line of his jaw.

Hair dusted that wide, solid chest, too, and a trail led from beneath his navel into the low-riding denim. It made Scarlett's mind stray to all of the wicked, wicked things she wanted to do with what lay at the end of that trail.

Instead of wearing briefs or latex, or any kind of fetish wear at all, he wore those faded blue jeans, ones that were worn from actual use and not as a nod to fashion. His feet were clad in equally scuffed cowboy boots.

And there, she realized with delight. There was her opening.

She curved her lips up in a predatory smile, feeling herself slipping into the role. When Scarlett reached the man, she caught a whiff of his scent. She was glad that she'd planted her high heels firmly on the ground when the combination of soap, spicy aftershave, and raw male hit her senses.

This was it—*he* was it. She couldn't have explained it, but she wanted him more than she'd ever wanted any other sexual partner in her life. Her experiences with the submissives that she had topped before this had all felt generic and unsatisfying.

But with this man . . . she had the feeling that it would all be different.

She waited for him to raise his eyes to hers, something only a poorly trained or very stubborn sub would do. Thanks to Luca's warning, she knew he was the latter.

As she'd suspected, he did, and she again felt the power of their inexplicable connection surge when his incredibly blue eyes met her own gray ones.

"I'm Mistress S, sub. And we have a problem."

Logan felt a wicked surge of excitement as the small Mistress planted herself in front of him, hands on her hips. Very sexy hips, he noted yet again, ones that flowed into a slender waist and the curves of full breasts. He'd felt a deep sense of satisfaction to find that she appeared every bit as interested in him as he was in her.

Something in him again warned him to find a different partner for the evening, one who would be satisfied with administering a flogging, then sharing hard, impersonal sex.

Every other part of him wanted the woman currently standing in front of him, though he knew somehow that she was going to push him further than he was comfortable. Just having met her had thinned the barriers he always kept in place.

He hadn't been in the club for very long, but he was already feeling the pain from being trapped in the crush of people. A scary-looking Mistress—or Master, he wasn't quite sure—had started bearing down on him at the same time as the tasty treat in front of him, and he'd felt as if the walls had been closing in on him, stealing away his air.

But it was different with this one . . .

An experienced submissive, he could tell that she was a fairly new Mistress. The nerves were there, in her eyes, around the corners of her mouth. Still, despite the sweet features of her face, dominance seemed to seep out of her very pores, an exotic perfume that caught his attention like a dog with a steak.

And then there was that strange pull between them, the one that had snapped into place the second his arms had wrapped around her outside. The one that made every other Dominant woman in the room seem dull and unappealing.

It was an irresistible combination for a man who ran the show everywhere besides the bedroom.

And he couldn't ignore the fact that, since she'd introduced herself and glared at him with that bitchy expression that made his cock hard, he'd found it a little easier to breathe.

"What's the problem, sweetheart?" He grinned down at her, his expression deliberately cocky. He needed to keep his defenses up from the start around this one, to keep her from sneaking too far into his psyche.

He waited to see if she would dismiss him immediately for his rudeness.

She arched an eyebrow at his term but didn't comment on it, which left him mildly disappointed. Instead she nodded at his feet, looking like nothing so much as a wet dream of a stern schoolteacher.

"Bottoms go barefoot in Veritas, sub. Remove the boots."

Her voice was whiskey smooth with an undercurrent of sin, at odds with the girl-next-door face. Logan found himself wanting to fall to his knees and obey, to please her, and despite how much he wanted her, the notion didn't sit well with him.

A Mistress had to work much harder than saying a few

words and looking pretty to earn that kind of response from him.

He'd felt the punch of attraction when their eyes had first met, but now he was wary. What kind of hold did she have on him already, to make him want so badly to please her?

Shaken by the notion, he grinned insolently and shook his head. "Make me, baby."

Logan watched as heat flickered in her eyes, which, upon closer inspection, were stormy gray rather than the expected blue.

He watched as she shrugged one shoulder, a simple gesture that was nevertheless full of innate grace.

"We'll do it the hard way, then." So caught up in the siren's song of her voice, Logan was caught off guard when the little minx kicked her leg up with the smooth flexibility of a trained dancer and pressed her sharp stiletto heel against the thin denim of his crotch.

He froze when the perfectly positioned bootheel dug into the tender sac of his testicles, just enough to catch his attention.

"No need to get nasty, sweetheart." Though he wasn't overly concerned that she was one of those Mistresses who took joy in cock and ball torture, he was still uncomfortable enough from the feelings coursing through him to be a smart-ass.

"Take off your boots." Damn her. She looked completely calm and in control. Like she knew he would do as she said, simply because she had said it.

Their little standoff had drawn an audience, too, and the press of bodies around them made his throat constrict with the beginnings of claustrophobia.

"A hundred bucks on the little brunette."

Logan flicked his eyes around the gathered crowd to find

the speaker and glowered when he saw that it was Luca, the only acquaintance he had at In Vino Veritas. He would have snarled if Mistress S hadn't chosen that moment to dig that stiletto in just a bit harder.

"I warned you." She shrugged and smiled at him, and the smile made Logan's entire body clench with pure, undiluted need. She leaned forward, a calculated move, he knew, but still he found his attention caught on the creamy swells of her breasts, offered up as they were in the almost indecently low neckline of her black lace corset.

He wanted to get his hands on those breasts more than he wanted his next breath.

His attention was still caught on them when she lowered her leg, and he grinned as he hoped, prayed, that she would lean forward a bit more, just enough for him to see a hint of nipple that he knew would be rosy pink.

"I'd still be happy to give you the ride of your life—" Logan's words were cut off when the slender woman whirled behind him, her movements precise and controlled. He felt the sharp toes of her boots dig into the backs of his knees, and then he landed on his knees on the floor, his breath leaving his lungs in one uncomfortable jolt.

"What the—" He threw his hands out in front of him to protect his face when she pushed him down further and straddled his hips backward. Despite the surprise and the uncomfortable position, his cock pushed against the thin denim of his jeans as his body registered the heat of her naked legs pressing tightly into his torso.

Her ass was sweetly rounded and close enough to touch. He craned his neck to see. Her skirt had ridden up when she moved, and he caught sight of the rounded curves of her behind, a hint of the sexy panties she wore beneath.

With firm hands, Mistress S tugged off one of his well-worn cowboy boots and then the other. His socks followed. Standing, she caught his eye as she very deliberately stuffed a sock inside each boot, then handed the pair off to Luca, to tuck out of reach behind the bar, he assumed.

"What's your name?" she asked, her voice steady, certain he would answer . . . and he did, though he hadn't intended to.

"Logan." He could hear the wariness in his own voice, and rightly so—this woman was nothing like he'd expected.

"Well, then. Logan." Her words were stern. "I told you. Subs go barefoot here."

Logan felt twin desires pulling inside of him. He wanted to apologize, to earn her favor.

He also wanted to wipe that smug smile off of her face. She'd won this round—and he hadn't seen it coming, so points for her.

But he wasn't tamed that easily.

"You going to punish me now, baby?" He ran his tongue over his lips, deliberately provoking her. He knew what would happen now, and he was looking forward to it.

She would take him to a private room, or to one of the many pieces of equipment set up around the massive play area of Veritas. She would try to dig deeper, and he would deflect. She would flog him, and he would be able to lose himself in the pain.

They would fuck, and then they would go their own ways. He'd head back to Montana until his needs could no longer be assuaged with his imagination and his own hand.

The fact that he didn't care for the idea of leaving her was just a signal that he needed to do exactly that. She looked like she could draw out all of his secrets, and that just wasn't going to happen.

Still, he thought he just might die if he didn't get a taste of that creamy flesh spilling out over the top of her corset.

"Yes," Mistress S replied, her face calm, though those gray

eyes of hers reflected more than a hint of the turmoil that he was feeling himself. "I am."

Then the woman did something Logan never could have seen coming.

She turned on her slender stiletto heel and walked away.

CHAPTER THREE

S carlett kept her steps slow and deliberate as she left him, though her heart was pounding in a wicked rhythm against her rib cage—a rhythm born of excitement and anticipation.

What the fuck was that?

Forcing herself not to look back, Scarlett crossed the room, her goal a table that was far enough away that it was clearly a dismissal and yet would give her an unobstructed view.

Logan.

The name suited him, suited the shadow of a beard that covered his jawline, the attractive smirk that curled his lips, the challenge in his eyes.

She wanted another look at him.

But she would just have to wait. She was the one in control.

Hoping she was projecting outward calm, no matter how much anticipation was roiling inside her, Scarlett pulled out the tall chair, lifted herself onto it, feeling the stretch in the muscles that had once propelled her across a stage. Slowly, she crossed one leg over the other, a deliberate tease, knowing the fact that she hadn't yet looked back at him told him she didn't care one way or another what he did.

But she did. Oh, she really, really did. And so she finally let herself look across the room, back to where she had left him.

She hadn't given him leave to move. If he felt even half of

what she did, he wouldn't have. It was disconcerting how much she wanted him to still be there.

Deliberately torturing herself, she let her eyes skim the mosaic-tiled floors. And then there he was.

He was still in place, though he had risen to his feet, staring after her. As their gaze met, Scarlett felt something tangible pulse in the air between them.

Slowly, expression wary, he dropped back down to his knees as she watched. He even went so far as to lace his hands behind his head, which told her that he was far from new to BDSM.

But he didn't drop his eyes, instead leaving his stare fixated on her. Still, triumph washed over her, and Scarlett had to try very hard not to grin.

"That's my boy." Allowing the smallest of smiles to curve over her lips, Scarlett turned in her chair and gestured toward Rani, one of the serving subs, for a fresh glass of wine.

She didn't want it, not really, but she needed a distraction, something to occupy herself with while she, too, sat through the excruciating wait that she was setting for them both.

She wanted to fist her hand in that gorgeous golden hair, wanted to bite the taut cord in his neck and feast on his lips.

But submission didn't come easily for this sub, no matter how he liked his sex. He needed his defenses broken down. And though it was a lengthy process, she would do it.

A Domme gave her subs what they needed, after all.

The minutes ticked by. Slowly. Excruciatingly so. Scarlett contemplated sitting on her hands to stop herself from fidgeting, sensing that this sub would use any sign of nerves on her part as ammunition to keep her from breaking him down.

When a low male voice spoke beside her, Scarlett welcomed the distraction.

"Mistress." The man kneeling at her feet was young, probably close to Scarlett's own twenty-four years, with close-cropped chestnut hair and eyes she knew to be green, though they were lowered with proper deference.

His muscled body was naked save for a pair of black briefs that rode low on his hips. Scarlett let herself appreciate the view, as well as the manners.

"Brendan." With the toe of her boot, she tilted the man's face up. Luca had arranged for a scene between her and Bren, who was delightfully submissive to his core, while Scarlett had been in training.

He had been everything she wanted—on paper. But sometimes the spark just wasn't there.

It hadn't been there with any of her submissives. Not until tonight.

Scarlett found herself somewhat disappointed that Bren didn't raise his eyes to look at her, even though he let her turn his face in her direction. So well trained. So perfectly submissive.

It didn't do a thing for her.

"What do you have planned this evening, Bren?" Finally, he looked up at her, and when she saw the eagerness in his expression, Scarlett cringed internally, realizing her mistake and struggling to rectify it. "Would you like me to ask Luca to arrange a scene for you?"

Bren's face fell, and Scarlett could have kicked herself.

"If you are otherwise occupied, Mistress, then perhaps I will just observe tonight." No reproach, no overt jealousy.

She hadn't acknowledged it consciously until right at that moment . . . but she wanted that spark of fire in a sexual partner. She wanted someone who required something more from her, someone whom she had to break apart before building him back up.

She dared a glance at the sub she had left kneeling in the

middle of the club's floor. Logan was still in place—she doubted he'd moved even an inch. But his muscles were rigid, tension radiating from every line of his body.

His face was set in a ferocious glare and he stared daggers at Bren.

"Oh." Scarlett should have had her full focus on the sub kneeling before her, but she couldn't take her eyes away from Logan. He was breathtaking in his fury.

Alpha, indeed.

On his knees, Bren shifted, catching Scarlett's attention again. She schooled her face into kind dismissal.

She liked him; she really did. And their scene together had been fun—he'd been very patient with her neophyte nerves.

She might have even scened with him again tonight, if not for two things.

One, she was leaving tomorrow. If he was getting attached, it would be cruel to encourage him.

And two . . . Her gaze was drawn back to Logan, who looked like he might stalk across the floor at any moment and shove Bren aside for a chance to get her.

Yes, two was the ferocious alpha male who dared her to make him hers.

"Enjoy your evening, Bren." Scarlett nodded in dismissal, steeling herself against his disappointment. But really, he was better off with someone else.

She watched the muscles of his strong back ripple as he moved away and reflected that he would have no trouble at all finding another Mistress to play with. Or a Master, if he was interested.

But this Mistress was taken, at least for tonight.

Turning back to Logan, Scarlett started when she saw Mistress Avery stalking back toward him. Submissive poaching was not encouraged at Veritas or at any kink club.

But if he wanted to go with the other woman, she wasn't about to stop him. It was his choice—it was always the sub's choice.

His body was becoming impossibly tenser as the tall woman approached. Logan didn't look like he wanted a choice. He looked like he wanted an escape, and when he cast a quick, panicked glance her way, Scarlett dared a quick glance at her watch.

She'd planned on making him kneel for at least a half hour, to rouse his anger and make him think about how she wouldn't be an easy Mistress. It had been only twenty minutes, but he had looked to her for escape, for something he needed.

Well, she would give it to him. Though it probably wasn't going to be in a form he expected.

Projecting dominance wasn't so very different from the stores of energy needed for a dancer in a performance. She watched intently as Logan looked belligerently up at the other Domme who approached him, the statuesque blonde all but purring as she placed one spiked heel on his thigh and ground the shoe into the muscle.

"I like a man on his knees," Avery murmured, her smile hungry. Logan didn't wince, even though the spike being dug mercilessly into his leg had to hurt like hell.

He opened his mouth to speak, but Scarlett cut him off, closing in on the pair and standing, still and straight.

"He's spoken for tonight, Mistress Avery." Scarlett kept her voice polite and cool, though a part of her was wondering if the beautiful male creature at her feet would contradict her.

Though she had fixed her gaze on the other woman, from the corner of her eye she saw Logan looking at her warily. That was all the opening she needed.

Avery smiled, the expression of a skilled predator with her prey in sight. "I don't see a collar."

Scarlett smiled back coolly. She wasn't mad—she had no right to be. Avery wasn't speaking to her with condescension and wasn't being any meaner to Scarlett than she was to anyone else.

Mistress Avery was just a bitch—it was her thing. But bitch or not, Scarlett had no intention of handing her delicious sub over on a silver platter.

Mine.

"True enough. Though not all Mistresses need a collar to command loyalty," Scarlett agreed amiably, transferring her attention from Avery to the man who eyed the pair of them with apprehension in his eyes. If Scarlett had seen only that wariness, she would have backed off.

But twined with the nerves was desire—desire for her. And she had a responsibility to see it through.

"You may stand." Her voice was quiet, but Logan rose instantly, pushing away Avery's foot as he did.

"I will be in private room number three for the remainder of the evening. I suspect that Mistress Avery is about to request your company for the evening as well, and as always, the decision is yours."

Logan's eyes widened and his fists clenched, and Scarlett smothered her grin.

"If you are coming with me, then I expect you there within the next five minutes." It almost killed her to walk away when all she wanted to do was run her fingers over the muscles in his arms that flexed as he clenched and unclenched his fists.

Patience, Scar, she reminded herself. That inexplicable connection that stretched between them was palpable even as she walked away, heading to the private room to prepare for what she hoped was going to be an evening of mind-blowing pleasure.

Five minutes wasn't a long time, but at that moment, it may as well have been an eternity.

The clock ticked, and Scarlett fought back bitter disappointment. She knew that she hadn't imagined it, that delicious promise of the power exchange that they could play with, but . . .

Well, Luca had warned her. This was one ornery sub. And if she were going to be in Vegas longer, she would have relished the challenge of coaxing him around.

But she was leaving in the morning. Her night of pleasure wasn't to be, because she knew that every other submissive would taste flat after meeting the one she truly wanted.

"Well, then." Disappointment washed over her. Pinching her lips together and swallowing against the burn in her nose, Scarlett moved to the touch screen that was set into the wall. A few swipes of her fingers had brought up Logan's profile, which she supposed she didn't need now.

She had no business being so disappointed.

It wasn't a noise that made her turn her head, but more a sudden awareness that she was no longer alone. Her heart thudded in her chest as she looked toward the door, finding Logan leaning against it insolently, his thumbs hooked in his belt loops.

He raised an eyebrow at her but didn't speak, waiting for her to take the lead. Scarlett suspected that if he had realized that was what he was doing, he would have had some kind of smart-ass comment.

She wasn't about to clue him in. Instead she looked him up and down, noting the lines of the muscles that hadn't quite relaxed yet.

Of course, she enjoyed the view as she did. Who wouldn't? He was the most beautiful man she'd ever seen.

"I said five minutes. It's been seven." She made sure that her words were level, indicating only the slightest bit of stern disapproval. "I have no interest in a sub who can't keep track of the rules."

"Then perhaps you need to loosen up." With those insanely blue eyes broadcasting wicked intent, Logan sauntered—there was no other word for it—toward Scarlett. She knew he was trying to gain control.

She refused to answer; nor did she break eye contact. Her pulse accelerated, desire and nerves and wicked *need* coiling up inside her as he came close enough for her to feel the heat emanating from his skin.

Some bottoms were a challenge, offering Dommes the chance to break down their outer walls and get at the sweet submission that lay within. This one seemed more defiant than most.

If she showed even a hint of weakness, he'd be all over her, a shark scenting blood.

Not for the first time that night, she wished that she had more time to spend with him.

When she didn't answer, didn't back away, Logan took another step closer, looking down into her eyes.

"Mistress seems displeased." His words were cocky. "Perhaps I may make it up to her by licking her cunt?"

Scarlett sucked in a breath as the visual played out through her mind—Logan on his knees before her, his hands braced on the soft skin of her inner thighs. She knew that she shouldn't have been shocked, not with the warning that Luca had given her about this submissive. But his blunt words sent a shiver running down her spine, making arousal flush her skin.

She wanted him, enough to press forward at a quicker

pace than she would have liked. But she was running out of time, and the thought of not having him even once didn't sit well.

Not entirely sure of what was driving her, she nevertheless felt the primal urge to leave her mark on him—on his skin, on his soul.

First she had to take back control of the situation. She needed to do something to make him feel vulnerable.

"Your safe word is bunker?" She had looked up his information in Veritas's database before he had entered the room. It was an interesting choice for a safe word . . . a place for him to hide.

If she had longer, she would press him to tell her why he had chosen that word. But since they had only one night, she supposed it didn't matter . . . and he was promising to keep her hands full without pushing that particular issue.

Logan's expression was wary as her sharp words caught his attention. "Yes. Not that I've ever needed it."

Scarlett drew herself up as tall as she could. She was of average height for a woman, and the four-inch heels on her boots still just barely brought her to eye level with him.

But power wasn't all about size. And when she arched an eyebrow coolly at Logan, watched the flicker of nerves turn to blue flame in his eyes, she got the first punch of that headiness that came with a true power exchange.

"For this evening, you *will* use that word if you need to." She didn't ask him to; asking would cede a modicum of power back to him.

It was time to delve deeper. Watching the guarded expression that began to creep over Logan's handsome features, Scarlett felt herself grow weak in the knees, and that had never happened before for her—never.

This beautiful man had depth, had secrets, and she wanted

to unwrap him layer by layer. Enough that she had pursued him, even though she had a sense that her heart might hurt when she walked away from him at the end of the night.

It was time for her to start, really start, peeling away the layers of control that he was so very obviously hugging tightly to that broad, delicious chest.

"You have your safe word. The club safe word is red. Now, strip."

CHAPTER FOUR

Logan steeled himself against the pang of apprehension that reverberated through him as Mistress S stood, waiting.

Now strip.

He'd figured they would get naked tonight—had counted on it. Only in release would he find the solace that he came to Vegas for.

But the look in those wide, expressive gray eyes confirmed his suspicions that this woman—this lithe, sweet, gorgeous woman—had plans for him that might be a bit rougher on him than he'd anticipated.

He had never used his safe word. Never had to—he never gave a Mistress access to the places inside of him that he wanted to guard. Now it was a point of pride.

She could do anything to his body, and he would take it. But his soul was his own. It was the only way he'd found to survive.

The calm control on the young woman's face resonated with something inside of him. Where normally he would have had a smart-ass comeback, instead he found his fingers working the button at the waist of his jeans.

"How did you know my safe word?" He didn't much like that she did. His chosen word told more about his history than he'd have liked, secrets only Luca now knew, and he'd never given it to a Mistress before, since he'd never had any intention of needing it.

"A good Mistress will know everything about you, Logan."
Scarlett gestured to the computer screen on the wall, the one
she'd been looking at when he'd entered. "Plus Veritas has a
new system. All of your information is stored in there. Easier
for me to understand the basics about you so that we can move
on to more . . . pleasurable pursuits."

Her words made his cock swell as he pushed his jeans
down his hips, around his ankles, and let them fall to the floor.
He'd been hard since she'd laid him flat and removed his
boots with her own hands, but now, as her gaze worked him
over from head to toe, he felt a searing attraction that brought
his erection to the point of pain.

Her eyes darkened as she watched, and he knew that she
liked what she saw. He wasn't modest—he had a good body
from all of the physical labor he did back on the ranch.

But this—this thing that sizzled between them—it was
more than just physical attraction . . . and it brought him out of
his comfort zone.

He knew what drew him to submit sexually—after he'd
gotten back from overseas, he had tried to exert rigid control
over every aspect of his life, and only in sex was he comfortable letting go of that discipline at all. But what drew her to
dominate? He'd never cared before, but he found that with
this raven-haired angel in front of him, he wanted to understand her better.

What was this to her? A one-night stand, or something
more?

He found that, for the first time, he wanted more than just
the next few hours. For some reason that was beyond him, he
felt a need to please her.

He couldn't have it. He didn't belong here. He couldn't
stay.

"Hands behind your head. Feet shoulder width apart."

Her voice was sweet but underlaid with that steel that made his cock pulse. He did as she said, forcing himself to be still as she circled him, looked him up and down.

Those delicate fingers reached out in a graceful yet clearly possessive touch. The feel of her hand sliding over his skin, even in that innocent touch, made him shudder.

She touched him gently, starting at his shoulders, then his stomach, down to his hip bones, as though she had a right . . . which he supposed she did. He'd given it to her.

But when she traced one fingernail down the raised ridge of scarred flesh on his back, he flinched away.

"Don't," he snapped. He should have had that in his list of hard limits—no touching his scar. No asking questions about his scar. But he didn't have a list of hard limits—not one he'd ever written down. He'd simply never let anyone take him past the point where he wanted to go.

His gut told him that if he tried his usual tricks with this pretty little Domme, she would tell him to run along and find someone else to play with, no matter what strange attraction vibrated between them. Like that other Mistress who'd approached him . . . Mistress Avery.

Any man with half a brain would be terrified of that woman. And more than that . . .

He wanted this one, this firecracker whom he couldn't keep his eyes off. He knew that when he was back at the ranch, when he needed something to get him through the long months until he was strong enough to brave a city again, he would palm himself and think of her.

Mercifully, Mistress S didn't push, didn't ask him about his scar, though he could see her filing it away in her brain for future use. There was safety in that, because in the future he would be gone.

She ripped that security blanket away with her next words.

"Get on your hands and knees. I'm going to get familiar with your body."

"What?" Logan couldn't stop the question in time.

What did that mean, exactly?

She gave him that look again—that bitchy one that said he'd better get moving. The one that made him even harder.

But beneath her bitchy tone, he sensed there was need riding her as much as it was him. Maybe that was why he did as she said, though his every sense was on alert. He fixed his eyes straight ahead—he might not have been the most obedient submissive, but he was an experienced one who knew the rules.

Closing his eyes, he simply listened as she walked back and forth, the heels of those boots that accentuated her long legs clicking on the tiled floor, lulling his thoughts into that first wave of calm that came with even the most superficial submission. The slither of silk hitting the floor, then a liquid sound—something being poured—and then more steps, growing louder, approaching him.

He fought the urge to rear up when she straddled him. The slither of silk that he'd heard had been Mistress S removing her skirt, and now he could feel the heat of her through the thin fabric of her panties, pressing against the small of his back.

"Why did you choose me, Logan?" As she spoke, she poured a handful of warm liquid across his shoulder blades. As it trickled over the planes of his back, it made Logan imagine arousing Mistress S to the point where she became that wet herself.

No question, this woman was getting under his skin. He couldn't have that, no matter how much he might want it.

So he made sure that his words were cocky, a smirk on his lips as he replied, though the touch of her fingers as she spread the warm, scented oil over his skin made him want to groan with pleasure.

"You're way hotter than that scary Domme." He hissed as the heels of those wicked boots dug into his rib cage.

Good. He wanted her to punish him. Maybe if he goaded her enough, she would do as he'd expected—take one of the floggers from the wall, beat him until they were both sweaty and quivering with need. He could lose himself in the beautiful pain, and afterward in what he was sure would be the hottest fuck of his life.

But . . . wait. . . . She was sliding off of him, humming her disapproval. She circled him, each step slow and sure, then crouched down in front of him, grabbed his chin in her hand, and forced him to look her in the eye.

Damn, but she had beautiful eyes. Large, expressive, a beautiful stormy gray color. They were surrounded by long, thick lashes that seemed gold and caramel and ebony all at once, which told him that she wasn't wearing any of that goop that women painted on.

He could get lost in those eyes.

But he couldn't afford to.

She pinned him with her stare, and he felt like a cornered animal, turning wary and defensive.

"What are you looking for, Logan?" She looked like she truly wanted to know, not just to break him down, but because she was interested.

"Whatever pleases my Mistress." The glib answer slid from his lips before he could think it through. A defense mechanism. Logan was startled at the trickle of shame that worked its way through him when she pursed her lips in disappointment.

The hint of defeat was gone in the blink of an eye, replaced by grim determination. "Well, then. You'll love this."

*　　*　　*

Scarlett unclipped the length of chain from her corset and swiftly gathered Logan's hands behind his back. She attached it to the buttery yellow leather cuff on one of his wrists, then the other, binding his hands behind his back.

She was glad she'd done it quickly when he reared back on his knees and looked over his shoulder at her. He was wily, and he was smart, and he'd outmaneuver her if she gave him half a chance.

It was tempting to let him do it, to grab onto the lust that hung heavy in the air, to sink into it. To let herself get burned by the electrical current of passion surging between them, because she knew it would be worth it.

Despite the temptation, she knew she would be cheating them both if she did. Plus he was starting to piss her off, though that didn't completely detract from the need that was riding her.

Reaching for the chains on the heavy wooden bench that sat on the edge of the room, Scarlett secured the ends to the length that held Logan's hands behind his back. Glaring at him—he was making her temper rise with his refusal to cooperate, and with it her level of arousal—Scarlett stalked across the room to where she'd dropped her toy bag.

Though vanilla sex had never really done it for her, she suspected that even without toys, any kind of joining with Logan would be off-the-charts hot. But that wasn't what either of them had come here for.

It was damn hard for her to be the strong one, to resist, when all she wanted was to fist her hand in his hair and plunder that smart mouth.

Focus.

Slowly, purposefully, she bent down to open the bag. The

four-inch heels meant she had to reach farther, but even though she wouldn't be doing splits in the air anytime soon, she was still pretty damn flexible.

Scarlett stifled a laugh at Logan's groan. The whole point of bending in this ridiculous way was to let him see the outline of her ass, clear enough through the lace panties that she wore.

To give him a hint of the reward he could have if he submitted.

"Mistress . . ." Logan's voice was a rasp, and the desire she heard there made her knees weak. "Mistress, let me touch you."

Scarlett remained silent as she pulled the two items that she wanted from her bag. Ripping open the foil package, she removed the condom, tossed the wrapper aside, then straightened back up and returned to Logan.

The sight of him, naked, bound, and at her feet, nearly brought her to her knees. He was just gorgeous, even though he was a far cry from the kind of man she'd see in a magazine. He was raw, and rough, exuding masculinity—he made her think of the outdoors, of manual labor, of sweat and hot, hot sex.

But no hot sex just yet. She had work to do, though ignoring their connection was becoming harder every minute.

"Don't move." Dropping to her knees in front of him, Scarlett bent and, without warning, pulled the head of his cock between her lips and began to suck, keeping her stare locked on his own.

His taste flooded her mouth, and she held back her own moan. It was addictive—she already wanted more.

She wanted it all.

"What—oh God." Logan's body jerked as he tried to pull away from her, then again as his hips pressed forward. Gently, Scarlett sank her teeth into the tender skin just below his corona, and he froze at the warning.

Though he held still, he couldn't seem to keep back the noises of pleasure. Scarlett placed her full attention on her task, though she wanted to take her time, to savor the salty taste rolling around on her tongue, wanted to savor the feeling of his heat pulsing in her mouth. But she needed to bring him to the brink, as fast and hard as possible.

She never let her submissives come in her mouth. Ever—it was a rule.

But with Logan—she wanted to drink him down, wanted to possess every bit of him that she could have.

"Mistress—oh. Please. *Please.*" The sudden hitch in his breath told Scarlett that he was on the verge of coming.

He cursed, long and loud, when she forced herself to slide her mouth off his cock and wiped her lips with the back of her hand. His taste remained on her tongue, teasing her as she quickly rolled the condom down the impossibly hard length.

"I didn't take you for a cock tease." Logan glared at her, his skin flushed, his jaw clenched.

"Don't be bitchy," she commented mildly, then followed the condom with a silicone cock ring. Securing it snugly at the base of his cock, Scarlett inhaled deeply, savoring the sight of his erection, which looked nearly painful, it was so engorged.

When he swore again, she stood, then bent and tucked a finger beneath his chin. His eyes spat fire as she tilted his face up, causing her pulse rate to accelerate, but she was pleased that, despite his rage, he didn't pull at his bindings.

"We're going to take a little break now," she told him softly, arching her back to give him a good view down the front of her corset. A strangled sound emanated from his throat.

"I don't need a break," he replied mulishly, not bothering to hide the hungry gaze that devoured her ample cleavage. "I can take anything you give me."

"I hope so." Scarlett took one step backward, then another. Oh, it was hard to walk away from him, even though she knew she would come back.

"I'll be back once you've had some time to think."

The woman had left him chained to a bench, slick with oil, with a boner that, thanks to the cock ring, couldn't recede.

He shouted after her, ground his teeth, and raged inside his own head, and then Logan sat back on his heels, stunned.

Mistress S might look all sweetness and light, but he'd never met a dominant woman with such iron balls. He admired it—and desired it.

She was everything that those hopes he'd shoved down deep inside him long ago—the ones he'd had before he'd ever gone overseas—had hungered for all these years.

It made him want badly to please her. And in that moment, with need and confusion clogging his mind, she could have demanded more of him than he'd ever given, and he would have had no choice but to respond.

Despite his best efforts, he responded to everything about her, body and soul.

Silently, he knelt, refusing to even shift his weight from knee to knee to relieve the pressure. She would come back—he trusted that. Any Domme worth her salt would never have left him truly alone but would have stayed close by, monitoring the scene from the screen on the wall outside the private room, the one that could be accessed only by a temporary code that belonged to whoever had reserved the room for the night.

This Domme radiated confidence, power, knowledge. She wouldn't be far. He just had to wait her out.

He whipped his head around when the door opened. A

sudden, overwhelming sense of relief washed over him when she stepped back inside the room, her lips curled into an imp-ish smile, a glass of red wine in her hand.

Man, but she was beautiful.

He opened his mouth—to say what, he wasn't sure—and then he saw the reason for her smile.

A male submissive walked behind Mistress, his gaze on the floor as was proper, his posture unassuming.

His very proper submissive manners didn't mask what even Logan could tell were classically handsome looks, a body maintained from something besides workouts at the gym, and an expression of peace at being under a Mistress's command.

Panic welled inside of Logan, something he'd never be-fore felt when in the middle of a scene.

"What the fuck is this?" He growled, and for the first time, he pulled at his chains, pride be damned. He wanted to get free, needed to get to her, needed her to accept him before she decided on this other sub.

"I'll serve you. I'll do whatever you want." Logan didn't even care that the desperation was evident in his voice.

She was his, damn it. He could serve her better than some clean-cut kid ever could. And that damn kid didn't even have the decency to look smug.

Mistress S led the other sub halfway into the room, close enough that Logan could see everything clearly, but far enough away that he craved her heat. "I thought you said that you would do whatever pleases me, Logan."

With a gentle hand, she pushed the shoulder of the other sub down to his knees, then pulled a plush velvet chair over beside the other man's still form.

"I'll eat your pussy. I'll make you scream." Logan's voice was a growl, accompanied by the metallic clank of his chains.

She regarded him calmly before sinking regally down into

the chair, but even through the red haze of his anger, he could see the emotions she was trying to keep from him.

He'd pissed her off, and because she felt the same desperate need that he did, she was pushing him.

She crossed one leg over the other, the move both wanton and prim. Logan fought back a shout.

"On your hands and knees, Bren. Make your back as flat as possible." The other man didn't even blink at the strange request, assuming the position with more grace than he looked capable of.

Logan bared his teeth when his Mistress set her glass of wine down carefully on the back of the other man—Bren.

Bren's muscles quivered when the glass came to rest on the hard planes of his back. Mistress S murmured with approval, and Logan didn't have to guess why—he would have had to be blind not to notice and grudgingly appreciate the way the other man controlled himself, made himself perfectly still.

Didn't mean he liked it. No, he didn't like it at all. Furious, and yet still aroused, he clenched his jaw shut and sat back on his heels, trying to rein in his temper.

"It pleases me to have a sub willing to serve me, Logan. They don't have to do it perfectly . . . but they do have to try." As she spoke, Mistress S nudged Bren's rib cage with the heel of her boot. He moved under the touch, just the slightest bit, but it was enough to send a small wave of red wine over the edge of the glass.

Mistress S looked directly at Logan as she picked up her glass, and he felt as though she could see straight through him.

He wanted her, more even than he wanted to go back home.

"I am happy to reward a sub for trying, even if mistakes

are made. But I require an honest effort." Her eyes sparked, the color of banked coals before they burst into flame. Returning the heel of her boot to Bren's side, she whispered something to him, pressing her shoe into his flesh to guide him until he faced her, still on hands and knees.

A sense of foreboding washed over Logan when he realized that this brought the other sub's face at a level with Mistress S's pussy. His temper flaring, he pulled at his chains, snarling at the resistance of being bound.

He would be the one to bring her pleasure, to taste her sweetness. Him and no one else.

"Be still," Mistress S snapped; it was the first time she had raised her voice to him. He heard her own frustration in the words. "Bren has done as I asked. He deserves a reward."

Logan wanted to shout when she dipped her fingers into the glass of wine, then painted them over the creamy expanse of her inner thigh. She repeated the gesture on the other leg, and he watched, riveted, as the ruby-colored liquid rolled over the smooth skin.

He was suddenly parched, and those trickles of wine were the only thing that could quench his thirst.

"Are you thirsty, Bren?" Her voice was soft, intimate. Logan could have killed the other man for being on the receiving end of the exchange.

"Yes, Mistress." Bren was infuriating. Even now, even with the Domme's pussy inches from his mouth, he kept his eyes focused on the floor, the picture of self-control.

But the other man wore only black shorts. His erection pressed against the snug fabric, demonstrating just how affected he was by the beautiful brunette whose legs framed his face.

"Have a drink, then." Mistress S shifted her hips to the edge of the chair, closing her legs slightly, which brought the spilled wine within reach of Bren's mouth.

"Thank you, Mistress," the other man said solemnly before inclining his head . . . and swiping his tongue over the woman's skin.

"Damn it. Mistress. Let me do it. I want to do it." Logan pulled at the chains, his mouth dry with need. He could do it—he could do more than lick wine from her thighs. He could bring her more pleasure than she'd ever known, because he *wanted* her more than she'd ever been wanted before. He was sure of it.

"You know your choices, Logan." His Mistress's voice was slightly breathy—she wasn't unaffected by the tongue working slowly, purposefully on her skin, even though Bren was doing as he was told and licking only her legs.

Or maybe, he realized as her eyes met his, maybe she was affected because of him, because he was watching. Just as he was affected by her.

"You may use your safe word. Or you may do as I wish you to," Mistress S managed.

That safe word was on the tip of his tongue—he couldn't let her do this. Wouldn't let her. Couldn't stand to watch another man touch her.

But he understood the lesson she was teaching him. This would go her way, or it wouldn't go at all.

If any other Mistress had tried this with him, he . . . Actually, he wasn't sure what he would have done. No other Mistress had been so determined to work past his skilled deflections before.

Was this one worth it?

As he watched her head tip back, watched the low lights bounce off her dark hair and the flush of pleasure paint her skin, he knew that no matter how much it troubled him to give in, the second she had stumbled into his arms, he wouldn't have been able to do anything else.

Though his brain still screamed, *Mine, mine, mine*, he inhaled, then exhaled, then forced himself to again sit back. His body was still a long, tense line, but Mistress S smiled at him with approval.

"Thank you, Bren." Placing her hand on the other man's chin, the Domme urged his face up and smiled at him. "I'm very pleased with you. You may go find Master Luca. I believe he has found you a Mistress to play with for the night."

"Anything for you, Mistress." Bren smiled, though Logan saw the disappointment in the expression, then nodded, rising gracefully to leave the room. Logan followed him with his eyes and saw the slight tension in the other man's shoulders.

Unless he was very, very wrong, Bren would have given anything to be where Logan was right now. Somehow the knowledge helped to smooth the worst edges of Logan's anger.

The woman who commanded his full attention locked stares with him, then made her way back across the room. Bending down in front of him, she caught his hair in her hand and tugged sharply.

She had him so off balance, all Logan wanted to do was make the world stop spinning. Before he could overthink it, he lunged forward, pulling the chains tight behind him, and claimed her mouth. His teeth nipped into her lower lip, and then his tongue traced over the seam of her lips. She tasted like wine, like the strawberries that grew in a wild tangle back on his ranch. His ego soared when she moaned into the kiss.

The kiss was like nothing he'd ever experienced before. It was heat; it was desire; it was need. It threatened to consume them both.

He would have gladly gone up in flames. But she had other plans.

The sharp crack of pain when she reared back and slapped him across the cheek stunned him and made his cock ache.

"You stubborn ass." Finally, the calm facade had disappeared, and her temper was a tangible thing. Whirling, she made her way to the tan leather bag that lay on the floor, retrieved a blue glass bottle, and returned.

Without ceremony, she moved out of his line of sight. The disturbance of the air told him that she was now kneeling behind him, and he understood even before he heard the liquid sound of oil being poured.

"No!" He shouted the word, panicked. He tried to shy away when the warm oil was poured over the small of his back but was pulled up tight by the chains. "I can't . . . I don't want that!"

"You have your safe word." Ruthlessly, she worked the oil down between his buttocks. "If you want control, then you should train as a Dom."

"Please. No." Again, Logan's safe word was on the tip of his tongue—twice in one night. The idea of what she was about to do was abhorrent to him, though not because he thought it wouldn't feel good.

If she did this, she could make him lose control without him being able to do a thing about it.

He wanted to please her, more than he'd ever wanted to please a Domme before. But he couldn't submit completely.

And yet the safe word just wouldn't come.

"Subs don't get to say no unless they're using their safe word, Logan." Her words were slightly breathless, her stubborn finger still sliding between his buttocks, not an easy task with the way he was bucking. Nerves lit in the wake of her touch, melding with the overwhelming desire he'd been feeling since they'd met.

She was a good Domme, reminding him that the choice was ultimately his, even as she ensured that he knew what the reward for submission would be.

"I am going to dominate you, Logan." That damn finger of hers finally reached its goal. Mistress S pressed the top against the pucker of his anus, causing Logan's hips to jerk. "You can't do anything about it."

The finger pressed forward, working against the tight muscles until his body gave and opened for her. Logan swore as the discomfort twined with the undeniable pleasure from her touch.

"Good. That's good." She pressed a kiss to his spine as she pushed forward, then slowly pulled her finger back. "Give in to it. I'll make you feel good."

Logan shuddered as she thrust her finger in and out again. He felt his excitement rising high and fast.

With her free hand, she reached around him and slid his cock ring off. His arousal rocketed to a level that felt so good it hurt, and he knew he wouldn't last long.

And then that damn questing finger found the tight bundle of nerves inside of him. He jerked away as she slowly rubbed the tip of that finger back and forth, as the sensations became too much.

"No. No!" The word was a reflex. He couldn't have this—he couldn't be vulnerable to her like this.

But as she worked that spot, as his balls drew up tight and heat gathered at the base of his spine, Logan realized that his Mistress had been exactly right. She dominated him utterly, her touch sweeping him past the point of holding on to control and into a mindless haze of pleasure.

"No . . . Oh please. Please." He could do nothing but ride the sensation as she edged past his control and forced his orgasm from him. With nothing else to hold on to, he leaned back against her surprising strength as his hips bucked once, twice, three times, his liquid heat jettisoning into the condom he wore as he climaxed.

She held him as he convulsed, the orgasm racking his body. When the tremors finally subsided, he leaned back, out of breath, sweat coating his skin.

She pressed back against him, supporting him for a long moment. Then she eased out from beneath his weight, stood, and circled around to face him once again.

Logan was horribly uncomfortable. He felt raw, exposed, and he couldn't look her in the eye—couldn't look up at this beautiful, incredible woman who had not just gotten around his walls but had smashed them to bits.

Logan was the kind of man who found pride in managing the things that life threw at him. But as he knelt before this woman who had upended his world, he didn't have the faintest idea of what he was supposed to do.

She didn't let him wonder—she told him. "We're not done yet."

CHAPTER FIVE

Scarlett trembled as she reached for a damp cloth to clean the jasmine-scented oil from her hands. In front of her, Logan knelt stoically, gorgeous, glistening with oil, bewildered yet still powerful.

Now that she had made it past the outer shell of his control, she wanted to continue to peel back the layers until she found his very core. Bending, she unhooked the length of chain attaching his wrists to his ankles and the one linking him to the heavy wooden bench. Offering him a hand, she helped him to his feet.

"That was beautiful," she told him, and she hoped he could hear her sincerity. Logan being pushed past the barriers he had erected around his innermost self had been stunning, and she knew that the scene would be imprinted on her mind forever. "You deserve a reward."

She watched as a shiver worked its way down Logan's hard frame. Her mouth went dry at the sight of him.

Lacing her fingers in his, she pulled him to the chair she had sat in while Bren licked the wine from her thighs. With one hand on his chest, she pushed him to a sitting position, then placed one high heel between his legs and kicked them apart. While running her hands from his knees up his thighs, she looked him directly in the eye.

"You will behave." She decided to leave his hands bound, to add to his feeling of helplessness, but left his legs untethered in a gesture to show that he had earned a tiny share of her trust.

"Yes, Mistress." He was still meeting her eyes boldly rather than looking down, but Scarlett had the impression that, rather than an act of defiance now, it was because he wanted to see her.

So she said nothing, instead removing the used condom, then wiping him down with the damp cloth. When she tore open a fresh foil wrapper and began to roll the latex sheath down the cock that was already stiffening again, Logan trembled beneath her touch, and Scarlett felt her heart melt.

This was bad. She had no illusions that she'd broken him down to the core. But she'd be damned if she'd deny herself just a bit of possession, just for tonight.

Scarlett slowly hooked her fingers in the sides of her panties, then tugged them down and stepped out once they'd pooled on the floor. Bracing her weight on the arms of the wide, soft chair, Scarlett climbed into Logan's lap, spreading her thighs wide so that she could straddle him. Her stomach did a slow flip when he buried his face in her neck, then pulled back to look directly into her eyes.

"Why did you do that?" His voice was raw, solemn. Scarlett knew he was referring to the way she had ignored his request to stop, the way she had pushed him past what he wanted into what she thought he needed.

She wasn't omniscient, and for a moment her breath caught in her throat—had she done the right thing?

Trust your instincts. Luca had told this to her time and again as he'd trained her.

"You were trying to control the situation." The fierce possession in Logan's eyes made Scarlett want to look away, but she forced herself not to break eye contact. "As your Mistress, I can't allow that. It's the entire point of a power exchange."

She breathed out a sigh of relief when Logan again nuzzled his face into her shoulder. When he spoke, the warmth of his breath tickled the side of her neck.

"And why did you choose me? Why not Bren? He's clearly an easier sub."

Scarlett smiled wryly to herself, then reached down and clasped Logan's erection, which was now fully firm, despite the fact that he'd just come. Rubbing her thumb over the tip, causing him to hiss in a breath, she chose her words carefully.

"Easy isn't always better," she finally said, positioning the head of Logan's cock at her entrance. She wanted to slam down on him and ride him hard, to put her feelings to work as physical sensation, but she knew that delayed gratification would be worth it.

"And I don't feel the same connection with Bren that I do with you."

A guttural cry issued from Logan's throat as she slowly sank down completely on his length, and her sigh of pleasure mixed with his. Wet as she was, she was still small and he was . . . well, *not*. She had to work her way down, twisting and pushing, until her body accepted his full length.

It was *perfect*.

"Mistress." Beneath her, Logan was still, though he couldn't quite control the quivering of his thighs beneath her. She knew how he was feeling exactly.

Joining with him like this was the most intense thing she'd ever experienced in her life.

"Will you tell me your name?" That he managed to ask while he was inside of her told her how much he wanted to know, how much he wanted that extra connection between them.

"Shh," she whispered, laying her cheek to his shoulder and inhaling the scent of his skin. She wanted to tell him, yearned for that extra connection as much as he did.

But she shouldn't. Names would just add more intimacy, and as it was already, she knew that it was going to kill her to walk away at the end of the night. She had never believed in

love at first sight, in any kind of instantaneous connection—
not until tonight.

That tonight was all they would have ripped her apart inside, even as she slowly began to move, rocking back and forth
on his cock.

But she needed the opportunity in Montana. She wouldn't—
couldn't—walk away from it, especially not for a man.

Then he thrust up into her from below, and her maudlin
musings were burned away as the sparks between them flickered, then burst into full flame.

The heat licked at the soles of her feet, still clad in the
boots, and traveled up her legs, bursting into an inferno in the
pit of her belly as she rocked her hips down against him.

"Mistress." Logan's voice was hoarse. He looked up at her,
caught her stare with his own, and Scarlett felt a shudder rack
her body as something inside of her recognized something inside of him.

If this was all she was going to have, she didn't want to
hold back. Burying her face in his neck, she urged him onward
with lightning-fast movements of her hips.

He pulled at the chains that held his arms behind him,
then leaned back and set a harsh pace with his hips. She found
herself wishing that she hadn't chained him, but there was no
time, no time, no time, and then she was rocking back against
him, meeting his every brutal thrust with a rock of her hips,
stoking the flame.

The room was silent apart from their heavy breaths and
the slap of their flesh as the blaze turned to wildfire. His cock
touched an extra-sensitive spot inside her. Scarlett couldn't
take her eyes from his as her climax whipped through her, and
he watched her every movement greedily.

Only once she was done shuddering did he redouble his
efforts, his movements designed solely to reach his own plea-

sure. Then he pushed into her hard, his mouth open in a silent shout as he came.

Their gazes held as they rode out his pleasure, the connection between pulling tight.

Trembling, Scarlett dipped her head, pressed a kiss to Logan's sweaty forehead without thinking, licked her lips over the salt his skin left on her mouth.

That was . . . That was . . .

She didn't have a word for what she felt. She especially didn't have any words for the fact that she wanted to stay just as she was for hours, days, weeks.

"Mistress . . ." Logan whispered against her neck, burrowing his head in. Nestled together like this, it just felt . . . right.

It was terrifying. She couldn't delude herself . . . At the end of the day, she knew what she wanted—a forever relationship, a family.

She'd approached Logan, yes, but she hadn't anticipated how very real this would all be. She couldn't pursue anything with him when she was about to leave town.

And yet the idea of leaving him was terrifying.

Silently, she climbed off his lap, coaxed her hands not to tremble as she pulled the used latex off of his cock. She felt his intense stare following her as she disposed of both condoms they had used, washed her hands, then returned with a clean, damp cloth and a bottle of water.

She kept her eyes focused on her tasks as she wiped him down, unhooked the chain from his wrists, massaged his hands to encourage the blood flow. Cracking the lid off the bottle of water, she handed it to him, waited for him to drink.

"Thank you." Logan's eyes met hers over the edge of the plastic bottle as he drank. A sudden sorrow whipped through Scarlett, like a keen blow from an emotional flogger as he waited quietly for her to do something, she knew, or say something.

She couldn't be a coward. This scene was her responsibility. But she weighed her words carefully as she slowly retrieved her lace panties, then her skirt, and shielded herself with her clothing.

Turning back to Logan, she watched quietly as he stood, drained half the bottle of water, then offered the rest to her by tilting it in her direction.

"I won't see you again, will I?" he asked when she refused, the shaking of her head almost frantic. He didn't look any happier than Scarlett felt, but the resignation in his eyes told her that he'd accepted it.

"No." Reluctantly, Scarlett shook her head, chastising herself as she did. Being this upset was ridiculous. Yes, the sex had been mind-blowing, but she'd met this man only tonight. She was *not* about to turn her life, her plans, inside out for a man. It might hurt now, but in a few days she would be fine.

"You've pleased me greatly tonight." Unsure of what to do, Scarlett crossed to the chair where Logan stood. She felt like she should make some kind of grand gesture, but what, she had no idea.

"May I?" When he held out his hand for hers, she cocked her head, curious.

When he lifted it to his lips, turned it over to place a warm kiss in the center of her palm, her knees threatened to give out on her.

"Thank you," he said again, walking backward to the door. "For everything."

And then he was gone, leaving Scarlett feeling decidedly out of control.

Afterward, Logan slumped over the bar in the main area of the club, wrapped his fingers around an icy brown bottle of beer and hoped that the chill would help to wake him up.

Get a grip, Brody, he chastised, tilting his head back to take a long pull of the glacial liquid. *It was just a scene. Just sex.*

But that wasn't ringing true. Somehow, despite his best efforts, the coolly elegant brunette with the face of an angel had stomped his barriers to the ground. She'd made him feel things he hadn't wanted to feel and had made him *like* it.

Trying to gain control of himself, to reerect the walls that the woman—damn it, she had refused to even tell him her real name—had sent crumbling to the ground, Logan cast his gaze around the club, looking for a scene that would hold his attention, take his mind off of what had just happened.

Instead he found his stare drawn back to the door to the room he'd exited. He watched, waited for Mistress S to exit.

When she did and the crimson lights of the main room played over the raven tones of her hair, Logan felt his breath catch. She looked so sweet, even dressed in the bustier that offered up her creamy breasts, the skirt that showed off those long, long legs.

How had she managed to skillfully unearth those feelings that he'd long ago buried?

"Goddamn it." Setting down his beer, Logan scrubbed his hands over his eyes. When he opened them again, Bren—that motherfucking bastard—was again kneeling in front of Mistress S. She had her hand cupped under his chin and a smile on her lips.

He knew, *he knew* that she'd said she didn't feel a connection with the other man. But possessiveness washed over him in a flash of blinding white.

She was *his* Mistress. He didn't want her touching anyone else.

Before he could think his actions through, Logan pushed away from the bar, then crossed the room in large, purposeful strides. Mistress S turned just before he reached her, and her eyes widened for the briefest of seconds.

And then his mouth was on hers, his hands working her hair loose from the smooth, controlled knot where she had it tamed. Her felt her startled intake of breath when his tongue pressed against the seam of her lips, demanding entry, then the soft sigh as she started to kiss him back, the need to dominate clearly warring with the pleasure of his touch.

As he took her mouth fiercely, his movements leaving no time for protest, a roaring filled his ears, the result of his blood heating, rushing through his veins. He groaned, sank his teeth into her lower lip, and tugged gently at her hair as he fought the urge to devour her whole.

He wanted to please her more than he'd ever wanted anything. And yet, somehow, by being just the way he was, he thought he was doing just that.

Logan hadn't nearly gotten his fill when Scarlett broke the kiss, gasping. He felt a hint of smugness when he saw that her pupils were dilated, her lips swollen—no matter how cool she played it, he affected her just as much as she affected him.

Then she pulled her knee up between his legs. He had to admire her strength and balance as she held it there, pressing it into his crotch just hard enough to cause his painfully engorged balls to tighten even further.

Fury suffused her ivory skin, but mixed with it were signs of the same need and lust that were tangled so tightly inside of him. Satisfaction hit his veins like the burn of whiskey to the back of his throat.

Lowering her leg once he stilled, she then stepped back, her spine straightening, that domineering expression he'd already seen so many times tonight warning him that he was in trouble.

Anticipation—she wasn't done with him yet; he didn't yet have to say goodbye—warred with apprehension.

"I'm going to go easy on you, because emotions are running high for both of us after that scene." Not taking her eyes from Logan, the Domme gestured for Bren, who was still kneeling, to rise. "Bren, please open my bag and remove the paddle. The one with the holes."

Logan sucked in a breath, anticipating the bite of pain. The holes in the paddle allowed the air to pass through more freely than a solid one, allowing for a faster swing and a harder blow. Though he wondered what she would have pulled out if she *wasn't* going to go easy on him, as she'd said, he found himself impressed.

She wasn't very big, but this Mistress was fierce.

He thought he just might be crazy about her.

"Unzip your pants. Bare your ass, then bend over that barstool." She spoke like she was sure he would obey. His reflex was to tell her that she'd have to make him.

And then his mind flashed back to the inside of that private room. To the way she'd bound him, aroused him, and milked his climax from him despite his resistance.

Looking at the determination in her eyes, he knew that if he didn't do as she said, she would have no qualms about doing the exact same thing out here, where everyone could see. It had been bad enough to be stripped down, raw, exposed to this one woman.

Slowly he turned, undid his pants. The metallic rasp of the zipper grated against the suddenly hushed air of the club as he lowered his jeans to his knees, then bent over the stool.

He had no problem with nudity—never had. But this wasn't just being naked in public.

The damn woman was poking at his boundaries again, and he hadn't even managed to shore the barriers back up. And he sure as fuck didn't care for it. Even if he already cared for her.

"You will use your safe word if you need to," Mistress S

commanded, and Logan felt his temper rising. "And you will say yellow if you need a break. Don't forget to breathe."

Logan ground his teeth together, then goaded her. "Put a little muscle into it, sweetheart, so I know you've started."

He heard her hiss out a breath, then the whistle of the paddle sailing through the air.

Smack!

It took everything in him not to shout as the wood connected with the flesh of his right ass cheek. The pain radiated outward, fireworks followed by a wicked burn.

Motherfucker.

The woman had one hell of a swing.

Smack! Smack, smack! She alternated, landing two blows on each side of his ass. Logan felt his cock rising, hardening, as he fought past the pain and into the pleasure that accompanied it. The sharp sensation helped to clear his head of his anger, to reach for the pleasure with both hands.

Smack! The Domme centered this blow, flogging the sensitive skin where his legs met his ass. No longer able to stay silent, he choked out a low groan as he shuddered.

"Let me see you again." He didn't care who heard him, didn't even look around to see, staying frozen where he was, facedown over the barstool.

He'd never been able to handle more than one night in the bustling city, the claustrophobia making him yearn for the wide-open skies of his ranch.

But for this woman . . . he would stay a second night. A week, even. He would stay until he couldn't bear it for another second.

"I can't." He felt her presence behind him, heard the quiet words, meant just for him.

"What did I do wrong?" In the past Logan had always been the one to pull away, and it stung to be on the receiving end of the rejection.

He'd been belligerent, stubborn, even mean for a good portion of the evening. But his gut was telling him that those things were why she had chosen him rather than Bren.

Easy isn't always better.

So then what was it? Was he imagining the chemistry between them?

"Apart from being the most cantankerous sub I've ever come across?" she asked wryly. He felt her hands on his face, her fingers cool in contrast to his skin, which was on fire. She coaxed him to look up at her, placing one finger against his lips to keep him quiet.

"You've done nothing wrong. I would love nothing more than to break you down and build you back up again." Her words sent a shiver skating down his spine.

He had no doubt that that was exactly what she would do, and he believed her fully capable of it.

"But I can't." Bending, she replaced the finger on his lips with her mouth, granting him the most chaste of kisses, but that small touch made his mouth go dry.

He closed his eyes as she stepped back, listened to her murmur to Bren as she collected her bag. The staccato click of those sexy-as-hell boots slowed as she passed him, and his heart leapt as he wondered if she had changed her mind.

And then it quickened again. Logan listened as she walked away, each press of those spiked heels into the tiled floor like a knife to his heart.

CHAPTER SIX

When the time had come to say goodbye to the Vegas Veterinary Center, where Scarlett had spent so many hours over the last two years, it felt bittersweet.

She was sure she was doing the right thing by trading in the familiar scuffed floors and smells of antiseptic and dog hair for hay and manure. But closing a chapter of her life was harder than she'd anticipated.

"You're absolutely sure this is what you want?" Dr. Roxy Snow, one of the three partners of Vegas Vets, tucked a strand of wildly curling light brown hair behind her ear. Little vertical lines appeared between her eyebrows as she frowned, studying Scarlett up and down. "We would still love to have you here full-time. With the time you put in during school, you could be a partner within a couple of years."

Scarlett winced as temptation rose. Staying would probably be the safer offer, and she knew it. She would have a decent starting salary, good benefits, wouldn't have to say goodbye to her friends, like her roommate, Beth, who had cried all over her T-shirt not half an hour earlier.

If she stayed, she could go back to Veritas tonight. Could see if Logan was still there.

But it wasn't for her. It hadn't ever been, not really. Her dream had hatched only weeks after the director of her dance school had sat her down and told her, quite bluntly, that while she had the drive, she didn't have the talent—or the figure—to ever be more than part of the corps of a ballet company.

The dream had gotten her through a dark time, when she'd had no direction, no idea of where to go or who to turn to.

So she couldn't turn her back on it now.

"I'm sure." She grinned at Roxy, who was only a few years older than Scarlett. She would miss her, would miss all of her friends, like crazy.

Would also miss the connection she'd discovered the night before. Which was ridiculous. She didn't even know the man, not really. Even if she'd paddled his ass.

To cover the flush that was rising on her cheeks—Roxy knew nothing about Scarlett's preference for kink—she huffed out a deep breath. "Wow. I can't believe I'm actually doing this."

"No changing your mind, then, huh?" Roxy's mouth twisted with disappointment. "Damn it. I figured. But I had to give it once last shot."

"I'm sorry, Rox." And she was. For the last few years, Scarlett's world had been more stable than it had ever been, and leaving that calm to head back into the unknown was terrifying.

She said none of that, though, instead stuffing her hands into the pockets of her shorts. "I'll be back in a year. You won't even notice I've been gone."

A childish shriek sounded from the back room, and Roxy rolled her eyes good-naturedly. "*Someone* will notice that you're gone, that's for sure. You ready?"

"As I'll ever be." Scarlett felt like an invisible fist had palmed her heart and was squeezing tightly as a skinny, carrot-topped nine-year-old girl barreled into the exam room where she and Roxy were sitting, a squirming tricolored Chihuahua clutched tightly in her arms.

"Rox, can I dress Chewy in—" The girl stopped dead in her tracks when she saw Scarlett, then squealed, shoving the dog at Roxy and making a beeline for Scarlett. "Dr. Malone! You're here! I knew you wouldn't leave without saying good-bye!"

"Of course not, Layla." The fist squeezed tighter as the young girl wrapped her arms around Scarlett with glee—glee that Scarlett knew would turn ugly as soon as she actually had to leave.

Putting it off another moment, Scarlett simply leaned in to the hug, absorbing the scents of baby shampoo, sweat, and wax crayons that emanated from the girl's skin. She met Roxy's eyes over Layla's bright head and grimaced along with her friend.

Roxy was technically Layla's aunt, though she'd been her guardian for so many years now that she'd assumed the role of mom. Layla had spent her early years bouncing between her alcoholic mother and various temporary foster homes, and when she'd discovered that Scarlett had been a foster kid, too, she'd become as attached as Roxy would let her.

Scarlett knew that she had to choose her next words very carefully, to keep the little girl from feeling like she was being abandoned yet again.

"I'll just take Chewy out to do his business." Roxy smiled encouragingly as she turned to the door of the small exam room. She fixed Layla with what Scarlett had termed *the mom eye*. "No giving Dr. Malone a hard time, okay?"

"Right, Rox." Layla rolled her eyes, Roxy rolled hers back, and all three of them broke into laughter.

Then Roxy was gone, and Scarlett was left with a little girl who had already been abandoned far too often in her life.

Before she could even open her mouth, Layla slid from her arms and flopped into the spindle-legged chair across from her, her arms folded over her chest, a sign that she was feeling defensive. "I don't understand why you have to leave me."

Scarlett paused, considering her words. Layla was old enough to understand intellectually that Scarlett wasn't leaving *her* specifically at all—and to use it to dredge up guilt to get her own way.

But Layla's past also had to be taken into account, and the knowledge that behind the bravado there was likely a very real sense of hurt and fear panged her.

Leaning forward, placing her elbows on her knees, Scarlett decided not to use any cutesy voices or to circumvent the question. So she looked Layla right in the eye, her expression serious.

"You want to go to college someday, right?" She already knew the answer, but she waited as Layla squirmed in her seat.

"Yes. I want to be a vet, like you and like Rox." Layla eyed Scarlett suspiciously. "What's that got to do with anything?"

"Well, think about this. Suppose that there's a school right next door to Roxy that you could go to. It's a really nice school, and you could be happy there and stay with everyone you know. *But* there's another school that's not next door to Roxy at all. And you know that the school that's close to home could make you a good vet. But that other school? It could teach you how to read animal's minds." Scarlett waggled her eyebrows to emphasize that she was making that part up.

"You can't talk to animals." Layla's voice was full of frustration, like she already knew where this was going.

Scarlett smothered her smile. "No, I can't," she agreed. "But suppose you had these two choices. You know which one you want. But which one is the right one to choose?"

Layla's face melted into a frown. "I don't like this. Maybe I don't want to choose."

Oh, baby. Scarlett melted even more, remembering the scared little girl she'd once been herself.

"I have a secret for you." Leaning in closer, she placed her lips close to Layla's ear. "I don't want to choose either. But being a grown-up means that sometimes you have to do it anyway."

Pulling back, Scarlett watched as Layla's lower lip began to tremble. Tears pricked at the backs of her eyes.

Oh, this just *sucked*.

"So you're choosing the place where you learn to talk to animals. Except you can't actually talk to them." Layla pulled a strand of her hair from her ponytail and chewed on it thoughtfully.

"Right."

Layla nodded then, as though her mind was made up. She pinned Scarlett with a stare that seemed way too grown-up for her nine years.

"So I won't see you for a while. But you *will* come back." It wasn't a question, and Scarlett found that she had to smother a laugh as she took in the imperious expression on Layla's face.

"Of course." Perhaps she'd been worrying too much. It seemed that this former foster child was going to do just fine.

But others weren't as lucky as Layla, to escape the system that at times made it seem like no one wanted you, no one loved you. After her goodbyes to Layla and Roxy, Scarlett took a drive by the building where she hoped to be able to change that, in some small part.

Pulling up in front of the old abandoned warehouse, Scarlett got out of the car, then sat on the hood, cross-legged. The hot metal of the hood burned her skin, but she ignored it as she stared up at the building.

Most degrees in veterinary sciences placed an emphasis on smaller animals—house pets. But in this very building, Scarlett wanted to create a place where everyone was welcome—small animals. Large ones.

As well as children who got no affection at home, and who would be affected deeply by having someplace to go where they could volunteer and feel the kind of unconditional love that came from four-legged creatures of all kinds.

That love was what had gotten Scarlett through her own years in the foster system. And she wanted to pay that forward, in a big animal hospital on the edge of the city where she could treat animals of all kinds, even foster some of them from time to time.

But she wanted to do it right, and for that she needed more education dealing with larger animals.

She had applied to several different internships, but in the end had chosen one that had fallen into her lap—serendipity, she'd thought.

Luca was a good friend, and as a businessman, extremely well connected. When he'd mentioned that he had a friend on a ranch in Montana who could work with her one-on-one, it had seemed perfect.

Scarlett had thought it somewhat strange that the veterinarian—Dr. Logan Brody—hadn't wanted to meet her in person, since she would be living in his house for the next year, working by his side. But the phone interview had gone well enough, and something about the internship had clicked in a way that the others hadn't. And Luca had recommended him.

It would be good for her to leave Vegas, anyway. She had started to cling too tightly to routine, and it was time to push past her comfort zone.

Still, saying all of these goodbyes kinda sucked.

Swallowing thickly, Scarlett pressed a hand to the side of the building in farewell. "Stay abandoned for another year, you hear?"

Climbing back into her car, she fought through the knot of

emotion gathering at the back of her throat. She wasn't second-guessing herself. She rarely did.

But goodbyes were hard. And she had one more to do.

Scarlett winced when Luca thumped a bottle of wine down on the table at Starbucks. He didn't give it a second glance as he settled back in the wooden chair and took the paper cup she offered him, though Scarlett knew that if it was from her wine snob of a friend, the bottle likely cost somewhere in the high four figures.

Luca Santangelo, she knew, had billions of dollars sitting in his fat bank accounts, and if he broke a priceless bottle of wine, he'd just buy another.

Scarlett watched as he eyed her mocha Frappuccino, her eyes narrowing as she dared him, just dared him to comment.

"That'll go straight to your hips." He grinned as he slugged back half of the drink Scarlett had ordered for him—dark-roast coffee, black. He had vices, many vices, but comfort food wasn't one of them.

And he also knew that Scarlett hadn't had as much success as she'd wanted in the world of ballet, because her figure wasn't "ideal." He regularly commented on this, but not because he agreed with those shadowy figures in Scarlett's past.

He thought she was plenty slender—even too much so. If her curvy hips and full breasts meant she couldn't dance, well, then it was their loss.

And so she wasn't upset by his comment, knowing it had come from Luca's heart.

"Fuck you," she replied mildly. She wasn't nearly as thin as she'd been as a ballerina, but she was a lot happier, so she considered it a fair trade. "It's my weekly treat. And I'll run it off anyway."

Yes, she was definitely happier, not stressing about every single bite that she put in her mouth. But she still had to battle to remind herself that apple slices could taste every bit as good as French fries.

"Didn't you have quite a treat the other night?" Luca pushed the bottle of wine aside so that he could get a better look at her face. Scarlett tried to will any emotional reaction from her expression, but Luca was a damned experienced Dom, and she knew she wasn't fooling anyone.

"That's not open for discussion," she warned, hiding her face behind her cup. She'd managed to avoid thinking about Logan for a good chunk of the last few days, since she'd been so busy packing. But Luca's reminder brought it all back, and now it felt like a heavy weight had settled in her stomach.

She had been sure that her disappointment would fade within a few days. So far, she'd been wrong.

Luca eyed Scarlett thoughtfully. She glared right back. The man might have trained her, but since they were both Dominant, they were equals, despite her lack of comparative experience.

Of course, they weren't at Veritas. But Scarlett was pretty sure that Luca would respect the boundary anyway.

He studied her for a long moment, those dark eyes taking in things she was sure she didn't want him to see. Walking away from Logan the other night had been one of the hardest things she'd ever had to do, and she was still feeling decidedly unsettled.

"I'll miss you, kiddo," Luca finally said, his face heartbreakingly handsome when he smiled. He was the type of man she was usually attracted to, Scarlett mused—swarthy good looks, a slick smile, a dirty sense of humor. Yes, she usually preferred that kind of man, not cowboys with scruff dusting their jaws, with tight asses in even tighter jeans, with challenge in their eyes.

Damn it.

"I'll visit," she said mildly. She'd have to if she wanted to experience her kind of sex. Montana didn't boast any major cities, and though she'd combed online sites, she hadn't found any hits for BDSM groups there, either. "And it's only for a year."

But right at that moment the thought of visiting Veritas—of playing in the club without Logan—made her want to stick a straw in the wine that Luca had brought and start slurping.

"Whenever you make it back, I have a submissive who is quite desperate for another scene with you." Luca grinned wickedly, wiggling his eyebrows. "In fact, after that paddling you administered in the bar this week, I suspect there's going to be an outbreak of broken hearts when I tell the subs that you're gone."

Scarlett rolled her eyes. Normally, she would be pleased that her skills had been admired.

But *normal* wasn't a word that applied to what had transpired between herself and that big cowboy.

She really didn't feel like telling Luca that, though, so she pretended to consider it when he told her it was Bren who was asking after her. She felt a flicker of surprise, not that the submissive had made any secret of his interest in her, but that he was so quietly persistent.

If she hadn't met Logan the night before, she might have been intrigued.

But she had. So she wasn't.

"I'd rather not start anything I can't finish right now," she finally said, hoping that she sounded convincing. The way Luca arched his eyebrow at her told her he wasn't buying it, but he let it slide the way he never would have if she had been a sub.

"Fair enough." Draining his coffee, Luca kicked back in

his chair, arms behind his head. Scarlett was amused to see most of the females and a few of the men in the shop not so surreptitiously eyeing the very large, very sexy man. "It's okay. I won't tell anyone that you're secretly pining away for me."

The smirk on his face made Scarlett consider, quite seriously, dumping her Frappuccino over his head. Finally deciding that would be a waste of whipped cream, she bent over, ostensibly to tug on the top of her boot, but really to let him see the tops of her breasts, which were displayed fairly chastely in her V-neck T-shirt, but she knew he would look.

He did and had the grace to smile wryly when she smacked him on the knee. "Babe, I'd eat you alive."

"I don't doubt it. You need someone strong like me, though . . . but someone who wants to let you be the bossy bitch you are in the bedroom," Luca replied, his lips curving into a smirk. "In fact, if you'd just let me matchmake, I know the perfect person for you."

"No. No more." Scarlett held up a hand, saw something uneasy flicker through her friend's eyes. She blinked, sure she'd imagined it, and then her cocksure friend was back, placing his feet in her lap, right in the middle of Starbucks, owning the small coffeehouse the way he commanded every place he went.

"I'm not going to see you for a while," he started, wiggling his feet in her lap. "So before you run off to Montana, let's have a good talk. I want to make this visit count."

CHAPTER SEVEN

The bottle that Luca had given her—a going-away gift from all three owners of In Vino Veritas—jostled on the passenger's seat of her Honda Civic as Scarlett maneuvered the vehicle over the gravel road that led through the front gate of her destination.

A weathered wooden sign with FOLSOM FARMS carved into it arched overhead, the posts gnarled, rough, and looking almost as though they had grown right out of the ground.

At the end of the rutted lane, with one hand on the pricey wine for safety, Scarlett pulled up in front of the large house that would be her home for the next year. Her mouth fell open slightly as she climbed from the car and got a good look at the structure . . . and at the massive dog lying on the front porch, an animal that was hairy and gray and nearly as big as she was.

The dog lifted his head, looked at her, and returned to his nap. Scarlett smiled, amused, and looked back at the house.

Made of the same rough wood as the front gate, the house wasn't as big as it had seemed at first glance. But almost the entire front of the building was made of glass—windows that stretched floor to ceiling—and the way the glass reflected the setting sun and the blazing sky cast an optical illusion, making things seem more open than they really were.

And they were plenty open already. Shading her eyes, Scarlett took a moment to stretch out the kinks from her long drive and to get the lay of the land.

So much land. Open, untouched, stretching out under the

endless Montana sky. The vast emptiness was fiercely beautiful—and more than a little unnerving, after the neon lights of Vegas.

"Hey there, big guy." When the massive dog finally roused himself, trundling over to say hello, Scarlett crouched down, eager for the company. "You must like having all this space to run around."

The dog sniffed her hand and promptly flopped down to the ground, rolling over to beg for a belly rub. Charmed, Scarlett buried her hands in the soft fur and indulged him.

"Oh, I see. You're more the type to just laze around and survey your kingdom." Scarlett laughed when the dog shook the fur out of his eyes and rolled them in delight. "Well, thank you for letting me come here to look after all of your royal subjects."

"That's Mongo. You've got his number already." An amused male voice made her jolt. "It's his house. I just live here."

Shading her eyes again—she'd left her sunglasses in the car—she rose to her feet and dusted her free hand on her jeans before holding it out. She'd been looking forward to meeting the supervisor of her veterinary internship in person for months.

When her eyes locked on the man who was staring at her, looking equally shell-shocked, she understood the pained expression that Luca had given her over coffee yesterday.

A jolt went through her as their eyes met. Damn it. That inexplicable connection between them was every bit as tangible as she'd remembered.

"I ... What ... ?" Uncharacteristically lost for words, Scarlett let her stare linger on the man whom she had last seen with a hard, lickable ass bent over a barstool.

"*You're* Dr. Logan Brody?"

Scarlett took a step forward—to do what exactly, she

wasn't sure—and wondered if she should throttle Luca or thank him.

Now she knew why he'd looked uneasy for a split second yesterday . . . He'd been at the club that night. He'd seen what had pulsed in the air between Scarlett and the beautiful blond man whom she'd topped.

Knew he'd sent her off to *live* in close quarters with that cowboy for the next year. And he hadn't said a damn word.

"S stands for *Scarlett*, then." Under her scrutiny, Logan stuffed his hands in the pockets of his worn jeans and stared back, his expression unreadable. "Or maybe for *sadist*. My ass is still sore. You have a hell of a swing."

"You said you wanted to feel it," she shot back, then found herself blushing. She *never* blushed.

But here it was, out in the open. And oh, what a cluster-fuck.

Her one-night stand, the man she'd admitted to wanting to break apart and build back up, was her boss for the next three hundred and sixty-five days. And though he had to have come to the same realization, he was just standing there, a hint of an insolent smile curling his lips.

In fact, he looked like he was enjoying the hell out of that notion—like he was relieved that their power struggle had finally flipped in his favor.

Scarlett's gaze raked over him hungrily. So many times in the last few days, she'd replayed their time in the club, wondering if she'd made the right decision by leaving without making plans for more than what they'd already shared. She'd wondered if she would ever see him again.

She wasn't upset about this turn of events, even though it complicated things greatly.

Logan looked mouthwatering, his jeans faded, ripped, and tight in all the right places. A slim-fitting black T-shirt stretched over the chest that she'd had her hands all over, and the boots she'd taken off of him herself were back on his feet.

Her fingers itched to touch him, to run her hands over those broad shoulders. She took another step forward, her new cowboy boots crunching on the gravel, and watched as a shutter that was damn near visible dropped down over his face.

It stopped her in her tracks.

He had let her top him inside the walls of Veritas, but out here—out here the rules were different. This delicious alpha male was her new supervisor, a fact that tilted their power exchange way off its axis.

"Bags in the trunk?" Logan finally asked. Scarlett strained to hear some kind of inflection in his voice—anything to let her know that he was feeling even part of what she was. But his face was set as he pulled her two suitcases from the car without even straining, though they had to weigh upward of sixty pounds each.

"I've got it." He waved her away when she reached for one, scowling until she backed off. Shrugging, she followed him into the house, though she did sneak a peek at the way his arm muscles flexed under the weight of her luggage.

But when he walked up the stairs ahead of her, her face was put right on level with the fine spectacle that was his ass. The fact that she'd seen that ass naked, touched it, *owned* it had Scarlett digging her nails into her palms in an attempt to keep her hands to herself.

"This one is yours, if it suits you." By the time Scarlett had followed Logan into a large, sparsely decorated bedroom, she was vibrating with lust. Realizing that he expected a response of some kind, she turned in a slow circle, taking in the wooden dresser, the patchwork quilt.

The wrought-iron headboard. An image of Logan spread

on the bed with his hands bound to those bars had dampness surging between Scarlett's legs.

She swallowed desperately. Oh man, this was so awkward. Mostly because all she wanted to do was jump him, and yet he stood there, as cool and composed as if they'd never met.

If he hadn't commented on his sore ass, she might have wondered if the man she'd met in the club had an evil twin.

"Well. I'll let you get settled in." Logan nodded once shortly. "I'll make some dinner. Come on down when you're ready."

He might have left like that, leaving Scarlett utterly bewildered, but he hesitated, then crossed his arms over that wide chest.

Body language 101, or so Luca had called it. Arms crossed over the chest . . . Logan was feeling just as disconcerted as she was.

What should she do? Be professional and pretend that what had happened between them . . . well, *hadn't*?

That was ridiculous. It *had* happened, and there was no going back. So Scarlett decided to take matters in hand. It was going to be one hell of a long year otherwise, because she wasn't going anywhere. She wanted this internship experience.

And it would be what they made of it. It didn't *have* to be awkward.

No, it could be downright delicious instead.

Bad, Scarlett. Bad.

But she couldn't look at the man and not remember how he'd felt inside of her.

"Are we going to address the situation?" Slowly, Scarlett pulled her arms from the sleeves of her fitted denim jacket. The posture arched her back, brought her breasts forward.

Logan's gaze flicked down, took in the view she was offering. He shifted, and Scarlett's eagle eyes watched his cock swell against the front of his jeans.

"You really want to start out this way?" He looked into her face, his expression set in stone, and for a long moment Scarlett felt her heart leap into her throat—he was going to reject her, and this was going to get even more awkward, if that was possible.

But how could he ignore it? That pull between them?

When she looked into those cerulean eyes and saw a hunger that mirrored her own, she understood that he was just as confused as she was. She couldn't help it—she smiled, a slow curve of the lips.

"You fight dirty." Logan growled, his gaze raking her up and down. Scarlett felt as though his hands had touched her in all the places his eyes had looked.

And with those words, the admission of the need vibrating beneath his sneer, that delicate balance of power shifted yet again. Triumph, relief, washed through her.

Scarlett drew herself up tall and placed her hands on her hips. "On your knees."

That twist of his lips faded for a moment—with shock, Scarlett assumed—and then it was back.

"We're not at Veritas, little girl." He took a step toward her—crowding her, trying to take some power back. "You don't give the orders here."

Scarlett didn't move.

"But if you want me, all you have to do is say so." Another step—now he was close enough that she could feel the heat emanating off his skin.

And she felt that connection snap back into place like it hadn't been three days since they'd rocketed each other into a state of bliss.

"I said, on your knees." He didn't move; neither did she.

Her mind raced, trying to think of a way to make him submit that didn't involve physical force.

His chin tilted up with defiance, pride, and it hit her. A big, stubborn alpha like this—she hit him in his Achilles' heel.

"I'd have thought a big, tough cowboy would be man enough for a real Mistress," she taunted, twisting her lips into a wicked smile. "But maybe you can't handle anything more than a little playmate who has no idea how to top you."

Logan's spine stiffened, and victory lit her up when she saw the flash of anger in his eyes.

Challenge accepted.

"You're kind of a bitch, aren't you?" There was no heat in his words—it was merely an observation he offered as he finally sank to his knees, shifting to look up at her.

"Arms behind your head," she said quietly, savoring the rush of power that came from obedience—from *this man's* obedience. "Head down."

Another pause, a mutinous glare, and then he did as she said. Scarlett looked at him for a long moment, noted the tension and the desire stringing him tight.

She also noted that his cock had swollen to full hardness as they'd interacted, telling her that, at his most base level, he wanted this. In fact, it looked like he wanted it so much that it was damn uncomfortable.

"Don't move. Not even an inch." She'd just let him think on that for a few minutes. And allow time for her to compose herself, to think about what all of this meant now.

She'd been kicking herself for days over leaving him behind, never dreaming that he hadn't lived in Vegas, too. And here fate had smacked a second chance down in her lap.

She just had to reconcile that with how badly she wanted to learn while she was here.

"I heard you the first time." Logan glared at her, and Scarlett raised an eyebrow to hide her amusement.

She turned to the purse she'd tossed on the bed, rummaged through it, then returned to Logan with a bandanna.

"Don't you dare," he spat as she folded it into a long strip. His muscles twitched, like he was fighting the urge to stand.

"When I tell you to kneel, I expect you to embrace the posture fully. That means no fighting it. Not even with words." He narrowed his eyes at her; she returned the expression, then pressed the folded cloth over his mouth.

"Fuck!" Logan tried to pull away, but Scarlett hooked a leg over one of his shoulders, pressing the softness of her belly against his face, offering him the heat of the place that ached between her legs.

The distraction paid off. Logan stilled, his nostrils flaring. Scarlett flushed a bit, knowing that he was scenting the musk of her arousal.

She pushed through the small wave of discomfort at the sudden intimacy between them, since he'd done what she wanted. While he was distracted, she swiftly slid the gag over his mouth, worked it between his lips, then tied it snugly behind his head.

He growled, his eyes throwing little daggers her way.

"Do it completely, or don't do it at all," she reminded him. "And if you choose not to do it, sniff three times loudly to get my attention." Turning her back in a purposeful dismissal, Scarlett reached for the zipper on one of the suitcases that Logan had lugged upstairs for her. She felt Logan's presence behind her, demanding her attention, and it took everything in her not to turn around.

Instead, she focused on keeping her fingers from shaking as she pulled out her toy bag. She'd thrown it in at the last minute, unable to leave it behind, even though most of her things were going into storage . . . and even though she hadn't anticipated having much use for it for the next year.

Now the feel of the familiar, supple leather beneath her fingers calmed the voice in her head that was screaming that it was a bad idea to start her internship this way. What had happened to getting off on a solid professional footing? But instinct had taken over, scenting her mate, and she was pretty sure she couldn't have stopped herself if she'd tried.

She wasn't trying very hard.

Opening the small bag, she selected a length of hemp rope that was soft to the touch yet would still chafe if he pulled against it.

She watched Logan's gaze flick up to her briefly when she approached him, rope in hand, but he dropped his eyes again just as quickly.

Scarlett remained silent as she circled behind him, knelt, and took a moment to look her fill.

Even from behind, he took her breath away. Broad shoulders, a back rippled with muscle that caused his T-shirt to pull tight . . . not to mention the taut globes of his ass, outlined clearly in the faded denim.

That entire magnificent body tensed when Scarlett removed his boots, setting them neatly aside. Logan's breath huffed out when she traced the edge of her thumbnail down the center of the soles of his feet, hard enough to keep it from tickling, waking up all the nerves.

"Huh." A grunt, then a short shudder worked through Logan's frame when Scarlett wound the rope around his ankles. She had to focus on this, for though Luca had taught her some rope skills, it wasn't something she was well practiced with.

But as she wound the rope between Logan's legs, up over each hip, then behind him to secure his hands behind his back, she watched the rope outline his body and felt a deep satisfaction. It was not so different from seeing a sub's skin reddened from her hand.

It was a visible mark of possession. It made her blood flow hotter in her veins.

"Think you can hold that pose awhile longer?" It was a rhetorical question, since she'd bound him so that he couldn't move. But she wanted to poke at his pride a bit more, to remind him that he was here, like this, because she wanted him to be.

He nodded, the movement a sharp jerk, lifting his focus to her face. Though his lips were pressed together, his eyes were full of banked . . . anger, certainly. But also need.

Scarlett held on to the latter as she turned away and began to unpack her suitcases, leaving him as he was, bound on the floor.

A strangled shout emanated from behind her, then a thump that could only mean he had knocked himself over onto the floor. Her heart leapt—instinct told her to turn around, to right him, to make sure he was okay.

You know he's fine, Scar. He knows how to let you know if he needs to stop.

She knew she was pissing him right the hell off. And she also knew that that was maybe not the smartest move, since he was now her boss.

But the damage had been done the second they'd set eyes on each other outside of Veritas. All they could do was go forward. And to do that, they needed to figure out each other's boundaries.

Breathing deeply to calm herself, she picked up a stack of T-shirts, then turned.

Logan was lying on the floor now, still bound, every muscle in his body tensed to what must have been the point of pain. The anger, the helplessness in his eyes made Scarlett's pulse skip a beat.

Trust your gut.

"Three sniffs," she reminded him, then carried the shirts to the wooden dresser. She had to step over him as she went, and his body jerked as she did.

Better hope those knots hold, Scar. That's one pissed-off cowboy.

Scarlett moved back and forth in the room as she unpacked, acting as though Logan were no more than a big box on the ground that was in her way, though she was hyperaware of him at every moment. Her footsteps seemed to soothe him into calmness. The tension melted out of his body, finally leaving him with nothing more than a wary look in his eyes.

Finished unpacking, Scarlett methodically zipped her suitcases back up before stowing them away in the closet. Then she clasped her hands on the rope behind Logan's back and helped him back to a kneeling position. She checked the color of his fingertips—still pink, still healthy—before untying his gag.

He spat it to the floor as she made her way to the bed. Sitting down on the edge of it, she kicked her legs back and forth playfully, her eyes looking him over, trying to assess his mental state.

The wariness was still there, but when she'd ungagged him, a big dose of defiance had returned as well. Heat churned in Scarlett's gut when she realized just how much work this man was going to be.

Good thing she was up to the challenge.

Those deep blue eyes of his met hers, glared into them. She smiled in return.

"You look nervous, Logan." She kept her tone light and lilting. "Would you like to tell me about it?"

Logan leered at her in return. "I'm afraid my Mistress won't let me taste her pussy."

Scarlett wanted to crow with triumph—even here, on his turf, as they were fighting to establish dominance, he'd referred to her as his Mistress.

But she smothered the elation behind a massive show of disappointment. God, this was going to be one tough stallion to break in, but he was sure going to make her life interesting while she did it.

And suddenly that was clear to her. Whatever this was between them, it was big enough, strong enough, that they weren't going to be able to tuck it away on a shelf for the next year.

They were just going to have to find a way to reconcile work and . . . *this*. She couldn't see any other way. He would lead her outside on the job, and she hoped he would allow her to control things when they played in the bedroom.

Heart tripping with anticipation, Scarlett bent forward, ran her fingers over his lips.

"Fate has given us a freakish second chance to explore this thing between us," she said mildly, though her brain substituted the word *Luca* for *fate*. "So are you going to be an asshole, or are you going to let me in? Because I'm not looking for something casual. I'm looking for a partner."

Her nerves hitched a bit as she spoke. Even in the BDSM lifestyle, not a lot of men—or even women—were thrilled to hear those words from a potential partner. And while it was absolutely what she wanted, she hadn't expected to feel so much for someone *now*.

But it was the truth, and Scarlett couldn't expect honesty from a sub if she held it back from him.

She wanted the white picket fence, and she wasn't going to settle for less. Not that it would happen in the end with Logan— they barely knew each other—but this thing between them seemed like it had the potential to be so much more.

And it was best to start as you meant to continue.

Scarlett expected some smart quip from Logan—expected him to use her vulnerable words to try to wrestle power back. Her heart thumped in her chest when he opened his mouth to speak, then closed it again, his expression tinged with confusion.

"This is my ranch, my home. I'm the boss here," he said finally, and he seemed surprised by his own words. "I don't know if I *can* let go."

Scarlett wanted to grab him, kiss him, and hold him tight forever.

Instead she kept her lips to herself as she methodically released him from the ropes.

The second she did, he was on her, framing her face in those large, work-roughened hands, claiming her lips with his own.

For a long moment she let herself be swept away in that kiss, which reminded her of everything that had transpired between them the night they'd met. It filled her with need, every bit of her.

But instead of opening her mouth when his tongue demanded entrance, she managed to get her bearings, then sank her teeth sharply into his lower lip.

"Fuck me!" Logan sprang back, slapping a hand to his mouth. He stood, anger vibrating from every inch of that long, rangy form. "What the fuck was that for?"

Scarlett stood, too, keeping her hands at her sides, though she wanted to cross them over her chest. She couldn't show him any weakness, any defensiveness.

But that kiss had shaken her. How could someone she barely knew make her feel this way?

"Go to your room. You're going to pleasure yourself with nothing more than your hand." The surprise on Logan's face at her words made her bite the insides of her cheeks with dark amusement. "You'll think of me when you come. You'll have to figure out what I expect from you before you'll be allowed inside me again."

The expression crossing Logan's face was indecipherable.

"Help yourself to whatever's in the kitchen tonight," he finally spat out. "And we start work at six a.m. Don't be late."

Then he was gone.

CHAPTER EIGHT

ogan couldn't sleep.

How could he, when his cock was still hard as a rock, even hours later, and arousal haunted every breath that he drew?

He was still stunned that he'd knelt for her when she'd commanded it—here, in his own home. His instinct had been to refuse, to see if he could seduce her on his own terms.

I'd have thought a big, tough cowboy would be man enough for a real Mistress.

The way she'd phrased that . . . She'd told him that if he wasn't strong enough to submit, then he wasn't the man for her. It had played right into the desire, the all-consuming need that had seized him the second he'd seen her.

Though his brain had shouted at him to stop, his body had obeyed.

"Exasperating woman." Shoving the quilt aside, Logan let his hands curl around the length of his arousal. Forgoing dinner, he'd locked himself in his room as soon as Scarlett—as soon as *Mistress*—had given him leave to go. He'd stripped and fallen into bed, allowing his mind to run over and over the events that had just occurred, but he was still resisting her order.

You're going to pleasure yourself with nothing more than your hand.

As the familiar sounds of the ranch settling in for the night wove around him, his body ached for the release that Scarlett had commanded. But how could he settle for his hand when he already knew just how soft and warm and wet she was?

The memory sent another wave of need through him, painful in its intensity, and Logan groaned as he tightened his grip on the base of his cock.

He wanted her—he wanted everything she promised, everything she could give him. But he had nothing to offer in return.

He just didn't let people in as much as she demanded. He couldn't.

He was tied here, to the wide-open spaces, the big skies that let him breathe, that let him find as much peace as he'd ever been able to.

No matter what she said she was looking for, she wouldn't stay. No one did—and she was a city girl. Had big plans to open an animal hospital back in Nevada—that was the entire reason she'd agreed to the internship with him.

And he wouldn't—couldn't—blame her for going.

But what would it be like to have an actual relationship with a woman again? He'd dated a bit to keep up appearances in town, and then there were his once-yearly visits to Veritas. But he hadn't had a *girlfriend* since before . . .

Since before the need for all this wide-open space had worked its way inside of him.

But he could so easily picture Scarlett here, her eyes focused on nothing but him as she stripped him naked, then bound him to the fence that bordered the horse corral. He could picture that willowy body of hers arching as she commanded him to turn, to brace himself for her blows.

He couldn't hold back anymore. With a groan, Logan pulled the bottle of lube from his bedside table, squirted some into his palm, then began to pump the erection that was by now swollen to the point of pain.

Yes, he could picture it so perfectly in his mind's eye. It would be twilight, and the sky would be painted with streaks of blueberry and rose. It would set the scene perfectly as she wielded a deer-hide flogger, raining blows over his back and his ass to warm up the skin, to awaken the nerves.

He could almost feel the flogger now, shooting pinpricks of pleasure and pain through the cock that jerked beneath his hand.

She would begin to flog him harder, the stinging bites flicking over the sensitive spot where his legs met his ass or between his thighs. He would want to come from that alone, but she would make him wait.

In this fantasy, because he was hers, she would slide a silicone ring over his cock, the way she had back at Veritas. She would help him to sit, maybe on a bale of hay covered with a blanket.

Then she would lift her skirt and let him taste her. She would command him to make her come before darkness fell, if he wanted to be inside of her.

Logan's breath began to come in fast pants. The lubricant turned his fist into a warm, wet cavern, pulling at his cock in a facsimile of a cunt, but never coming close to the pleasure of the real thing.

If he was hers, once he'd licked her to climax, she would straddle his lap. She would position the head of his cock at the entrance to her pussy, would take him in, giving that little wiggle that showed she had to work at it, but that she wouldn't settle for any less than all of him.

She would begin to move on top of him, those slender but surprisingly strong thighs working her up and down on his erection, bringing his climax closer and closer. He would be bound; he wouldn't be able to do anything but take it as her pussy milked his release from him.

She might even reach behind him, slide her fingers between the cheeks of his ass. She might rub it over that tight bundle of nerves that made his orgasm gather in the base of his spine before exploding out of his cock.

And because he was hers, he would let her. He wouldn't have to hold back from being vulnerable.

She would know him inside and out.

The fantasy plus the reality of his fist hitting all the right spots in a way that only someone's own hand could do was too much. Frantically, he grabbed for the T-shirt lying on his pillow with his free hand, covered his cock and the hand that he was using to jerk himself off at high speed.

He couldn't hold back the shout as he thrust into his fist once, twice, the worn cotton catching his release. He lay still for a long moment, his breath shuddering in and out.

Unless he could think of a way to fully submit to the fascinating woman who would be living in his house for the next year, this was all he could have—his fist on his own cock and the ghost of Scarlett in his head.

The thought had unease roiling in his gut. But sleep managed to find him, and he finally drifted off.

Tossing the T-shirt aside, he pulled the covers back up. He pictured Scarlett's face, her lips curved in a sweet smile that told him he'd done well.

And when he dreamed, he dreamed of her.

The low growl of her agitated best friend sounded in Scarlett's ear as she answered her cell phone while climbing into bed. "You were supposed to call me when you got in."

Unable to look at the floor without imagining Logan bound up in her rope, she turned the light off and rolled over, fixing the phone to her other ear.

"I was a bit preoccupied," she replied, her voice all sweetness and light. "Did you forget to tell me something? A really big something?"

"I didn't forget anything."

Scarlett could have reached through the phone and wrapped her hands around Luca's neck.

"You knew. You knew that my internship supervisor was at Veritas that night, and you didn't warn me." Scarlett inhaled deeply, then let the breath out, trying to calm herself down. "If you weren't so goddamn big, I'd drive back to Vegas and shove a six-inch dildo up your ass while you sleep. This is so ... so ... incredibly *weird*."

Yeah. Especially because you tied him up, then sent him to jack off by himself as soon as you were in the door, Scar.

Well, there were things that even best friends didn't need to know.

"So what you're saying is that if you had known who Logan was that night, you wouldn't have approached him like you did?" Luca asked her, all traces of teasing gone from his voice.

"I—" Scarlett wanted to lie. She wanted to say that she would have just found someone else to play with, because she needed to keep things professional.

But the truth was, no matter how many other delicious, available subs had been in the club that night—and there had been plenty—she would have wanted Logan. Would have chosen him out of all the rest, even knowing what she knew now.

The connection between them had been a palpable thing, tugging them together.

"Precisely," Luca replied, his voice full of deadly calm. "And just try to put any kind of dildo anywhere but in my hand, and I'll flog the creamy skin of your delectable ass so hard that you can't sit down for a week."

"Try it," Scarlett snapped back. They sat in silence for a long moment, Scarlett fuming, and she assumed Luca was doing the same—you didn't threaten an experienced Dom with a sadistic bent unless you were either very far away or very crazy.

As her temper cooled a bit, Scarlett realized that she was both.

"Sorry," she finally muttered. "I'll withhold the dildo. But I'm still annoyed. Why didn't you tell me?"

"Fate did this, not me, pet." Under normal circumstances, Scarlett would have bristled at the nickname—she might have trained with Luca, but she was a Dominant too—but she knew he didn't mean it to belittle her. "So you need to calm down."

"But you gave me the referral. Even if Logan and I hadn't met, you knew that I was coming out here to live with a big, gorgeous submissive. You could have warned me."

"I gave you the recommendation before you beat Mistress Avery off of him." Luca's voice still held a hint of irritation. "And it's not my place to share details about someone else's sexual preferences, Scarlett. If you don't understand that, then I haven't trained you very well at all."

Scarlett sucked in a shocked gasp—Luca's blow had hit home.

It was an unspoken rule in the lifestyle. If you ran into someone you knew in the club on the street, you pretended you didn't know them. Even if you'd had someone's cock in your mouth the night before, if they served you your coffee at the local Starbucks the next morning, you didn't breathe a word about their preferences unless they gave you permission to.

"And for what it's worth, I didn't anticipate that the two of you would—ah—*connect* the way you did," Luca continued. "Fate's a sneaky bitch sometimes."

"No shit." Flopping onto her back, Scarlett raked a hand through her hair. Kicking off her covers, she stretched one leg out above her at ninety degrees, then clasped a hand around her thigh and brought it in toward her chest.

Ever since she'd first donned ballet slippers, stretching had helped her to relax. And right now, with confusion and irritation and an unholy ache between her thighs, she could use all the relaxation that she could get.

"So what's the problem, exactly?" Luca asked. "Apart from the fact that he's your internship supervisor. You've already got your degree. You're Dr. Scarlett Malone, veterinary superstar. He can't take that away from you, and he wouldn't. You're coworkers who have the hots for each other. And now you're together in that big ranch house. And barn. Lots of places to tie someone up in a barn. Maybe do some branding."

"For fuck's sake, Luca." The laugh barked out of Scarlett's throat. "Only you would want to use a cow brand for scarification. No, thank you."

Letting her thoughts turn over in her head, she pondered Luca's question. What was the big problem? Shouldn't she have been happier that the universe had given her a second chance with the man she wanted more than anyone she'd ever met?

And she was happy. But mixed with that joy was pure terror.

"I already have feelings for him," she admitted finally. His face, full of wariness as he lay bound on the hardwood floor, flickered behind her closed eyes. "Which doesn't make any sense, I know. But I want him . . . Well, it's more than simple want. And . . ."

Scarlett hesitated. That dominant streak in her hated to admit failure, but she knew that doing so would allow her to be a good Domme.

"I don't know if I'll be able to take him where he needs to go," she said softly, feeling her pulse stutter. "He's got so many walls up. And I want to help him tear them down. But . . . I don't know if he's going to let me in."

And if he doesn't, he'll break my fucking heart.

There was silence on the other end of the line. Finally, Luca responded.

"We never know, do we?" His voice was raw and open in a way it hadn't been earlier. "Even in the vanilla world—love is about taking a chance on someone."

The word *love* made Scarlett's body tighten.

"I don't lov—" she started to say, but Luca cut her off.

"And speaking as someone who knows you both. If anyone can get that stubborn asshole to submit, Scar, it's you."

CHAPTER NINE

"Now, that's a nice visual, baby."

Scarlett almost dropped the towel she'd been wrapping around her body at the sudden presence behind her. She did screech and jump about a foot. Though the air of the bathroom was still thick with steam from her shower, she could make out Logan's rangy form clearly.

Fully dressed, he leaned against the doorframe, arms crossed, eyes fixed on Scarlett. A quick burst of temper that he'd intruded when she was showering, while she was naked and vulnerable, snapped through her.

He needed to learn some manners. If he was going to spy on her in the shower at five thirty in the morning, then he damn well better have a mug of coffee for her in his hand. A *big* one.

"Remember what I said about manners, sub?" Arching an eyebrow in a look of pure challenge, Scarlett let her towel fall to the floor.

Logan blinked in surprise as she stood, ramrod stiff, and let the droplets of water trickle down her body.

It was to his credit, she supposed, that he didn't reach out to touch her, or gape like a fish.

"You're not the boss here," he said finally. Scarlett got a twisted pleasure from watching him struggle to pull his stare up to her face . . . and to keep it there.

For payback, she left the towel on the floor and continued the conversation buck naked.

"When it comes to work, I'm not the boss," she corrected him, arching her back a little to push her breasts forward. His stare flickered down, then back up as he hissed in a breath. "But if we do this, anything outside of work, I am your Mistress."

"You fight dirty," he growled, uncrossing his arms and fisting his hands at his sides. After flicking a cautious gaze at her expression, Logan let his stare rake over her entire naked frame, up and down.

"If you can handle it," she added, not bothering to hold back her smirk when he scowled. Daring to push him a little further, she left the towel on the floor, then made her way toward the door. She had to brush up against him to get through the doorway, and she arched her hip into his pelvis as she sauntered by.

A pained hiss escaped his lips when she rubbed over his cock, which was hard and pressing against the front of his jeans. Scarlett felt a dark thrill of satisfaction.

"When I said we start at six, I was referring to a normal day," Logan called after her, and Scarlett stopped, whipping her wet hair to the side so that she could look back at him. "Today I have a few things to show you before we break for breakfast. I'll see you downstairs at twenty to."

"I can't get ready in ten minutes." She'd never considered herself very high maintenance, but she'd anticipated having at least the time to apply enough makeup that she felt armored against everything that Logan tended to bring out in her.

With this ornery sub, she needed every tool she had at her disposal.

"On the job . . ." he said quietly, and Scarlett's stomach did a slow roll at the reminder.

When it came to the ranch, he was the boss. And though it pained her to cede the point, she'd agreed.

"I'll be down in ten," she snapped. She was more annoyed

that Logan had somehow gotten the upper hand in this one, even though she'd managed to thoroughly disconcert him by letting that towel drop.

He was sneaky. And as she slid into her bedroom and closed the door, she realized that she'd just have to be sneakier.

Though Scarlett didn't wear a lot of makeup when she was outside of the club, she almost always wore at least some. Making the decision to leave her face bare gave her a few pangs—her skin was clear, but she still liked the look of it better with a smooth coat of foundation. And she was pale, washed-out without a bit of eyeliner and some lip gloss.

But as she smoothed a hand over the wet hair that she'd pulled back into a severe bun, she reminded herself that she was making a deliberate statement.

She'd be willing to dig down deep into the depths of her soul to explore this connection between them . . . if Logan would go there with her.

Besides, she thought on a mental shrug as she pushed through the swinging door that led into the kitchen, the cows wouldn't care.

Logan was sitting in a chair that he had turned around backward and straddled. He looked good enough to eat.

Scarlett swallowed that thought. With a meaningful glance at the clock that hung over the sink, she arched an eyebrow as she entered, though her naked face made her feel vulnerable.

"See? On time."

"Good." He stood, moving across the kitchen to snag his cowboy hat from its place on the counter. When he placed it on his head and turned back to Scarlett, she saw the alpha in him come out to play.

Watching him assume that mantle of power was sexy as hell, showing her that he was strong, strong enough to be with her.

Her mouth went dry as she watched him transform into the hardworking rancher, the doctor, and a sexy-as-sin man all at once.

Her pulse skittered when he reached into his back pocket because the motion pushed his pelvis forward and drew her eyes to the outline of his cock.

"Get your eyes off my dick," Logan drawled, and Scarlett looked up, flushing. He'd caught her. "You can see more of it later, if you're lucky."

But she refused to be embarrassed. He was a good-looking man; they were well aware of their mutual attraction. Still, she was unnerved that she'd let go of her control enough to do something as silly as ogling his package.

She had to find some kind of balance to make this work.

"I'll decide that," she reminded him, then nodded to the black-and-white bandanna that now dangled from his fingers. "Trying to gag me will not tip those odds in your favor."

"You'll need this. Every day. Protects you from the dust." Stepping into place behind her, Logan began to tie the bandanna around her throat.

"Ask me," Scarlett whispered, her voice husky even to her own ears. "Ask for permission."

She cringed as she spoke. Damn it. She was supposed to let him be the one in charge right now. It just didn't come naturally to her—and maybe that was how he felt when she insisted that he submit.

She couldn't see him during the pause that followed, couldn't read from his face what he was thinking. Wondered if she'd made a fatal error.

"May I help you with this?" There was a taunting edge to

his words, but that was it—just an edge. As if he was clinging to the control he had while he could.

"Call me *Mistress* first, then proceed." Scarlett held her breath in indecision—would this insistence on formality push him too far, break the magic of the moment?

To her surprise, he bent over her shoulder, pressed his lips to the seashell curve of her ear.

"Mistress," he whispered, his hot breath fanning over the sensitive lobe. A shiver zipped down her spine, and it wasn't soothed when he laid the folded strip of cotton over the width of her throat.

Strong fingers followed its length over the soft skin of her neck. When he reached the nape of her neck, he tied it in a precise knot.

"Ready?" Logan tilted his hat at an angle, looking like an ad for old-fashioned cigarettes. Scarlett's lips quirked—did he mean the question to have multiple layers?

She was ready to start her internship, yes.

But she wasn't at all sure that either of them were ready for *this*.

"Come on." Logan's words came out harsh enough that Scarlett found herself jerking back from the tender touch. It was hard to make out the emotions playing across his face beneath the wide brim of his hat, but she suspected that even if she'd had a clear view, she wouldn't have seen much.

As if he'd pressed an off switch, all of the aching need that had passed between them vanished. Logan nodded as though she truly were nothing more to him than a new intern he'd just met, then made to leave the kitchen.

But he did motion for her to go first, a gesture that wasn't lost on her.

The second she stepped outside, Scarlett was struck anew

by the vast openness of the land. So much open space after the confines of city living made her shiver, a bit of strange unease working its way in.

"Does it ever freak you out, being out here all alone?" Turning, Scarlett saw that Logan had strode on ahead of her. Sighing with exasperation, she hurried after him, repeating her question.

Tilting back the brim of his hat, he stared at her, features set in stone. He looked cold enough that Scarlett would have taken a step back, if she hadn't already discovered another side of this man entirely.

"I'm not sure what you mean, exactly, by *freak me out*, since I'm no longer twenty years old." Scarlett's mouth fell open as the barb struck her. "But assuming you mean, do I wish I lived closer to people, then no. I don't. I like to be alone."

Resuming his pace, he continued to point out the various buildings as they passed them. "Chicken coop. Storage shed. Stables, with tack room."

Mind playing catch-up, Scarlett kept pace with him, staying right by his elbow, which, given the sidelong glance he gave her, was annoying the hell out of him.

Good. He deserved it after that comment about her age. She was young, sure, but she was certainly not immature.

"If you like to be alone so much, then why did you offer up an internship?" Scarlett scowled to herself as she tried to keep up with Logan's long-legged strides. "Pardon me, but that doesn't seem like the smartest of ideas if you're looking for solitude."

Having reached the door to the stables, Logan stopped abruptly, turning to face Scarlett. Tipping his hat back again, he scrubbed a hand over his face, then looked her in the eyes, expression set.

"I didn't offer it. Luca called and said he knew of someone

who could really use the experience out here and that he highly recommended I take her on."

Scarlett's mouth fell open, and embarrassment heated her skin.

"You . . . Oh my God." She wasn't used to being disconcerted, and she didn't much care for the feeling. In that moment, she could have cheerfully whipped Luca with his strongest whip.

The damn Dom had engineered this whole thing. He'd wanted Scarlett out here, with Logan. For a full year.

Scarlett wanted to be here.

Logan was the only one who wasn't in agreement. But still . . .

"Why on earth did you agree if you don't want someone here?" Her words were barely more than a whisper. What he'd told her had pulled the rug out from under her feet.

She'd given up so much to come to Montana—a potential job, an apartment and roommate she loved, all of her friends.

Logan released an exasperated breath, then removed his hat entirely. His free hand raked through his hair, and Scarlett found herself distracted by the way the early-morning sun shone off the golden strands.

"Luca and I go way back. Pretty much anything he asks of me, I'll do." His stoic expression was infuriating—Scarlett felt like she'd been sucker punched in the gut.

Furious, she planted her hands on her hips and glared up at Logan. The early-morning sun was harsh, blinding her, but she didn't care.

"What the hell am I supposed to do now?" Frustration laced her words. "Why did you tell me this? I was counting on this internship. And now you tell me that you don't want me here."

Scarlett thought of how she'd behaved since arriving—

carrying on with their fledgling relationship—and shuddered.

Logan looked taken aback, the startled expression melting into a scowl. "Don't twist my words around." He took a step toward her, catching her under the elbows, and Scarlett felt that clutch in her heart that occurred whenever he was around.

"I'm not twisting anything. You just told me that Luca made you take me on. Oh God. He didn't set you up to come on to me in the club, did he?" Horror dawned even as she clung to reality.

She wouldn't put it past Luca to interfere to that extent, but he'd told her he hadn't and she believed him. More than that, she felt, deep down in her gut, that there was no way to fake this kind of attraction.

Logan growled low in his throat, and the fingers holding her elbows squeezed. "I'm going to pretend that you didn't say that." His voice was quiet; Scarlett felt ashamed.

"I'm sorry. This is all just a bit of a shock—" She bit off her words, and nearly her tongue, when Logan shook her, just the tiniest bit.

"Just shut up for one damn minute." Those amazing blue eyes blazed down into hers, and Scarlett felt her stomach do a slow roll.

"I said that I like being alone. I do. And I said that Luca had put me up to this internship. That's true, too." His words were gravelly and he sounded sincere. Scarlett tried to look down, but he caught her chin and forced her to look back up— something she'd done to him before, which emphasized this strange push-pull of their relationship.

"But I never once said that I don't want to have you here." Releasing her so abruptly that Scarlett felt as though she'd been dropped from fifty feet, Logan slammed his cowboy hat back on his head. With one arm—*stop ogling his biceps, Scar-lett*—he gestured toward the rest of the yard.

"Explore on your own. I'm going to cook. I'm hungry." Striding away, he called back over his shoulder, "Be in the kitchen in half an hour, or you don't eat."

Scarlett was left standing speechless in the yard. Who, she wondered, was going to come out on top of this one?

As soon as she entered the house, the smell of bacon and eggs and, best of all, coffee greeted her. She hadn't bothered to come forage for dinner last night, too wound up to eat, so it was the first time she'd seen the kitchen.

The counters were a dark blue beneath walnut cupboards. Very masculine, it might have seemed too dark, too closed in, if not for another one of those gigantic windows, letting in the spectacular light.

She'd intended to say something to Logan right away—it had even been on the tip of her tongue—but the view of the bright blue sky, stretching over the jagged mountain peaks, was astounding.

"Takes a while to get used to it." Scarlett turned when Logan spoke, and she caught the barest hint of wistfulness on his face—one of the few times she'd seen him unguarded.

The walls seemed to come back up between them when she started to step toward the small oilcloth-covered table at which Logan sat. She took her time, observing the way he'd laid out breakfast ... observing him.

Despite their arguing, he'd made not just scrambled eggs, but omelets with large chunks of onion, mushrooms, and to-matoes. The bacon was perfectly fried, and there were even slices of orange, fanned out prettily, along the edge of the plate.

Not what she'd expected from this rough, tough, pissed-off cowboy.

"Well, this is unexpected." Before she had a chance to chicken out, Scarlett reached across him to the plates and broke off a piece of bacon, which she pressed to his lips. "I was expecting a box of Cap'n Crunch."

Logan's eyes narrowed with suspicion as Scarlett offered him the bite of food. He continued to look at her, face set, as he opened his lips, chewed, then swallowed.

"We're not on personal time right now." He reached for his own piece of bacon, and Scarlett tentatively pushed his hand away, her confidence growing when he didn't push back.

"We most certainly are," Scarlett insisted. Taking his fork in hand, she scooped up a bite of fluffy eggs, held it to his lips. "It pleases me to feed you."

"Shouldn't you be making me serve you?" His eyes roamed her face, and though Scarlett really, really wished she had some makeup on—particularly in the unforgiving bright light of early morning—she held herself still and let him look.

Though the continual shifts of power between them made her more uncertain than she'd ever been, she steeled herself to push through, wanting to show him that being a bit vulnerable wasn't the end of the world.

Shaking her head slightly, Scarlett slid into his lap, thighs spread wide, facing him.

"A power exchange doesn't necessarily mean I'm looking for a slave, Logan, though that does work for some people." The next bite that Scarlett picked up was for her, a slice of juicy orange. "And I think you'll find that many Dominants find great joy in nurturing their sub."

She nibbled at the lush piece of fruit, and the juice ran down her hand. Without asking permission, Logan dipped his head, licked up the stream of sweetness from her skin.

He looked at her after, waiting for her reaction. That was good. So Scarlett didn't chastise him for acting on his own. But then, before she could even recover from the sensation of his tongue rasping over the tender skin at the inside of her wrist, he moved his hands up to cover her breasts.

Scarlett lifted her hand and lightly slapped his cheek, just hard enough to get his attention. He wrapped her wrists in his hands, holding her firmly in place.

Scarlett's pulse began to pound as she looked him in the eye, saw a man every bit as alpha as she was reflected there.

What was it about him that drove her so crazy, in the best possible way?

Submitting had to be a choice for him, she understood in that moment, and it was one he wouldn't make lightly.

All she could do was show him that she was strong enough to take care of him.

"If you can't keep your hands to yourself until I give you leave to do otherwise, sit on them." She didn't struggle, didn't try to wrench her hands away. She simply waited, doing her best to appear calm despite the complicated feelings swirling inside of her.

When he finally, slowly, let his hands fall to his sides and bent his head, his surrender was so beautiful that Scarlett wanted to wrap her arms around his shoulders, to bury her face in his neck and never let go. And that she wanted to just hold him even more than she wanted to undo his jeans and take him inside her was yet another reminder of how very different he was from every submissive, every other *man* she'd ever come across.

Instinct told her that pushing the emotional side of things too hard, too fast might make him shut down. So she swallowed down the enormity of what she was feeling and returned to their game.

Picking up another piece of bacon, she lifted it to his lips. "Eat."

For another ten minutes, they ate in silence, Scarlett feeding Logan bites in between her own. A couple of times he swiped his tongue over the sensitive tips of her fingers as she pressed segments of orange to his lips, and he shifted beneath her every few minutes, which pressed his hardening cock up against the growing dampness between her legs.

By the time eight o'clock came, Scarlett was quivering with need, and she could feel Logan's erection, thick and hard between them. She could have had him in that moment, she knew. She could open his zipper, pull his impossible length out. Could take him inside her and rock them both into bliss.

But she'd promised. When they were on work time, he was the boss. So though it hurt to push the lust aside, she swung off his lap, put some distance between them.

"What next . . . boss?"

CHAPTER TEN

Logan didn't keep an office—the very idea of sitting in a closed building for hours at a time made him shudder. Though his predecessor had kept an office in town, Logan did his work on location and kept his cell on him—people in the small town and the surrounding farmland knew to reach him that way if they needed his veterinary skills.

Today had been utterly silent on the vet side of things. It wasn't entirely unusual—it was early fall. Not yet calving season, not breeding season, and not winter, when the animals tended to get sick.

He'd used the opportunity to push Scarlett hard at the chores, all the things they would be responsible for doing together for the next year. He hadn't expected her to balk at anything related to the animals—Dr. Scarlett Malone had come with excellent references from her professors.

But he had expected some sort of protest, or complaint, or *something* when they'd swept out the big barn, mucked out the stalls. When they'd rearranged the tack room and hauled bales of feed from the back of his truck.

He'd had seasonal workers twice the size of slender Scarlett who'd bitched and complained nonstop about the backbreaking work.

But this one? Nothing but questions, questions, and more questions—all of them eager.

If he'd met her in person during their interview for the internship, he could have avoided her at Veritas that first night they'd met—he would have known who she was. Now the one woman who intrigued him more than any woman ever had was living with him—in his personal space—for the next year.

There was no way to avoid her, and damn it, he didn't want to. But without that easy out, there was also no way to keep her from delving inside of him, from pushing him into places he didn't want to go.

By the time late afternoon rolled around, Logan's head was spinning. He had been sure that beneath that tough-as-nails Domme exterior there must have been something soft or weak. Something he could use as an excuse not to submit further to her.

But Scarlett seemed to give all of herself in everything she did. And rather than finding a reason to pull away, he was more fascinated by her than ever.

"We're done for now." Rocking back on his heels, Logan swiped his forearm across his sweaty, dusty forehead, watching Scarlett feed one of the horses.

"You're just a big handsome man, aren't you? All the ladies must love you." Though Logan had no idea how she'd fit it in the pocket of those tight pants of hers, Scarlett pulled out a carrot, offered it in her palm.

"Careful! He nips!" Logan sprang forward to knock Scarlett's hand out of the way. The horse—a big coal black Arabian named Loki—had attitude to spare.

Logan simply blinked when the nasty-tempered stud gently nipped the carrot from Scarlett's outstretched hand.

"He'd never nip me. He's hoping for a date." Scarlett rubbed a hand over Loki's nose, then turned to grin at Logan, her expression tired but full of delight. "It's great to be able to spend so much time around these big guys, you know? At school a lot of the training focuses on dogs and cats. But this guy, he's just so beautiful."

Both Loki and Logan rolled their eyes, but while Loki's gesture was in agreement, Logan's exasperation was because he was out of answers.

"The last person who offered Loki a treat like that nearly got his arm chomped off." Logan stuffed his hands in his pockets and regarded Scarlett from under the brim of his hat. She looked beautiful, even after a day of sweaty, dirty work. And with no makeup, a smudge on her nose, and a new rip across the knee of her blue jeans, she exuded calm, competent control.

He was beginning to see just how much he would do for her, open himself for her.

It scared the shit out of him.

"I said, we're done for now." Logan repeated it, with an extra layer of harshness in his words. "Your time's your own for the night. Spend it however you like. Dinner will be on the table around seven. You can eat or not, your choice."

"Why don't we go into town for dinner?" Scarlett suggested.

Logan gaped. He knew he did. "Why on earth would we do that?"

She furrowed her brow adorably, but Logan's mind was too caught on the question to fully appreciate how cute she looked. "I drove through Hanover Creek on the way here, but I haven't actually spent any time there. I should find out where the grocery store is, the gas station. I can't just keep eating your food." She frowned then, clearly perturbed.

Logan could care less if she ate his food. Truth be told, it was kind of nice to have someone to eat with . . . though he damn well hoped she wasn't planning to perch in his lap and hand-feed him for the next year. It was unsettling.

But this . . .

He went into town whenever he needed to. As she'd said, he needed groceries, needed to fill up his truck.

But he always took the quickest trip possible—no lingering over meals at restaurants for him. And he always prepared himself mentally for the onslaught of people who would be in the aisles, on the streets, brushing against him.

Brusquely, he shook his head. "Not tonight. I'm not in the mood."

He would have to have been made from stone not to miss the disappointment that flashed over Scarlett's face, though she smoothed out her features quickly.

"All right." Tucking a stray strand of her dark hair behind her ear, she turned as she spoke. "Why don't I go throw some sandwiches together for supper? It's been a long day. And tomorrow I'll head into Hanover Creek myself, load up on some groceries so I'm not always mooching off of you."

Logan watched her walk away, cursing that he felt so unsettled.

He shouldn't feel obligated to take the woman into town every time she had a whim. He couldn't live like that.

But neither was he comfortable with disappointing her already, before their fledgling relationship—whether professional or sexual—even got off the ground.

He strode forward a step, then stopped, planting his hands on his hips. He didn't want to look weak in front of her. She wasn't into weak men.

But more than anything, he wanted to please her.

"Fuck me." Before he could change his mind, Logan stalked into the house, into the kitchen. Scarlett didn't turn when he slammed into the kitchen, staying where she was, gathering sandwich ingredients at the counter, but he noted that her shoulders tensed.

Damn it. He'd already disappointed her. That wouldn't do.

"Get your bag, or whatever else you need," he ordered gruffly, fighting against the nerves that were rising up in his throat, threatening to choke him. "Meet me at the truck in five."

"We don't have to go." Scarlett's voice trailed off as she turned around to face him.

"You said you wanted to go. We're going." He rocked back onto his heels. "Come on. We don't have all night. This isn't the city. Things close early around here."

Though she seemed a bit afraid to show it, Scarlett couldn't keep the wide grin from erupting over her face. She rose onto her tiptoes, bounced, and Logan was struck yet again by how her every movement seemed like she was dancing.

"I just need to get my purse." She did a little spin, and Logan was surprised at the chuckle that slipped past his lips as she raced from the room.

Damn it, but the woman was fascinating on so many levels.

Still, unease danced ghostly fingers over the back of his neck as he headed out to his work truck and climbed into the driver's seat. The engine gave a cranky whine as he turned it over, emitting clouds of exhaust as Scarlett exited the house. She'd taken her hair out of the tight bun she'd had it in all day, and now the dark, silken strands streamed behind her.

When she climbed into the cab of the truck, her perfume hit him—she must have just sprayed some on. Damn it, she smelled like cake.

How was a man supposed to resist something so sweet?

Logan felt her looking at him as he started the truck on the long, rumbling path of his drive.

"Thank you," she said finally. He grunted, but was shocked into silence when she leaned across the wide bench seat and pressed a simple kiss to his cheek.

It was a chaste gesture, that kiss—just a slight brush of her moist lips over his cheek.

But it rocked him to his core. Words failing him, Logan simply grunted.

They drove in silence, and Logan was surprised that the twenty minutes it took to get to Hanover Creek, the nearest town to his ranch, passed fairly quickly. Not to mention painlessly.

Scarlett didn't try to make small talk when it wasn't called for, didn't try to fill the empty spaces with meaningless chatter like so many women, chatter that drove him to the brink of insanity.

He filed that away. It was just one more thing that he liked about her.

That file was getting rather full.

Instead he focused on his breathing, on staying calm as the gravel beneath the truck's tires turned to pavement. He kept his eyes dead ahead as he drove down the main street of town, parallel parked the big black truck between a big red truck and a big blue one.

He was out of the car and around to Scarlett's door before she could open it herself. He thought she might be one of those women who were all tied up in feminism, in opening doors for their own damn selves, but she simply smiled at him in thanks, a slow curve of those pink lips that made him want to kiss her.

"This is Main Street," he said, stuffing his hands in his pockets to keep from reaching out and touching her. "There are only two restaurants, and they're both here. So is the grocery store, down at that end." He pointed to the far end of the street.

"We passed the gas station as we drove in." He gestured back the way they had come, watching as Scarlett took it in with wide eyes. A grim part of him wondered if she was going to turn her nose up at the tiny town, which was rustic on a good day and unrefined the rest of the time—a far cry from Las Vegas. "We have a barber shop, a couple of women's clothing stores, a drugstore. And a really crappy movie theater."

She'd see now just what she'd left behind to come here— she'd probably had no idea. And as soon as she saw, she'd head back to the city.

Even as he thought it, Logan knew that he wasn't giving her enough credit. If he had to choose a single word to describe the woman who had turned his life upside down so quickly, it would be stubborn.

She wasn't going anywhere, not until she'd accomplished what she'd set out to do.

"Well, if there are only two restaurants, should we flip? Or do you have a preference?" Logan found himself staring at Scarlett with more than a bit of disbelief.

Yes, he knew he needed to give her more credit. But unless he was really reading her wrong, she wasn't at all startled by the appearance of the run-down town that she would call home for the next year.

If anything, she seemed . . . excited. Even enthusiastic at the prospect of being given the grand tour of Hanover Creek, as if it was all she'd wanted when she'd asked him to take her here.

Was it really that simple to please her?

Belatedly, Logan realized that she was waiting for an answer.

"Pizzeria is only good on Tuesdays and Thursdays, when Mama Pizzoli is working." Logan rubbed a hand across his chin, the bristle of his stubble scratching the skin. "The rest of the time her kids do their best to run the place into the ground. But Maxine's is solid. Chicken fried steak, burgers, pie. Or salads, if you'd rather."

Scarlett arched an eyebrow at him, and Logan realized instantly that he'd stuck his foot in it. He'd meant that most women he'd met ate things like salads with cut-up chicken on them when they went out to eat, rather than indulging in thick, juicy steaks like he would choose. He certainly didn't think she needed to be eating that way. She looked damned good to him.

"Not all women prefer rabbit food over meat, cowboy." Then she sauntered off down the sidewalk, leaving Logan staring after her.

He'd accidentally made a comment that she could have taken offense to, and she'd shrugged it off.

He just couldn't keep up with her.

"Hold up." Striding after her, Logan fell in next to Scarlett as they passed a storefront with windows that were boarded up. She stopped in her tracks, moved to the window, and peered in.

"What was this place?" Rubbing her fingers over the glass, squinting, Logan realized that she was trying to make out the shapes of the decals that had been scraped off.

"That was the office of Dr. Wilkinson. He was the town vet until I took over his practice ten years ago." Logan slid his hands into his pockets, remembering how he'd helped the older veterinarian board up the windows by himself. "He and the missus packed up and moved to Florida, and I didn't want to have an office in town. Too big for a clinic, anyway. Too big for lots of things. So it's sat untouched ever since."

Scarlett studied the building, running her fingers over the boards at the base of the glass. "So this is still yours?" A light went on in her eyes, and Logan watched as the wheels started to turn.

"It is." He replied slowly, his gut clenching. "Why?"

"How do you think a veterinary hospital would fare here?" She mused out loud, sending a skitter of panic through Logan's veins. "There are lots of surrounding towns. More animals than people."

Needing to deflect before she went further into her idea, Logan tried for a jovial tone. "Trying to put me out of business already, huh? Should have made you sign a noncompete contract."

Scarlett started, her skin flushing. "That's not what I meant. I was just curious. Ignore me."

But now the picture was in Logan's head, too, and it stuck there as they continued toward Maxine's.

Of a woman—Scarlett—who didn't *want* to leave. Who could—and would—make a life here, with him.

It was a pipe dream. He'd never ask her to give up so much. Still, he was far enough into the fantasy that he didn't notice the crowd of people streaming out the front door of the movie theater across the street until they were on him, around him, in his space.

Stealing his air.

"Hey, Dr. Brody!" A young woman of perhaps nineteen smiled flirtatiously at him, swinging her blond ponytail as she brushed past him. When she looked back over her shoulder, she seemed uncomfortable with what she saw, because she hurried on, moving away from him.

They were all moving away—the crowd couldn't have been surrounding him for more than a few minutes. But it was long enough. Logan felt himself freeze into place, limbs locked, voice caught in his throat.

Shit. He didn't want Scarlett to see him like this, his breath starting to rasp in and out, faster and faster until it was out of control. But, of course, she chose that moment to turn back around, those expressive gray eyes narrowing in on him with laser focus.

"Logan?" She took a few steps back as he bent, placed his

hands on his knees, tried to get himself back under control. Then she was moving faster, had her arms out to embrace him, to offer him comfort.

"Don't touch me!" He flinched away, throwing his hands up in defense. "Not now!"

Mortification was hot on his brow, at odds with the cold sweat that beaded his skin.

He gasped for air, thought of his house. Of the acres of land, of the bright blue sky in the morning.

Finally, his breathing slowed, and he was in control of things once more. He stood slowly, awkwardly, shame stabbing him painfully.

These panic attacks—this loss of control—he hated them with every fiber of his being. And he'd learned how to control them, for the most part, without the little blue pills he kept in his bedside drawer just in case.

Yes, he'd learned how to control them. When he was alone.

"Can I get you anything?" There was her voice, soft and cool and always so damn calm. *She* didn't have panic attacks, no, not the always-in-control Mistress Scarlett.

Though it wasn't fair, he snarled at her and shrugged her hand away.

"Just get back in the truck." Pulling the keys from his pocket, he tried to swallow back the anger and misery and even guilt from the flash of hurt in those wide gray eyes.

Well, what had he expected? He should have anticipated his loss of control and her reaction to it.

Scarlett's jaw set firmly and she followed him to the driver's side.

"What are you doing?" Irritable, he tried to step back out of her reach, but she was like a mosquito, pecking at him until she captured the keys.

"You're in no shape to drive. Get in the passenger's seat." Planting her feet, Scarlett simply stared at him, and he saw it written all over her face that he wasn't going to win this one.

Fighting back another snarl, he did as she said, pressing his forehead to the cool glass window the second he was seated inside. He closed his eyes as she started the truck.

She left him alone after that.

She'd seen part of him that he hadn't wanted her to see—a big part, a dark part—and he'd handled it badly. And the truth was, now that his anger had started to fade, he wanted to wrap his arms around her, to put his head on her chest and feel the comforting beat of her heart. Lose himself in the comfort that she offered and that wasn't usually here when he went to pieces.

He couldn't get used to it. But maybe he could have handled that differently.

What the hell was he supposed to do now?

She caught up with him back by Loki's stall, where he was hauling a sack of grain so heavy that his biceps burned.

She seemed to understand that he was battling personal demons, not speaking, not pressing him to tell her.

Logan watched from the corner of his eye as she made her way to Loki and trailed her fingers over the stallion's snout. He wanted to yell, to get out his anger that she'd seen him so vulnerable.

He hadn't known her long, but he already knew that she wasn't going to stand for that.

But maybe . . . maybe she could help take his mind off of it. With that in mind, he dropped the sack of grain with a thud and leaned up against one of the stall doors, watching her with fresh hunger in his eyes.

"Care to tell me what that was all about?" Scarlett's voice was casual, but Logan knew she was anything but.

"No." He kept his answer short, to the point. He didn't want to talk. He wanted to lose himself in her body and forget the feelings that were tearing him to pieces. "I don't."

In the blink of an eye, she morphed from a sweet veterinarian into his Mistress, and he couldn't seem to do a damn thing to keep his traitorous cock from hardening as he watched the transformation.

"Looking for trouble, are we?" Scarlett sauntered to him, brushing the palms of her hands over the thighs of her jeans. Damn it, she shouldn't have been so beautiful, with her hair a mess, with sweat on her brow . . . from running after him, he realized, and though he wanted to cringe, he held it inside.

This couldn't work. Working together, *being* together.

Screw it. He wanted to lose himself in her. And he wanted it now.

"I'm looking to be inside you." Logan took a step back when Scarlett moved toward him, the gleam in her eyes making him nervous in the best possible way.

She didn't stop in her slow pursuit. He could keep deflecting, but it wasn't what either of them wanted.

After so many years of being solitary, stoic, after endless empty couplings, it felt so damned *good* to hand over the reins, to let someone else take control, more than he'd ever let anyone before.

He might question his decision the next morning, but right now, he needed her to do whatever she wanted, to aid in emptying him of the painful feelings and fill him up with pleasure.

"Is that right?" Rising to her tiptoes, Scarlett exhaled, and Logan felt the warmth of her breath fan out over his chin. Her breasts were pressing against his chest, and he thought of that morning, in the bathroom, when she'd dropped her towel and he'd gotten to see all of her—

Snap.

"What the—" Something hard and cool had snapped around Logan's wrists. He shook his head to clear it of his little fantasy, looked down . . .

And saw that she'd snapped a cuff around his wrist. No matter what he actually wanted, instinct kicked in.

"Oh, no, you don't." He jerked back before she could attach the second cuff.

He shouted out loud when her hand slid down the front of his pants. There was a sizzle of heat as her warm palm brushed over the rigid length of his cock and then—

"Oh." Logan held his breath as she grabbed onto his balls and squeezed, just hard enough to get his attention.

She had it. He froze in place, the cuffs circling one wrist dangling in the air.

"Easy, now." Scarlett used her body to press him in the direction she wanted him to go. He scowled down at her. She was talking to him like he was one of the freaking horses.

She nudged him into an empty stall, turned him to face the back. Then, with one hand still holding his family jewels, she used her free hand to guide the arm with the cuff up to the large metal loop fastened at the back of the stall.

The loop was meant for tying a rein, or a lead, but Logan saw immediately where she was going with this.

"Scarlett." He wasn't sure if the way he said her name was a plea or a protest as she guided the free cuff through the loop. "Please. I just want to be with you."

"I'm taking my hand out of your pants now," she informed him. "And I'm going to cuff your other wrist. You will behave."

A woman who was over half a foot shorter than him, who

was a slender little reed compared to him, had just wrangled him into place. Other men might have found it demeaning, but Logan...

He thought it was hot as hell.

When the cool metal closed around his other wrist, Logan felt need work through him.

He wasn't looking for something permanent—or even something that could last for one year. But he still couldn't stop from wanting whatever Scarlett would give him.

A gorgeous man with his arms chained in front of him, bent slightly and waiting for her touch... Scarlett couldn't think of any visual that could possibly be sexier.

If only he didn't have that haunted demeanor surrounding him. It was because of just that, that she didn't just acquiesce to his demand, that she wouldn't let him pull her down to the hay and make love with her.

Though it nearly killed her to not offer the kind of comfort he sought, she reminded herself that she should give him what he needed instead.

And what he needed was to feel overwhelmed, to be pushed until his mind was blank.

But sometimes . . . and this was a surprise for a woman who didn't care for vanilla sex . . . sometimes she thought she might let him just pull her down and have his way with her, no toys, no power exchange. Just Scarlett and Logan.

But they weren't ready for that now.

"I wonder if you know what you look like when you submit," she said quietly as she ran her hands over his chest, then under his T-shirt. "If you could have any idea what that does to a woman, having a beautiful beast like yourself waiting for her command."

Logan shuddered beneath her touch but remained silent. Something had changed in him while they'd been in town. Something that, no matter what she was pretty sure he actually wanted, was making him now cling wildly to the last shreds of control.

She wasn't going to let him. She wanted all of him.

"Are you fond of this shirt?" she asked, reaching into her pocket for the knife she'd placed there earlier. It had been a going-away gift from her roommate in Vegas. It had all kinds of fun things that she might need out here "in the wild," to quote Beth . . . but it was pink.

"My shirt?" She could hear the puzzlement in Logan's voice. "Not really."

"Good." Flicking the blade out of her knife, Scarlett fisted his shirt in one hand, then slit the fabric down the back.

She was careful to not get the blade anywhere near his skin, but excitement surged inside of her at the sense of danger.

It was just so fucking *hot* that he would let her do something like this and not use his safe word. Trust—the ultimate aphrodisiac.

"Christ," Logan muttered, shifting as she peeled the cotton over those broad shoulders, then cut it the rest of the way off. When it fell to the floor, she dropped the knife, let her hands slide into his pants, where she felt the slickness of pre-come on the head of his erection.

He clearly thought it was pretty hot, too.

Quickly, Scarlett unzipped the front of Logan's jeans and urged them down over his hips. He was naked beneath the coarse denim, and she purred as her fingers caressed his smooth skin, savoring the muscles she felt in his legs.

"Step out." She helped him the rest of the way out of his pants, then took a moment to admire the sight in front of her before reaching for her toy bag.

Six feet, four inches of hard, tasty cowboy chained up, waiting for her to play.

Her nipples tightened beneath the sports bra she'd worn for work. She was a lucky woman, to have ended up here, with him.

Now, if only she could make him see that.

Opening the soft leather bag she'd carried into the barn with her after a quick detour to the house, Scarlett pulled out a flogger. Again surprised that she yearned to just lose herself in him, she forced herself to focus on his needs and establishing their roles.

This flogger was similar to the one she'd used on his ass at Veritas, but it carried a bit more of a bite.

She flicked it once, warming up her arm. The slender tails cracked through the air, the noise satisfyingly loud, and Scarlett shivered with anticipation.

"Brace yourself." Pulling back her arm, Scarlett let the tails of the flogger fly. They rained down over his back in a handful of biting kisses, reddening the skin they touched.

Logan's broad, muscular back tightened, and a soft moan escaped his lips.

"Are we still green?" She was referring to the code used almost universally in the lifestyle, modeled after traffic lights.

Green was good to go. Yellow—wait a minute.

And red, or in Logan's case *bunker*, meant stop.

"Green." The word was quiet, tense.

Inhaling deeply, Scarlett lifted her arm again, flicked her wrist, let the strands snap down on Logan's back. He jerked, snarled. She landed another blow, and he gave the same response.

Pausing, she cocked her head to one side, tried to gauge his mental state. As she waited, he looked back over his shoulder. She'd pushed him out of his head, for sure, and right into that mean place he went to, that knee-jerk defense against submission.

"That's all you've got, baby? Let me go and I'll give you more."

Heat licked along Scarlett's skin from the temper rising inside of her, and she glared, even as she reminded herself to be gentle. As she watched, Logan's eyes focused in on the supple ribbons of tawny leather, and his gaze sparked with heat.

"I like a bit of pain with my pleasure." He curled the corners of his lips upward. Teasing her. Taunting her.

The way he'd reacted to her paddle back at Veritas had already told her that. But here, now . . .

She thought that he might like pain because it made him angry, brought out the animal in him. And he used this to keep himself from getting too close to a Mistress.

To keep his secrets to himself.

She needed to force him past that. Needed to close that distance.

The easiest way to break down defense is to overwhelm the senses. Pleasure is the gateway to emotion.

Luca hadn't led her astray yet.

"If you think that's all I've got, you weren't paying attention the night we first met." Scarlett was amused to see a trickle of apprehension work its way down Logan's face. Smiling to herself, she moved back to her bag, sifted through the contents, and considered her options.

Chains rattled as Logan tried to turn, to see what she was doing, so she made sure to remain just out of his line of sight.

If he had time to brace for what was coming, to think about it, to get angry over it, he'd use that anger to shore his walls right back up. So she had to take him straight through to release, one that overwhelmed him, in order to make any headway.

Her body ached to strip him bare, to strip herself, to press up against him.

She ignored it.

Decision made, Scarlett carefully laid her chosen toys out on the scattering of straw that covered the floor, then rose with the two things she needed first.

Next she dragged a small stool over to bring her closer to his height. At five six, she wasn't *that* tall, but Logan still loomed over her.

The heels of her boots clicked sharply on the worn wood of the stool as she stepped up. Logan craned his neck, trying to see what she was doing, his entire body jerking in resistance when she placed the soft silk of the blindfold over his head.

"Take that off," he snapped at her, shaking like a dog trying to shed drops after the rain. "I want to see."

"We're not doing what you want right now." Scarlett was out of breath by the time she managed to get the blindfold securely fastened. "We're doing what you need."

"And you get to decide what that is?" Logan's voice was full of bravado, and if Scarlett hadn't been listening for it, she might have missed the slight tremor that lay beneath the bold words.

Whatever kept him from submitting fully, it haunted him, and her heart melted.

He'd asked her for this tonight. He'd turned to her for help. Which was why she had to ignore what she wanted and give him what he needed.

So yes, she was in control. He'd given his to her.

Steadying herself, Scarlett placed the noise-canceling headphones over his ears, holding them in place while he again cursed and shook. After selecting a Coldplay album, she clipped the attached iPod to the silk of the bandanna that was secured snugly behind his head.

Logan's body went rigid as she climbed down off the stool, and she knew that he understood the enormity of what she'd done. He couldn't see, could hear only what she wanted him to. He couldn't reach out to touch, could feel only what she gave him.

Kicking the stool away, she again took up the flogger. Now he wouldn't be able to see it, to hear the telltale hiss it made before landing. He wouldn't even be able to focus on the coming blows, because his mind would be occupied by the music playing in his ears.

Lifting the flogger, Scarlett let the supple ribbons fly.

Logan's body was completely tense and rigid—and she knew he was trying to hold on to some semblance of control. But she thudded blows over his shoulder blades and down his spine, heating his skin, waking up his senses.

It looked like the tension that he was holding so tightly on to was on the verge of easing, though he stayed silent.

Scarlett swung the next blow with more force, landing it right over the lower part of his ass so that he would feel the vibration all the way to his balls.

He shuddered, but still didn't utter a sound.

"Stubborn ass." She couldn't hold in the smirk. "You're going down, baby."

Tossing the flogger to the side, then scooping to stuff two more toys into the pocket of her jeans, she circled around him, studied his face. A fine sheen of sweat glossed his brow, and his mouth was set in tense, stubborn lines.

But he turned toward her, sensing her movement even through the blindfold and headphones, and that pleased her.

Baby steps, she reminded herself as she slid a finger between his cuffs and his wrists, checking to make sure that they weren't too tight, then gave him a thorough once-over.

His breathing was quicker than normal, but even. His

skin was slightly flushed, and while he sure didn't look relaxed, she could tell he was still with her.

Reaching into her pocket, Scarlett removed the next item that she intended to use on Logan. They were a set, two slender pieces of metal that looked like skinny pliers, each with a wooden ball weighing down the ends.

Standing on her tiptoes, she fastened her mouth over one of Logan's nipples.

"Oh!" He groaned, his voice louder than usual because he couldn't hear himself. He pulled at his chains as Scarlett sucked hard, then flicked her tongue over the hardening flesh.

Pulling her mouth off of his skin with a wet pop, she pinched his nipple between two fingers, then applied the clamp.

"Damn it!" That big body bucked, and while he was preoccupied, Scarlett paid the same attention to the other side, sucking his nipple to a point and attaching the clip.

Finally, he stilled, the lines of his muscles telling Scarlett that he was furious. After dragging the beaten wooden stool over and stepping up on it, she pulled one side of the headphones away from his ears.

"What color are you at, Logan?" She made sure that her warm breath fanned out over the lobe of his ear as she spoke, adding every extra layer of sensation that she could.

As if by instinct and not design, he pressed into her touch rather than away from it, but his reply was still full of tension.

"Green," he said curtly, and Scarlett nodded. She knew he wouldn't ever willingly use his safe word, but he'd confirmed what she'd noted.

Replacing the headphone, she flicked one of the heavy wooden balls dangling from the end of one of his clamps, sent it swinging, and smiled when he gasped. Then she circled behind him again, and this time she set aside the deer-hide flogger for a cat-o'-nine-tails. Like its name suggested, the wand was connected to nine long ribbons, each with a bead at the end to add bite.

His skin was flushed a beautiful rose, darker in the places where the flogger had struck. Scarlett loved seeing it, loved knowing that she was the one who had marked him.

But now was not about her pleasure. It was about pushing him through his barriers so that he could obtain his own relief.

Being careful not to swing too hard, Scarlett let the cat-o'-nine-tails fly. It had enough bite on its own—she didn't need to put much force behind it. She struck slowly at first, a blow on one shoulder blade and then the other, repeating the pattern on his buttocks.

When he seemed to be anticipating those slower strikes, she upped the pace, the flogger landing in what she knew would feel like a series of quick little nips—nips from very sharp teeth.

And as she flogged him, as she wiped away her own sweat with her free hand, she kept an eagle eye on his body language. She'd known he was stubborn since her first interaction with him, but now—

Now she was starting to see just what lengths he would go to, to protect himself. He held out far longer than any sub she'd ever seen before finally, finally, he started arching to meet the blows, his breath slowing, deepening, demonstrating that he'd finally hit that high, the rush of endorphins known as subspace.

To keep the transition from being shocking, Scarlett dealt five more blows, decreasing the intensity of each until the last was just a tickle against the now red skin of his back.

Bending to pick up the final two items that she'd laid out, Scarlett noted that her own arms were trembling.

Seeing this particular man, this one who held on to control so fiercely, reacting so strongly to what she did to him, made her ache.

Inhaling deeply, she once again moved in front of him. A quick glance told her that his fingers were still pink, his skin still smooth, despite the way he'd been pulling at his cuffs.

Setting one of the two toys on top of the wood that bordered the stall, she opened up the bottle she held and squirted oil into her hand.

Rubbing it between her fingers to warm it, she looked up at Logan. For the first time since she'd met him, he seemed to be waiting expectantly for her next move.

It was the endorphins of subspace that had made him so open, but that didn't bother Scarlett. It was why she'd pushed him the way she had.

One day she hoped he would let her in consciously. But for now, it was her job to push him there, kicking and screaming if it came to it.

"Here we go," she murmured, then clasped his erection in both hands.

"Fuck!" Logan reared back, then arched forward, pushing into her touch. He groaned as she interlaced her fingers around him, then started to slowly pump up and down the length of his shaft.

Lost in sensation, he sagged on the chains, shuddering every time she reached the tip of his cock and slid back down to the root. Liquid gathered on the fat head of his cock as she slowly picked up speed, working the pulsing length methodically, carefully.

"Damn." Watching Logan's head fall back, watching him lose himself in pleasure from the touch—*her* touch—had heat gathering between Scarlett's legs, and she knew that her panties were growing damp. Hunger smoldered within her, and for a moment she contemplated taking him in her mouth, tasting the salt and musk of his arousal.

But that would distract her, and this was all about him.

"Oh." Logan moaned louder, pushed harder into her grip. Swiftly, Scarlett reached up and removed first one of his nipple clamps, then the other, letting them fall to the ground as she returned her fists to his cock.

"Shit!" he yelled, his mouth set in a grimace born of both pleasure and pain, and Scarlett knew that the blood was rushing back into his nipples, a controlled burn. She began to stroke him faster, one hand returning to the base of his cock as the other slid off the top, a nonstop stroke over his swollen flesh.

"Yes. That's—oh. Right there. Yes!" Beyond himself, Logan's hips began to pump, thrusting into her firm touch, and she knew he was reaching toward his release. His breath quickened, his muscles trembled, and his cock stiffened in her hand.

Right before he could come, she pulled her hands away.

Logan howled, even as he thrust into the air. Scarlett grabbed the heavy sacs of his testicles in her hands, pulling them away from his body to help stave off his climax. His lips twisted in a sneer, his voice desperate as his body tried to find a way back into her touch.

"You fucking cock tease!" he swore, sweat beading on his forehead. He was clearly frantic, and Scarlett licked her lips, watching the strength of his big body, restrained by the cuffs. "Let me come. Please let me come."

Ahh. There are his manners. Such as they were. Her focus narrowing to include nothing beyond this man, this submissive—not even the wood and straw and still air that surrounded them—Scarlett took the final toy from where she'd placed it at the edge of the stall.

Flicking the switch, she let it hum against her hand, a low but pleasant buzz.

Except—he was almost there. She didn't want to tease anymore—she wanted to shove him off the edge of the cliff from which he refused to jump.

She turned the vibrating plug up to high, then doused it with a generous stream of lube. Working the liquid over the entire surface, she moved to stand behind Logan once again.

His ass was still a beautiful scarlet from the kisses of her flogger. It was hard, and tight, and she found herself wanting to pinch it.

Another time. Right now she needed to send him over the edge.

When she slid a finger through his crack, he stiffened, though his pelvis still rocked into ghostly hands.

When she pressed the tip of the plug to the pucker of his ass, he tried to pull away.

She followed.

"No! No, I don't want that!" He yanked on his chains, and Scarlett pushed. The plug pressed against the tight muscle, and Logan groaned, the sound frantic. Then the tight flesh gave way, and the long, slender wand was in, the base snugged tightly against the hard planes of his ass.

The vibrating of the plug sent Logan thrashing, his feet planted on the floor, his hips moving as if he were already inside Scarlett.

"Not like this! I want to be inside of you!" he snarled.

He had shown her why he didn't like to come like this the first night that they'd met—that tender bundle of nerves inside of him milked his release from him despite anything he said or did.

It shoved him past his own control and into hers. Which was why Scarlett ignored his pleas, pulled the plug out, and slowly slid it back in, even though she wanted exactly what he did.

To be twined together, no barriers. Just naked skin and raw need.

"Scarlett . . . Mistress . . . no!" Scarlett's pulse skipped as he pleaded. Even though she knew his safe word, hearing the word *no* was disconcerting.

But he groaned and shuddered as she pulled and pushed one more time.

Standing on her tiptoes, she removed his headphones and tossed them aside. Then she tugged at the blindfold, pulling it free, the iPod following the headphones down to the ground.

Logan's eyes went wide as vision and hearing were returned. His gaze narrowed in on Scarlett, looking her right in the eye.

"Please," he begged, and she didn't think he even knew anymore if he was asking for release or asking her to stop. "I want to fuck you."

Climbing back onto the stool, she traced a hand over the line of his jaw and savored the shudder. When she fisted her hand in his hair and tugged, he only moaned.

"You don't get to come inside of me until you let me in." Her eyes were fierce, claiming his, as she reached down and wrapped her hands around his cock.

"Mistress!" The word was a shout, and then he cried out again as he shoved into Scarlett's hands, liquid heat streaming into her palms as he came.

She let it fall, closing her grip on his softening erection. His body tensed as the shudders took him over, and the movement tightened his clasp on the vibrating plug.

To Scarlett's amazement, the cock that hadn't yet fully softened went rock solid yet again in her palms. Before she could even move them to stroke down his length, another body-rocking climax shot through him, and she watched, stunned, as Logan threw back his head, closed his eyes, and released the most earth-shattering groan she'd ever heard.

"No more. Please," Logan whispered. He tried to fall to his knees, his body twitching with aftershocks. Breaking herself from her trance, Scarlett hurried down from the stool and moved to his back, switching off the vibrator.

Logan moaned softly, and Scarlett bit her lip to keep from wrapping him in her arms. She had a duty to care for him now, but if she'd come to learn anything at all about this man, it was that he would be furious within moments.

He wouldn't welcome an embrace, so she wouldn't press one on him.

He was silent as she dampened a cloth with a bottle of water that had been in her bag, then washed her hands and slowly cleaned his skin. His expression was unreadable but fixed on her, and Scarlett felt her own fast pulse skittering through her veins.

Swallowing thickly, she returned to his ass and slowly removed the plug. He hissed as she did, and she knew the burn would be waking those nerves up all over again.

Setting the plug carefully aside, she moved the cuffs that still bound him. *Click. Click.* Releasing one wrist, she drew the circlet of metal through the loop on the stall wall, then released his other hand.

"Fuck!" With a great snarl, Logan pulled away from her, putting distance between them as fast as he could. "I told you no!"

Scarlett watched, her face set in an impassive line, as he scrambled for his jeans, then his cowboy boots. Picking up the shreds of his T-shirt, he tossed it aside as soon as he noted its ruin.

There were so many things that Scarlett wanted to say. She

wanted to soothe him, to assure him that everything would be all right.

But she'd accomplished her goal—she'd touched that place deep inside of him, the one he kept so carefully guarded. Just a touch, but it was a start. And at the same time she'd taken him out of his own head, given him the respite that he'd asked for.

After the intensity of what had just happened, Scarlett found that she wanted to wrap herself in his embrace. To savor the feeling of closeness.

And as he glowered at her, his body rigid with fury, Scarlett understood that what this particular sub needed right now was space and time.

"I'm going to go inside," she said, making sure to keep her voice even. She would return to clean up their mess later—she needed to get out of his space. "Do you need anything?"

"I need you to fuck me like you keep promising with your teasing." Logan spat out the words. His body was rigid with frustration, his fists clenching at his sides.

He was a lot bigger than Scarlett, and he was enraged. But she didn't for a moment think she was in danger.

"If you wanted a quick fuck, you shouldn't have become a submissive," she reminded him, biting back a grin when he hissed through his teeth. "I'm sure there are plenty of women around here who will give you just that."

But that's not what you want. She knew that by now. What he wanted was to submit, to give in to the right Mistress.

He just didn't think he could.

"You're playing with fire," he taunted, and stepped closer to her, once again dressed in his jeans and boots. Before Scarlett could react, he had his fist clasped in her shirt, and he dragged her up to meet his mouth in a fierce kiss that spoke of heated possession.

"I'm too careful to get burned," she whispered when he finally broke away. The kiss had singed her skin and told her that he wanted to own her every bit as much as she did him.

It made her soul sing.

He snarled at her words, glaring down at her, then spinning on his heel and stalking away. Scarlett watched him go, her fingers pressed to her lips.

He was breathtaking, the jeans riding low on his hips, the muscles of his chest and back highlighted in the vivid colors of the setting sun.

"Damn." As he went she realized that, although it was a rule of hers not to ever lie in a power-exchange relationship, she inadvertently had.

She was careful, absolutely. But if she failed—if she couldn't get this particular man to submit, fully and completely . . .

She wouldn't just get burned. She'd be consumed.

CHAPTER ELEVEN

Scarlett bit through the crisp skin of her second apple as she reached the top of the stairs and entered her room, closing the door behind her. The scene had left her ravenous, but her emotions were in such a tumble that she wasn't sure she could eat much else.

Letting the tart taste spread out over her tongue, she crossed the floor to the massive window that looked out over the ranch.

Logan was pacing back and forth across the yard, every now and then throwing a mangled tennis ball for Mongo, who would retrieve it with delight.

His stiff steps showed Scarlett that he was in one hell of a foul temper. But he didn't appear to be on the verge of collapsing, so she decided to just leave him be.

She had her own care to see to, she mused as she methodically chewed her apple. Her body was sore, from the hard day of work that she wasn't accustomed to and also from the tension she hadn't known she'd been holding.

The scene in the barn had been more about emotion than sex, at least for her. But that didn't stop her body from being hungry, feeling tight, and aching with physical need.

Knowing that she could shuck off her jeans, lie down on her bed, and take the edge off by herself didn't sit quite right.

Now that she and Logan had started . . . whatever this was . . .

It didn't feel right to do anything unless they did it together.

"You need to focus on work this year, Scar." She lectured herself as she slowly—stiffly—stripped out of her torn jeans and her filthy T-shirt. When her fingers began to work at the knot in her bandanna, her mind flashed to the memory of Logan's strong, sure fingers tying it around her neck just that morning.

The big, stubborn alpha had blindsided her at a point in her life in which she'd been pretty sure she hadn't wanted the distraction of a full-time sub. No. She was lying to herself— deep in her heart of hearts, that was the one thing she'd always burned for.

A partner. Someone to call her own, something she hadn't had for years, if ever.

But the timing wasn't ideal. She'd had it all planned out.

Obtain doctorate of veterinary sciences. *Check.*

Spend year of internship on a ranch, honing her skills with larger animals. *Half check.*

Return to Vegas and open her own animal hospital with her newly acquired knowledge and her savings—one of the biggest perks about working with Logan was that room and board were free, on top of her salary.

She'd intended the animal hospital to serve two purposes— one was obvious. And the other . . .

She'd wanted foster kids in the area to have a place to come volunteer, to feel like they had a purpose when life beat them down. To feel the unconditional love of an animal, to give them hope.

Then, she'd thought—then she could search for that partner she craved.

But if she couldn't get her eye on the prize now, she was going to blow her list out of the water while she was still on point number two.

After tossing her apple core toward the wastebasket, Scarlett moved to the bathroom. Turning the hot water tap one full twist and the cold a half, she put the plug in the bottom of the porcelain basin and added a capful of the vanilla-scented bubbles she'd placed on the lip of the tub when she'd unpacked.

The water churning into the tub was so loud that she barely heard the knock at her door over the roar.

"Logan." There was no one else it could be. Her neglected body tightened up, her nipples puckering painfully as the unquenched desire in her body screamed at her to fling open the door and jump his bones.

"Down, girl." Scarlett couldn't help but laugh at herself as she wrapped her body in her worn terry-cloth robe. The bumpy fabric abraded the sensitive tips of her nipples, making her hiss a breath out through her teeth and heat pool between her legs.

She was pretty sure he wasn't here for sex. More likely, he'd be telling her to pack her bags and get out, that she'd pushed too hard, too fast.

With that thought settling like a stone in her gut, Scarlett tightened the tie of her robe and padded on bare feet to the door.

"Mistress."

The sight in front of her shocked her silly. Logan was still shirtless, wearing the same jeans he'd been in when she'd left him in the barn. But he'd removed his boots, which was a formal recognition of his submissiveness.

More than that, in one hand he clutched the wine she'd brought and in the other, a wineglass.

Just *one* glass.

Stunned momentarily speechless, Scarlett opened her mouth, then closed it again. Logan's head was bowed, and he just . . . waited, though his body vibrated with tension and need rather than calm.

Waiting for her to speak, she realized in a rush.

"You . . . you may speak." Her words sounded rusty, as though she hadn't spoken for a very long time.

Logan's gaze flickered up, met her eyes. She nodded, and he lifted his chin.

"I asked you to give me relief, and you did. Gave it the way I needed it. And then I yelled at you. So to apologize, I've brought Mistress some wine," he said, and though his body trembled, his words were steady.

He cocked his head toward the bathroom, where the rush of water and the vanilla-scented steam billowing out of the open door spoke of her unfinished bath.

"And . . . if the wine pleases Mistress . . . perhaps she will let me wash her back?"

Relief washed over Logan when Scarlett nodded, though he saw the careful consideration in her eyes.

He followed her into the room, his eyes pinned to the delicious sway of her ass, outlined in worn terry cloth. His fingers itched to touch her, but he wouldn't. Not yet.

It might kill him, though. He wanted to possess her with the thirst of a man thirty years in the desert without a drink.

If he'd come here to find her packing, he wouldn't have been surprised . . . but he'd have been inclined to use some of her toys to tie *her* up until he could convince her otherwise.

"Undress me." Her words snapped him from his thoughts.

"Yes, Mistress." Setting the wine bottle and the glass down on the bathroom counter, he moved in front of her, pressing himself against her. Every muscle in his body sighed with relief when he felt her heat warming his skin.

Hesitation played over her features. Then she spoke. "Call me Scarlett."

Triumph was a physical blow, nearly knocking him to his knees.

She had just given him a gift. He had to make sure that he deserved it.

In this position, he could draw her close, could rest her chin on his shoulder. It felt so blessedly normal—the first normal sexual interaction he'd had with a female for as long as he could remember.

Then he slid his hands between their bodies, his fingers stroking down the cleft between her breasts, eliciting a choked cry from her throat.

"Like this?" Logan pressed his forehead to Scarlett's as his fingers found her belt. They worked at the knot in the fabric, brushing over her lower belly, and she gasped against him.

He couldn't hold back the grin as he pulled the tie from its loops. He wanted more—wanted to hear her voice crest in pleasure, wanted to know he was the one who had brought it to her.

Locking her in his stare, Logan slid the soft, worn fabric of her robe from her shoulders. As it fell to the floor, he clasped his hands at her waist and lifted her up, placing her in the now knee-high water of the tub.

"Logan." Scarlett didn't sound shocked that he'd been so bold as to pick her up and move her . . . but unless he was way off, the reason that she was here, with him, was because she liked the fact that he wasn't a doormat, that he didn't look to her for his every reason to draw breath.

She'd had her chance at a pliable, perfect sub back at Veritas, with that Bren guy. Hell, looking the way she did, with that delicious dominant streak that she possessed, she could have most any sub she wanted, male or female.

But she was here. And she was using her quiet calm to chip away at his inner fortress, despite the fact that he was giving her quite a time of it.

He owed her . . . not everything, not yet. He couldn't. But . . . something.

His hungry gaze moved over her as she stood in the bath, the heated water pooling around her calves. To his eyes, she was perfect—a woman pulled straight from his fantasies. Her body was slender, but with full hips and breasts . . . her creamy skin, so pale in some places that he could see the amethyst of the veins running beneath . . .

The heart-shaped face that could soften with a smile or smirk while she wielded a flogger . . .

She made him hard and at the same time chipped away at the ice that surrounded his heart.

"I can't guarantee that I'm going to be quite so docile in the morning." He spoke honestly, and watched the amusement sparkle in her eyes. Linking his fingers in hers, he helped her balance as she slid into the hot water with a blissful groan.

"But right now . . . what you did out there . . ." Logan set his lips, ran his hand through his hair.

What she'd done out there was lay claim to parts of him that he'd done his best to forget even existed. And he was far from calm about it . . . In fact, it felt like an army of ants crawled under his skin when he thought about the way she'd controlled his body despite his efforts at resistance.

But the itching eased when he was around her. And he didn't even have to find the words to tell her, because she nodded with compassion.

He might want to throttle her again in the morning, but right now . . . looking down at his goddess, flushed from steam, so beautiful in her understanding . . .

He was inclined to worship.

"May I pour you a glass of wine?" Logan raised his eyebrows and waggled the bottle at her. When she nodded, he squinted at the label, then inclined his head, then continued.

"While I can't place the exact vineyard, I would say this is an artisan Riesling, nicely concentrated, possibly from Egon Müller. Elegant and sweet with a precise finish, though some might say it would be improved with a hint more acidity."

Scarlett's eyes widened, and those full, delectable lips of hers fell open with surprise. Logan bit back his smile as he turned around to pour from the bottle he'd opened downstairs. "Was this a gift from Luca?"

"Yes." Scarlett stretched the word out as Logan poured a stream of straw-colored wine into the glass. He knew that his friend Luca would likely shudder to see the seven-thousand-dollar-plus wine served in a vessel that had been purchased at a drugstore a decade earlier, but Logan didn't keep fancy things around.

He didn't need them—didn't need anything but that wide-open sky.

He turned back, savoring the sight of Scarlett's slender shoulders and damp hair as he handed over the glass, wondering if maybe he was starting to need something else, too.

"You . . . uh . . . you're into wine?" Scarlett's words were careful, like she was afraid of insulting him, and Logan couldn't hold back the laugh anymore.

"Not at all." Logan knelt next to the tub, reached for the bottle of girly-looking body wash balanced on the porcelain lip. "But I made a visit to Veritas right after the guys first opened. They'd been imbibing their new wares for a good portion of the day, in celebration. When I told them I was really more of a domestic beer kind of guy, they all set out to educate me. Especially Alex." The memory made Logan laugh again. No matter how bored he'd been by the properties of the various wines they'd carried at Veritas, some of it had sunk in.

"So you've known them a long time." Scarlett sat up straighter, the tips of her breasts just barely hidden beneath the bubbles. A good thing, too, because Logan's fingers itched to touch.

"I met Elijah and Alex that night, the grand opening of In Vino Veritas." Logan forced himself to keep his eyes focused on the woman in front of him, though when he saw where the subject was leading, he wanted to turn and run. "Luca . . . I've known Luca for twelve years. We were in the army together."

The words hurt to say—the memories from that time were something he never spoke of. Not ever.

But this woman wanted more from him. He might regret it in the morning, but right now . . .

He'd give her something, while he was able to.

"The army. Is that where you got your safe word from?" He felt Scarlett's stare on him, knew those eagle eyes of hers were soaking in every detail of his countenance.

Damn it. He should have known she'd pick up on that detail. Of course, the word held far more significance than just a simple army reference.

And right in that moment, when he felt so very close to her, he thought that maybe, someday, he could tell her all of it.

For now, though . . . nodding yes in answer to her question was more than he'd even thought possible before. And she didn't press, instead regarding him over the edge of her glass as she paused before sipping her wine.

When she moaned with pleasure, Logan felt his cock, which had been at least half erect since she'd stood naked before him, rise and stand tall, pressing uncomfortably against the front of his jeans.

"Oh, that's lovely," she murmured as she took another greedy sip, and Logan wasn't sure if she was referring to the wine or his erection. Then she pinned him with her stare, a butterfly on a board, and all he could see was her. "Well?"

She was making him stupid. He blinked. "Well, what?"

Arching an eyebrow, she shifted in the tub. This time her nipples appeared, peeping through the foam of the bubble bath, teasing him, and Logan couldn't hold back the moan.

Scarlett grinned at the sound. "Well . . . you told me something about you. Aren't you going to ask the same of me?"

"Yes." His pulse stuttered in his veins. Intellectually, he understood the exchange—he had shared with her, even though it was hard, so she was giving him something in return.

It still made him happy.

"Were you a dancer?" His words rushed out without warning. He might have wasted the question on something that didn't matter in the grand scheme of things, but he was dying to know.

Scarlett looked startled, so he continued.

"You just . . . have this way of moving. Especially when you're . . . topping me." The word stuck in his throat. No matter how much he knew that he was a sexual submissive, the rest of his being was so much in opposition of it that it was often hard to reconcile the two. "Innate grace. That's how I think of it."

Scarlett blinked, lifting the glass to her lips again. The stormy gray of her wide, expressive eyes shone wetly, or at least he thought they did, and then the moment was gone and she was handing the glass of wine to him.

"That's very, very observant of you," she said, and a predatory gleam came into her eyes, like she was about to eat him alive.

Logan suspected he would let her.

"I trained as a ballerina for most of my life. When I could afford the lessons, anyway." Again, that streak of sadness—and again, it vanished in an instant. "But by the time I was seventeen, it became clear that I didn't have the ideal body type."

"What the hell is that supposed to mean?" Logan was insulted on her behalf, and he knew his indignation showed.

As soon as Scarlett laughed, grinning at him, the sadness in her evaporated. Reaching out from beneath the surface of the water, she caressed his cheek, leaving water and bubbles in the wake of the touch.

"It means my boobs and hips were too big. I've come to terms with it." Her fingers trailed down to the wineglass he still held clutched in his hand, traced lightly over the rim. "You should taste this. It's delicious."

Logan let go when she pulled on the glass, his pulse accelerating as she sat up straighter, regarding him with all the imperial grace of a queen.

"Undress," Scarlett ordered, setting the glass on the side of the large tub. Her expression said that she knew he would do as she said.

Logan let his hands fall to the buckle of his belt, moving slowly to prolong the tease. She watched avidly as Logan slowly slid the leather through the loops of the worn denim, then tugged the fabric down, running the tip of her tongue over her lips as he slid the jeans down over his hips.

He knew just how she felt. It didn't matter that she'd had him naked and at her mercy less than an hour earlier.

He wasn't sure that he'd ever feel sated when it came to Dr. Scarlett Malone.

Completely naked, desire riding high, Logan held himself back, waiting for her next command, though he wanted so badly to just pull her from the bath, to lay her on the bathroom counter and fuck her until she screamed.

He knew she wasn't going to allow that, at least not yet. But he thought she might let him make her come . . . finally, after all of the time and attention she'd devoted to him.

And even though in that moment he genuinely wanted to serve her, it was hard to break old habits. If she let the dynamic between them focus on her for a while, then Logan could have a breather, a rest from the guerilla tactics that this Mistress had been applying to break him down.

When she crooked her finger at him, his body didn't give him any choice but to do as she said. Gaze caught in hers, Logan climbed into the bath with her, a tight fit for his height, even though it was a large tub.

More hesitant than he would have been even a day earlier, he slid his hands into the water and clasped Scarlett around the waist. She lifted her chin haughtily but didn't tell him to remove his hands.

"Lift me up." Bracing her hands on his shoulders, Scarlett dug her fingers into the muscle.

Logan hissed out a breath at the bite of pain. At the same time, his pulse accelerated, anticipating where Scarlett's devious mind had gone.

Bracing his weight on his knees, Logan seated Scarlett on the edge of the tub. The water sloshed around his hips, slopping over the side of the tub, bringing the smell of sweet vanilla to his nose. She spread her legs wide, and before he could even think it through, he found himself reaching out to touch the neatly trimmed dark curls that lay between her thighs.

"Ow!" He snatched his hand back when she slapped it, hard. It was only a small sting compared to the flogging that she'd administered earlier, but she'd caught him by surprise.

"Hands behind your back," she ordered.

Logan narrowed his eyes, feeling mutinous. "I want to touch you." His hands fisted at his sides. "I think I've earned that right today."

Scarlett smiled, a wicked curve of her lips. "I get to decide what you've earned and what you haven't." Laying a hand flat on her belly, she slid it down her pelvis, then over her labia, cupping her sex.

Logan groaned at the sight of her teasing gesture—the need to touch her had lit a fire in his blood.

"Now, it just so happens that this time I agree with you." Scarlett let her hands fall free, then picked up the glass of wine that was waiting on the ledge. With her free hand she shoved at Logan's shoulder, and she was none too gentle about it, sending waves rocking through the tub once more.

"Hands behind your back. I won't tell you again."

Logan's instinct was to refuse—he wondered if the need to push back would ever change.

But as Scarlett held the glass of wine over the vee exposed between her legs and Logan saw that his reward for compliance would be the chance to taste her—to *finally* taste her—he forced his hands behind his back and did his best to remain still, though every muscle in his body was tensed with the need to spring.

"Very nice," she murmured, tipping the glass over and letting the thinnest trickle of wine pour over her. Logan sank his teeth into his lower lip and laced his fingers together to keep from burying his head between her thighs.

"Ask me." With her free hand, Scarlett clasped Logan's chin in her fingers, giving him no choice but to look at her straight on. "Ask me for what you want."

"Damn you," he spat out, his mouth dry with need. Adrenaline spiked in his blood as what he so very much wanted came into reach. "Why? Why can't you just let me make you feel good?"

"You've answered your own question." Scarlett swiped a finger through the wine that was now steadily dripping into the bathwater. "You want my permission to do it. Crave it. It will be better for you if you have it."

Bending to press a damp, hot kiss to his forehead, which was beaded with sweat from the heat of the bathwater and his own restraint, Scarlett leaned back against the tiled wall and offered herself to him. "Now, Logan. Drink this wine. Use nothing more than your mouth, or you won't like the consequences."

Like a rubber band pulled taut, Logan snapped. Lunging forward so quickly that the water rose in a great, heated tidal wave, soaking his head as he reached for her. At the last moment, he remembered her order to use only his mouth and reluctantly laced his fingers behind his back again, then settled his mouth over her pussy.

Scarlett sighed once, long and deep, threading her fingers through Logan's now soaking-wet hair as he slid his tongue through her folds, wishing he could use his hands to hold her open, to drive right to her very center.

He lapped at her skin, the soft mounds of her labia, the creases where her thighs met her pelvis, determined to clean her of every trace of wine.

His tongue busily stroked, up and down, up and down. Logan looked up, made eye contact. Scarlett's gaze was locked on him as she slowly poured more wine, some stealing right into his mouth, the rest over the skin he'd just cleaned.

"Drink until I tell you to stop." Heat and arousal were flushing her features, making wisps of her dark hair curl around her face. "Don't waste any."

In truth, Logan didn't give a damn about the wine, or what it tasted like. Beneath the sweetness of the liquid was the spice that was Scarlett, and it spread over his tongue in a rush, satisfying a craving that he hadn't known before he met her.

Licking her from front to back, Logan began to slowly circle her clit with his tongue, all the while keeping his stare fixed on her face. He wanted to absorb her reactions—wanted to know what pleased her, he realized with a jolt.

When he ran his tongue around that hard nub of engorged

flesh, she inhaled sharply. Testing, he flattened his tongue, using it to lick the same area with a series of rapid, hard flicks.

She moaned, the low, deep sound like a siren's song. The hand in his hair tugged, and his scalp stung as she pulled.

"Scarlett." Logan rasped out her name, moved his head back and forth so that the shadow of beard on his jaw would rasp against her sensitive flesh. When he slid his tongue back into her folds, arrowing it inside her this time, her body bucked and she cried out.

Screw this. He wanted her weak, wrecked. Screaming his name. He didn't mind breaking the rules to get her that way.

"I want you to come." His hands found her inner thighs, then the soft, slick flesh between her legs. Using his thumbs to hold her open, he fastened his mouth on her clit and sucked.

"Oh my God!" Scarlett's hand slid from his hair, slapped against his back, her body bucking under his mouth. "Logan!"

He smiled smugly, nipping gently at her clit, which wrenched a shriek from between her lips. One of her legs slid over his shoulder, around his neck, drawing him closer as she let her lids close over those glorious gray eyes and threw her head back, her face awash in pleasure.

She pressed her pelvis into his face, her body demanding more. Logan slid the thumbs holding her open inside of her, letting them pulse in and out in a delicious tease.

"Do you like that?" he asked, taking a moment to nip at her inner thigh. "Ah, you taste like sin. I could get addicted."

An ungodly moan issued from her throat, and Logan felt the thigh around his neck tremble. And then she caught him by the hair again, this time pulling sharply enough to have him seeing stars.

"Shit," he muttered, trying to nuzzle back into her heat again.

"Logan!" Her breath coming in pants, Scarlett dug her

nails into his scalp, wrenching his head away from her pussy. *"Stop."*

There was no ignoring the command in her voice, even as her body arched toward him, telling him the opposite of what her mouth instructed. Her breath rasped in and out of her lungs. Swearing loudly enough that the sound echoed off the tiled walls, Logan set himself back on his heels and scrubbed his hands over his face.

"Why? Fuck me, why?" His voice sounded rough even to his own ears. His need was raw, like shards of glass slicing his skin, his mind clouded with the smell, the taste of *her*.

Of this woman, who overwhelmed him completely.

"Because," she started, glaring at him, and in that moment Logan understood that this wasn't an easy task for her either—she hadn't *wanted* to pull his mouth from her sex, to delay her climax.

"Because you keep trying to gain control. And that isn't going to work, not in this kind of relationship." Placing her bare foot flat on his chest, panting, she pushed until he leaned away from her. "But maybe you don't actually want to be with a Mistress. Maybe that's what your attitude is really about."

"No!" Logan practically shouted, the truth coming from deep in his gut. The thought of vanilla sex left him cold. He wanted—needed—submission.

He'd just never imagined that he, who lived such a solitary life, would find a Mistress who cared enough to push so hard, to dig her nails into his tough outer surface and pry the softer parts out from within him.

It scared the shit out of him. But if anyone could earn his trust, he would have bet on this woman, even if that meant betting against himself.

Realizing all of this didn't make it any easier to hold himself back. He glared at Scarlett, even as he fought the desire to suck one of her long, slender toes into his mouth.

"What do I have to do? When will you let me bring you pleasure?" His need to bring her to climax overwhelmed everything else.

Scarlett inhaled deeply, clearly trying to calm herself down. With a dark, wicked glint in her eyes, she again slid her hand down between her thighs.

Logan felt like a rabid dog on a tether, restrained by nothing more than a thin ribbon.

"You continue to pull back from true surrender by trying to control me, to control the situation." Scarlett slid her fingers inside of the pussy that Logan knew was hot and wet. He snarled, finally reduced to nothing more than his animalistic urges.

He leaned forward again, telegraphing his intent with the tense set of his jaw.

"Don't. Move." Scarlett glared fiercely down at him, then began to move her fingers in and out of her hot cleft.

Logan's body was strained to the point of pain. As he watched her begin to pleasure herself, saw the heat flush her cheeks, the words fell from his mouth like they belonged to someone else.

"What do you want me to do?" he bit out, the tips of his fingers digging into his thighs so fiercely that they left white impressions. "What can I do?"

Scarlett's eyes whipped open, the dark gray startling in its intensity. "Ask me."

"No." Logan ground his teeth together. This was about more than just this moment, and he choked on the word.

"*Ask me.*" Pulling her fingers from inside herself, Scarlett swung the flat of her palm, connected with his cheek. Blood surged, heating the skin where the blow had struck, severing his last shred of control. He could smell her arousal, the spicy scent so unique to her, could taste her on his tongue, could feel his need coiling tight inside himself.

He couldn't do what she wanted. The things in him that she wanted to own—if he released the lock, he'd never get that part of himself back.

He couldn't give her what she wanted. He just *couldn't*.

"No!" Lunging again, burying his face between her thighs, he fastened his lips on her clit once more and suckled with intent focus, needing to bring her to release, to bring her under *his* control so she would stop pushing, pushing, pushing.

She came within seconds, screaming as her body bucked against his, her legs locking around his neck to bring him closer even as she cursed at him.

Though his cock was still hard, though he hadn't touched himself, Logan felt like his own release ripped through him as he watched Scarlett bow beneath his mouth. For one long, beautiful moment, everything became crystal clear.

Bringing her pleasure . . . serving her . . . it could bring him peace. If only he could let go.

And then her shudders quieted, and the clarity of an instant before scattered as her head snapped up, her eyes full of white-hot fury.

And Logan realized that somehow, some way, he had miscalculated. More than that . . . he had made a very big mistake.

Scarlett's spine straightened as though she'd been shocked, and quick as a snake, she caught his cock in her hand and squeezed.

He hissed but didn't voice a complaint. As he looked into her eyes, he felt a thread of panic begin to work its way through his gut.

He might have pushed her past a point from which they could not return.

Pulling just enough to make him wince, Scarlett put her face directly in front of his. She was furious. He could see that; but more—she was disappointed.

Shame was like a thick mass that clogged his throat.

"I'm sorry—" he started, but one more squeeze of his erection had the words choking off at his lips.

"I'm sure that you are sorry now." There were so many emotions vibrating behind Scarlett's words that Logan felt the stone settling in his gut grow even heavier. "But what *I'm* sorry for is that it took this much, that we had to go this far, for you to see how unacceptable it is to treat what we have with so much careless disregard."

Temper flared within him. "Wait just a minute. I don't disregard a damn thing."

Releasing his cock, Scarlett placed her hands flat on his chest, then shoved him backward. He fell on his ass with a thud, and if there had been much water left in the tub, he would have emptied it.

Scarlett stood, and she was both beautiful and terrible, like a goddess standing on the pinnacle of a volcano.

"You want to hurt me," she said, so softly that Logan barely heard her.

Shaking his head, he scrambled to his knees. "No, no, never." *Not at all.* He wanted to worship her; he just didn't know how.

"You do." Calmly, Scarlett stepped out of the bath, every line of her body shouting that she was a queen and he, in that moment, her prisoner begging for mercy. "When I push you to your limits, you are supposed to use your safe word to communicate that you can't go any further. And that is something that I will respect. But disobeying me so directly simply to take back control is unacceptable and tells me that in your very heart, you want to hurt me."

She wasn't listening. He had to make her listen.

Pulling himself to his feet, he looked down at her, doing his best to rein in his temper. "That's bullshit and you know it."

He reached for her, and she thrust out one hand, palm facing him, a gesture that halted him in his tracks.

"I know that you have a hard time understanding the need inside of you, a hard time wanting what you want," she said softly, "and I'm going to do my best to help you understand."

Turning on her heel, gloriously, magnificently naked, Scarlett strode from the bathroom.

Confused and agitated, Logan followed her, not done arguing his point.

He stopped short when he found her bent over the bed, palms sinking into the soft quilt that covered the mattress.

"Since you're having trouble seeing things from my point of view, we're going to do some role-playing." Raising her heart-shaped ass higher in the air, Scarlett pressed her cheek to the bed. "You will spank me. Ten strokes, counting out loud. And if you don't put your back into it, you'll start again at one."

"No fucking way." Logan planted his feet and crossed his arms over his chest. "I don't strike women."

Scarlett lifted her head, looked into his eyes, and the depth of the understanding and the *hurt* he saw there nearly brought him to his knees.

"Are you using your safe word?" She wouldn't condemn him if he did.

After what he'd just done, he owed it to her, had to give her this without fighting.

Plus . . . he knew, he just knew, that if he didn't do this, she'd be gone.

"Fine." He bit the word out, then went to stand behind her. Appeased, she sank her face back into the bed, arching her spine, a graceful curve that he wanted to run his lips over.

If he tried right now, she would kill him.

"Have you . . . ? Have you ever been spanked?" he asked, his voice low. Needing the contact, he dared to reach out, smooth his hand over her flank, and she sighed, the sound making her flesh quiver.

His cock hardened, and he felt distinctly uncomfortable.

"Every Domme who wants to be certified at Veritas has gone through a mentorship program. And that includes a month-long stint as a submissive." Her voice held a hint of distaste, not, Logan understood, because she looked down on the role, but because it hadn't suited her at all. "I know what I'm in for here, Logan. Stop procrastinating. Spank me."

His hand slid off her skin and balled into a fist. He'd hit his share of men—had done far worse things—he'd been in the army, after all.

But the idea of hitting someone for sexual pleasure—no matter how alpha he was outside the bedroom, he just couldn't fathom it.

There wasn't anything he wanted to do less than lay his hands on Scarlett in this way.

He owed it to her, though. He wasn't going to beg. He was going to man up and do it, though he still wasn't entirely sure what her endgame was.

"Fuck. Brace yourself." Logan lifted his hand, took a practice swing that sliced through the air. Grimaced.

No matter what she'd said, he couldn't hit her with all of his strength. He'd hurt her.

He lifted his hand again, chewed on the inside of one cheek.

Then he let go and swung.

"One." *Crack*. The slap of his palm connecting with flesh reverberated through the room. Scarlett jolted on the bed but didn't cry out. When he snuck a peek at her face, he saw that she looked entirely calm.

For some reason, it irritated the hell out of him. Didn't she feel anything, when his world was turning upside down?

Bracing himself, he spanked her again and again, alternating cheeks the way she had while flogging him. She continued to hold still apart from a flinch every time the blow landed, though her breathing quickened, and the skin beneath his hand heated and turned pink.

He hated the flinches, hated the marks on her skin, hated everything about the situation. His anger grew until he was furious at her for putting him in this position.

"Ten!" He shouted the last number, then sprang away from her, his palms sweating, his body shaking. "Are you happy now?"

Below him on the bed, Scarlett sucked in a deep breath, then slowly stood. As if examining what her body had just gone through, she stretched, rising high onto her toes with her arms pulled tall above her head.

And when she winced, Logan felt like scum.

"I'm not happy unless you're happy," she told him, turning to look him in the face. She looked deeply sad and even a little vulnerable.

"Isn't that supposed to be my line?" Logan asked bitterly.

She pursed her lips. "You're angry with me."

"No shit, Sherlock." Logan was more than angry, he was so full of emotion that his skin felt like it was stretched too thin, unable to contain it all.

Scarlett crossed the few steps that it took to reach him and stood in front of him. Though she was close enough that he could feel the heat emanating from her skin, she made no move to touch him, to soothe him, and that told him how much he'd cracked the fragile connection that had developed between them.

"How you feel right now—that anger, that shame, that edginess? That's how I feel whenever you refuse to let me take you where you need to go. That's how I feel when you deliberately disobey me just for the sake of grabbing control back. That's how I feel when I have to punish you like this." She gestured with her arm, referring, Logan assumed, to what she'd just made him do.

His mind rejected her words. She was wrong, wrong, wrong. He didn't make her feel like this. He couldn't, not by just . . .

By disrespecting her in every way.

Logan was overwhelmed, agitated, felt like ants were crawling beneath his skin. He needed to get the hell out of there, but he didn't dare move until she told him he could go.

To his utter shock, Scarlett rose up onto her tiptoes and without speaking, pressed a soft kiss to the line of his jaw.

"It doesn't have to be this hard, you know." Sinking back down to flat feet, she regarded him solemnly.

Logan just stared at her, overcome.

She gestured to the door, her smile more than a little sad. "Go now. I'd like to be alone."

Clinging to the few threads of sanity that she'd left him with, Logan went.

CHAPTER TWELVE

Scarlett deliberately withheld all physical contact for an entire week. It almost killed her, especially when she saw Logan's muscles flexing as he worked around the ranch, or when she saw his tender side toward all creatures large and small when they started doing house calls together.

But she knew that she had to impress upon him the importance, the enormity, of what was between them.

And for the sake of his pride, he needed to come to her—it had to be his choice, not an order that he felt he had to obey.

Standing beside him on the dusty floor in the busy barn of a neighboring farm, Scarlett tried to focus on threading a length of rubber hose up the nose of a mare. The toffee-colored horse rolled her eyes unhappily but was clearly too miserable to try to get away.

They'd been called to the farm to take a look at a mare that was under the weather. Logan had ordered Scarlett to examine the animal, give him her opinion, and then provide treatment, all under his watchful eye. He hadn't strayed far from her in the past week, all the while observing her, teaching her.

But he hadn't said a thing about the relationship they had outside of work. He hadn't approached her sexually in any way.

Had she gone too far, making him spank her?

Was he waiting for her to lead, a submissive to a Mistress?

The thought upset her so much that her hands shook. The rubber tubing shook, sliding out of the horse's nostril, and Scarlett swore softly under her breath.

"Here." Logan caught the tubing before it could fall. Moving in so close that Scarlett could smell the soap he'd used that morning, he took her hand and placed it back on the tubing, helping to place the tube back in the mare's nose. Scarlett's pulse raced as, together, they fed the tubing into the horse's sinus.

"Yes. Like that." Scarlett might have missed it, but she thought she heard a small hitch in Logan's voice when her fingertips brushed over the back of his hand. "You have to get in far enough that you can pump, but not so far that you damage the sinuses and hurt her."

"Right." Scarlett hated that her voice was weak. But whatever else she was confused about, she knew that she hadn't imagined the connection between them.

But how the hell was she supposed to get through to him?

Was it even possible? Was she wrong about him entirely, and he truly was meant only for a Mistress who would be easy on him?

The thought of another woman laying her hands on him, touching him, made an inner snarl echo through Scarlett's head.

She wasn't about to give up on this submissive, no matter how stubborn a beast he was.

She just hoped that he hadn't given up on *her*.

A vibration at her hip startled her, jolting her from her thoughts. Her ringtone blared, and she flushed as she realized that she'd forgotten to turn the ringer to silent.

Logan's lips twitched with amusement as he listened.

"Save a horse, ride a cowboy, huh?" Logan snorted out a laugh. Scarlett felt her face flush even deeper.

Damn it. Why did the dynamics between them have to be so complicated?

"I'll turn it off," she answered hurriedly, letting go of the tubing.

"No. Go on and answer it. It's pretty appropriate, actually." Logan gestured to the pump end of the hosing that lay on the ground. "Just hand me that before you go so I can start to suction."

Scarlett was floored at Logan's casual reference to everything that had happened between them. What was he saying? That there *had* been something there? Or that there still was, despite his absolute avoidance of the topic for the last week?

Damn it. She might be a Domme, but she was still such a *girl*.

Throat dry, with no idea what to say, she scooped up the small handheld pump and handed it to Logan. Their fingers met again as she passed it over, and Scarlett felt her pulse skittering at the casual contact.

Flirtation over equine sinus trouble. *How romantic.*

"Thanks," she muttered, jerking her hand away. Tucking a stray wisp of hair behind her ear, Scarlett quickly strode out of the barn, pulled her phone out of her pocket, and stabbed at it to accept the call and silence the damn thing.

She'd taken too long. The phone went through to voice mail, then immediately started ringing again.

SANTANGELO, LUCA

"You can't expect me to be as available to you as one of your subs," she said mildly as she answered, rounding the corner of the building. "There's this wonderful modern thing called voice mail."

"Got you to answer, didn't I?" Even through the phone, Luca's voice was smug. "And now I can hear your reaction when I tell you that I'm coming for a visit."

"Rich man say what?" Scarlett stopped in her tracks. Luca was a big fan of his creature comforts—and he didn't count wide-open fields or cow manure on that list.

"You heard me the first time," he replied. "I just closed the deal on that chain of restaurants. I'm visiting each one to see what needs improvement, and there's a location in Billings. And what kind of mentor would I be to get within a half hour of charming Hanover Creek and not visit my favorite protégée and her stubborn submissive?"

"Ah. There it is." Scarlett sighed and rubbed her hands over her eyes. "You're nosy."

Part of her wanted to keep Luca far away from here, be-cause . . . well . . . because she felt like a failure, damn it.

And part of her was desperate for him to come and tell her how to fix the mess she had made between her and Logan, to tell her what to do to make it work.

"See what a good Domme you are?" Luca asked cheer-fully. "You can see my intentions, clear as day, right through the phone."

"Shut it, Santangelo." Despite herself, Scarlett laughed.

"That's *Master* Santangelo to you, babe." Even though he was joking, the underlying thread of authority in Luca's voice could be heard at the challenge, even through the phone. "Don't make me spank you."

"In your dreams." Scarlett's chuckle was abruptly cut off with Luca's next query.

"Since you brought it up, Scarlett dear, how *are* things with the reclusive doc?"

Scarlett's heart stuttered, and then she sighed. It was hard to force out the words—as a Domme it was her responsibility to understand the needs of her sub, to provide for them.

She was failing miserably, and admitting it left a bitter taste in her mouth.

"Not very well," she finally choked out. Threading her fingers in the loose tail of her hair, she tugged with frustration.

She would be crazy to say that Logan was the one . . . wouldn't she?

But the fact remained that she'd never felt like this before and wasn't sure she ever would again.

"He keeps trying to make me lose control, trying to make me give him the upper hand, and he fights me every step of the way when I try to lead him elsewhere. And I can't walk away. It's . . . We . . ." The frustration she'd felt a week earlier, when she'd forced Logan to spank her, welled up inside her chest. "I really can't convince you to tell me his story? Not even a hint?"

Normally, she would have enjoyed prying the details out of her sub, each reveal a triumph.

But with Logan she was ready to fight dirty.

"You know I can't, Scar. It's not my story to tell." Luca's words were thoughtful, and then he continued.

"But maybe I can help you get it out of him."

The phone call had changed something in Scarlett's demeanor. Logan could see that as soon as she strode back into the barn. She stood tall, certain, had that look in her eye that made him so apprehensive in the middle of a scene.

His heart thudded against his rib cage as he looked her over, noting how stunning she was, even in torn work jeans and a button-down plaid shirt.

She made him feel things that he'd never thought he could allow himself to feel.

Coming back up beside him, she picked up the bottle of disinfectant and cheerfully began to squirt it over the nozzle of the pump that he'd just finished using.

"You seem happy." His mind screamed at him to leave well enough alone—he'd managed to beat back his need to grovel in front of her for an entire week now, to go back to being just colleagues.

It was no business of his who had put that spring in her step, no matter that it planted a seed of jealousy in his gut.

"A friend is going to be in town this weekend, and I'd like to have them over for dinner." The smug challenge in her eyes when she looked at him told Logan that she knew he was fishing for information.

And yet he just couldn't leave well enough alone.

"You're asking?" His voice was accusatory, even though he hadn't intended for it to be.

"Your house," she said, shrugging. "Your rules."

Oh, really. Logan thought of the scene in the bath and just stopped himself from rolling his eyes.

It might have been better if he had, but instead he kept on questioning her.

"What kind of friend?"

"A friend from Vegas." Her eyes sparkled, and he knew she was baiting him. *Damn it.*

"A male friend?" The beast inside of him snarled.

A submissive?

Is this really over already, almost before it began?

Scarlett, squatting over the equipment, rocked back on her heels and looked at him sharply. Logan's mouth grew dry as that *look* came over her, the one that transformed her from Dr. Scarlett Malone, his competent and very attractive intern, to Mistress Scarlett, the woman who commanded his attention with her mere existence.

He blinked and the two merged, becoming impossible to separate in his mind. He wanted them both—he wanted *all* of her.

"Are you sure you want to do this?" Her voice was calm, but her eyes regarded him intently, and he knew that she was filing his every move, his every breath away in that sharp little brain of hers.

Logan scowled, hesitated.

Maybe it would be good if she got involved with another submissive. It would give him some space, a chance to get some control back over his life.

Why did that thought make him so damn miserable?

"Whatever pleases you." His words were curt in an attempt to hide what he was really feeling—until he figured that out for himself, he sure couldn't let her see.

She leaned in to him slowly, close enough that he caught that tantalizing smell of vanilla that seemed embedded in her very skin. Casting a quick look around, she fisted his T-shirt in her hand, pulling him down until he felt her breath mist over his lips.

"Scarlett." His voice was a warning—they were on a house call, definitely on work time, when he was in charge.

But he found that the more time they spent together, the more those lines blurred, morphing into something else entirely.

Besides, they weren't doing anything inappropriate. Never mind the thoughts that raced through his head when she moistened her lips with the tip of her tongue.

"What would please me is to have you say that and mean it." She pinned him with a stare, her gray eyes luminous in the dim light inside the barn. Logan's body tensed. The mare that they'd just treated was watching them contentedly, as if they were a reality TV show.

But as he looked up into Scarlett's eyes, he felt the worry melt away. Who cared what anyone else thought, as long as he pleased her?

"We will have a guest for dinner on Friday." Scarlett spoke as if he would accept it, simply because she decreed it so.

It was sexy as hell.

"You will be there with me." Releasing his chin, she leaned forward until he could feel the warmth of her breath on his lips. Still not inappropriate, but arousing as hell. "You will be there as my submissive."

Logan nodded warily, the jealousy that was lodged in his gut only partially appeased by her claiming of him as her sub.

"I will take care of all the details. All you need to do is show up when I command it—show up willingly." Her face was set in stern lines, and Logan sensed that this was it.

He couldn't fuck this up again. She might not give him another chance.

"Understood?" Her fingers dug into his chest, and the jolt of pain made his cock swell.

"Yes, Scarlett." Relief washed over him as he said her name. It felt good—it felt right.

And that was something to turn over in his head later.

"Good." Releasing him, Scarlett stepped back, dusted debris from her jeans before turning to pack up the last of their equipment. Logan eyed the sweet curves of her ass, outlined in thin denim, as she bent over, silently cursing that she seemed so calm, so serene—even though he knew she wasn't—while he was having a hell of a time not just grabbing the swells of those hips and taking her here and now.

Swallowing, trying to get his urges back in control, he looked up and felt a jolt of adrenaline when he saw a young ranch hand he knew by face but not name standing frozen in the doorway, his avid expression trained on the scene in front of him.

Logan scowled.

The cowboy winked, gave him a thumbs-up, and sauntered away.

CHAPTER THIRTEEN

On Friday night Logan knelt at the base of the stairs, head bowed. He wore nothing but a pair of black shorts that concealed absolutely nothing—shorts like that other male sub had worn back at Veritas.

His heart was racing and he felt terribly, horribly exposed. But that afternoon Scarlett had left the briefs on his bed, along with a note giving him instructions for the evening.

He felt raw, not just because he knew that she was about to put him through the ringer tonight, but because a stranger was about to invade his home.

His safe place.

He didn't let many people visit him here. Just when he couldn't avoid it—like when his good friend Luca asked him to take on a pretty little raven-haired intern.

But Luca had stuck with him through the hardest time of his life, had made him live when he hadn't wanted to. There was nothing he wouldn't do for his friend.

But it was taking everything he had to trust in Scarlett, to remember that she understood his needs and wouldn't let anyone defile his sanctuary. But he did—he trusted her.

Her heard her footsteps first and fought the urge to look up. *Tap, tap, tap* coming slowly down the stairs.

High-heeled red ankle boots came into view first, then shapely calves—calves that he'd had resting on his back.

Stepping lightly off the bottom stair, Scarlett circled in front of him, then lifted his chin with the toe of her boot.

"Look at me." Sucking in his breath at her words, Logan felt his mouth go dry.

Scarlett was dressed to kill. Though he wanted to behave, wanted to show restraint, his cock thickened, filled, pressed uncomfortably against the snug fabric.

She wore a dress that matched her boots, the color of a red rose, and the hem slashed across her at midthigh, leaving him with lots of long, toned leg to salivate over. It was skintight, hugging the curves that she had said were the downfall of her career as a dancer, and in that moment, Logan was fiercely grateful for them.

Her breasts rose, high and round, from the scarlet fabric that barely covered her nipples. The cream color of her skin contrasted beautifully with the dress.

Her lips were painted red to match the dress, and her hair had been pulled back in a severe knot on the back of her head, leaving no doubt about which side of the power exchange she fell on.

She was stunning.

"I'm pleased that you've followed my instructions," Scarlett started, but whatever she was about to say was cut off by the sharp ring of the doorbell. Bending just low enough to give Logan a good look down the front of her dress—a purposeful move, he was sure—she trailed a hand down his cheek, a small gesture of affection.

"You may relax. Stand up if you wish." He did, watching the sway of her hips as she sauntered to the front door.

Jealousy stabbed through him when he realized that whoever was on the other side—her *friend*—was going to see her dressed like that.

He sank his teeth into his tongue to hold back any words of resentfulness.

"Oh. Oh, you poor baby!" All traces of the stern Mistress

fell away as Scarlett swung the door open, then knelt and reached for something just out of Logan's range of vision.

Protective, he strode forward—and stopped abruptly when he saw that she had a canine bundle of fluff cradled in her arms.

"Put it down," he ordered, reaching down to clasp Scarlett by the wrists. "It could be rabid."

She shot him an annoyed glance. "Don't you think I would know that as well as you?" The puppy whimpered in her arms, and Scarlett shook off Logan's hands. "It's not. No extra saliva, no paranoia, no confusion. See?"

Scarlett held the dog out to Logan. It had matted gray fur, huge brown eyes, and a chunk missing from its left ear.

It shivered pathetically and tried to burrow back into Scarlett's chest.

"This poor guy needs a meal." Eyes wide, Scarlett looked up at Logan beseechingly.

"Once again with feeling . . . you're asking?" He snorted, fully aware that he had no say in the matter. Not that he really minded, not by now.

She huffed out a laugh, climbing to her feet with the dog held tightly in her arms. "We're not on the clock yet . . . sub." Cooing to the dog, she pushed past him, making her way to the kitchen.

The dog was getting hair all over her fancy dress, and she hadn't noticed. Or else she had, and she just didn't give a shit.

Logan felt one of those padlocks that he'd placed around his heart fall open.

If the woman could be so caring, so careful, with a stray dog that someone had dumped on his doorstep . . . how careful would she be with him?

"Do people drop animals out here often?" Turning on one of those impossibly high heels, Scarlett thrust the dog into Logan's arms, then went about the business of filling one metal bowl with water, another with a sample of dog food that a company had sent him. He couldn't hold back his grin when she cracked open a pack of ground beef and added a handful to the mix.

"You're ruining your hard-assed Mistress reputation." Logan scratched the dog behind the ears, then set it down in front of the bowls as Scarlett turned to wash her hands. "And not often, but yes, occasionally someone will drop an animal here. I don't mind boarding them while I look for a home—it's better than the animals being abandoned."

Mongo chose that moment to come charging into the kitchen, sniffing the air madly, his body quivering as he scented out the intruder. Spying the tiny fluff ball that was buried nose deep in his meal, Mongo let out a proprietary growl.

The newcomer sprang up, nipped Mongo on the nose, then returned to its business.

Mongo—all one hundred twenty pounds of him—yelped with surprise, then flopped down on the floor, rolled over onto his back, and stared at the pup adoringly, his tongue hanging out of his mouth.

Scarlett's and Logan's eyes met over the towel she was using to dry her hands, and they both burst into laughter.

"Not hard to figure out the dynamics in that one." She smirked as she made her way to Logan, seeming content that the puppy was filling its belly. To his surprise she pushed him down into one of the hard-backed kitchen chairs, then straddled his lap, facing him.

It was stupid, he knew, but the dogs set his mind at ease a bit.

It didn't always have to matter who was bigger, badder, more alpha. Sometimes nature just dictated that one was to dominate and one to submit.

Logan's cock paid attention when Scarlett wiggled herself into position on his lap. With her dress pushed up around her hips, her panties and his thin shorts weren't much of a barrier, and her damp heat surrounded him like a hug.

And then she wrapped her arms around him and hugged him for real, nuzzling her face against his neck. He realized with a jolt that she hadn't held him yet, not really—and knowing her, it was probably because she'd known he wasn't ready.

This time he surprised himself by hugging back.

"Thanks for indulging me with the dog," she whispered into his ear, and even though the feel of her lips against his ear made his cock surge, he found that he was content to just hold her and be held in return.

He couldn't remember the last time he'd *snuggled*. Since before he'd gone overseas, probably.

It was nice.

"Our guest will be here soon." Scarlett pressed her lips to his, momentarily fogging his brain. "If it wasn't going to be good for you, I'd be tempted to just ignore the doorbell."

Pleasure flooded through him at the thought . . . and then came the jealousy. Though by this point he knew it probably wasn't another sub—Scarlett wasn't that kind of woman, and what they had between them seemed real—she made him feel possessive.

"So this guest . . ." He started carefully, leaning back in his chair so that he could see her face. "Want to tell me anything more?"

Yes, Scarlett was not the kind of woman to flaunt another submissive under his nose. But that didn't mean that her friend wasn't *a* submissive, and to his way of thinking, any sub who didn't want Scarlett was soft in the head.

Grinding his teeth together, he waited for her response.

"Your jealousy is flattering." Resting her hands on his

shoulders for balance, Scarlett regarded him thoughtfully. "But since you need to trust me, I'm not answering. I'm going to let you suffer a bit longer."

"Of course I'm jealous!" The words burst out of Logan though he hadn't meant to say them. "I'm practically a recluse who has at least a decade on you. I'm submissive but can't seem to stop myself from putting you through hell."

The light slap across his cheek wasn't designed to hurt, but it startled him enough to rear back.

Scarlett had cocked her head, her eyes narrowed.

"So how old *are* you?" she demanded.

"Thirty-five," he answered reluctantly. Not *old* . . . but she was just starting out in life.

"Oh yeah, you're ancient," she agreed, her tone layered with sarcasm. "No woman who has spent years dealing with drunken frat boys could *possibly* be interested in a man with some maturity under his belt."

"Scarlett," Logan started, his words a warning. "I'm being serious. And I'm not in the mood for sarcasm."

She could have demanded that he get on all fours, could have paddled his ass for insolence. Instead she nodded, accepting his words.

Treating him like an equal, despite the roles in their relationship.

Right until that moment Logan hadn't realized that he expected his Mistresses to treat him like . . . something less. That some part of him craved it, and not in the sexual way in which some subs did.

The realization stunned him speechless, so Scarlett kept on talking without interruption from him.

"You don't give yourself enough credit. You're successful. Intelligent. Sexy as hell." She pressed an exaggerated, smacking kiss to his lips. "You're a real catch, Dr. Brody. So why don't you tell me why you've never had a Mistress for more than one night?"

"How do you know that?" He tried to pull back, furiously uncomfortable with the sharp turn their easy conversation had taken. "You don't know that."

"I do now."

Logan felt himself closing up under the weight of her stare. He couldn't tell her why he'd closed himself away from the world, or about the needs that kept him trapped out here in the middle of nowhere.

"Let's start with something easier, then." His tricky, persistent woman, acting like a pit bull with a bone in its jaws, tapped her finger against her luscious mouth, and he almost crushed his lips to hers to distract her.

That's what she would expect him to do. To try to grab control.

He wanted to do better.

"Tell me something about yourself." When he hesitated, she narrowed her eyes mincingly, then gently, so gently, wrapped her hand around his neck, a reminder of who was in charge. "I asked you a question, sub."

"I like to ride," he blurted out, squeezing his eyes shut. "I—when I'm on horseback, it feels like I can outride . . . memories."

Keeping his eyes shut, Logan waited for the shame to kick in. This was the deepest admission he'd ever made to anyone besides Luca.

Scarlett stayed silent, but he felt the softest butterfly touches brushing over his face, each press of her fingertips like the promise of a kiss.

He let her touch.

"Tell me something else," she demanded, running her fingers over his lips. He swiped his tongue over them, too, following her touch.

"I feel more for you than I want to." Opening his eyes, Logan found no disgust, no anger waiting for him on her face.

"In a relationship like ours, all of the power lies with the submissive. Remember that, Logan."

He opened his mouth to reply, though he had no idea what he was going to say. But the doorbell rang right then, the shrill buzz slicing through the tender moment. Both dogs yowled with excitement, the sharp yips of the stray punctuating Mongo's low rumbles.

"You answer the door while I put these guys in the dog run." Scarlett gestured toward the front door with one hand as she slid off his lap. Her lips twitched when she saw that even his difficult confessions hadn't eased his erection.

"You were wiggling around on my lap!" he protested, horror dawning when he realized he was about to answer his front door in nothing but teeny-tiny shorts and a big smile.

Anyone could be standing on the other side—a courier driver, a patient with a sick pet, even the town pastor.

Scarlett stood calmly, waiting, he saw, for him to make up his mind.

Grinding his teeth together, Logan drew himself up tall, then made his way to the front door.

If Scarlett wanted him to ride his horse naked through Las Vegas, he would try.

Because she listened.

Because she hadn't left.

Because whatever this thing was between them, it was growing stronger every day.

Cringing inwardly, Logan fixed a stoic expression on his face and swung open the heavy front door.

And sighed with relief when he saw that it was Luca.

"Come on in, man." Logan reached out a hand to his oldest friend, forgetting for a moment that he was wearing next to nothing.

Then he saw the figure behind Luca and froze.

"What's *he* doing here?" Logan couldn't hold back the snarl as he saw Bren, eyes cast down, waiting patiently for Luca to give him instructions. "I don't want him in my house."

"I don't believe you're giving the orders here tonight, sub."

Logan's jaw dropped as Luca—the man he'd been crammed ass to elbow with in the shittiest locations on earth—regarded him coldly, looked him up and down in a manner that told him he wasn't very impressed with what he saw.

Luca looked at him like a Dom would a sub, and despite every fiber of his being fighting the notion, Logan found his submissive training taking over.

His eyes went to the floor and he shut his mouth, though what he really wanted to do was slam the door in the other sub's face.

"That's better." Luca gestured to Bren, who stepped through the door quietly—always the perfect sub, Logan thought on an inner sneer.

Then Luca tapped him under the chin, sharply enough to hurt, forcing Logan to look him in the eye. "Your mistress says that you have a decent pain tolerance. But I feel compelled to remind you that you've never been under my whip."

Luca swept into the house, Bren following behind him. And Logan realized that, for the first time since he'd entered the lifestyle, he might have been maneuvered in over his head.

CHAPTER FOURTEEN

Scarlett kept a close eye on her submissive as she met Luca in the front entryway and proceeded to guide him into the dining room. Earlier that day she had set the table with a deep red tablecloth, a vase of wildflowers that she'd pulled from the fields behind the ranch, and fat white pillar candles that scented the air with sandalwood and candle wax.

She had intended for the setting to lend an air of formality to the evening, and if the others were feeling at all like she was, then she'd succeeded.

At ease in any situation, Luca followed her to the dining room table, sat in the hard-backed chair, and made himself comfortable. When he pulled Bren to him by the collar of his shirt, speaking in low tones that Scarlett couldn't hear, she knew that he was giving Bren his orders.

She was surprised and not entirely happy to see the other sub . . . but not, she saw, nearly as surprised or unhappy as Logan.

The longer she watched Logan, the more clear it became that his agitation stemmed from something deeper than jealousy or possessiveness.

At his heart Logan was an alpha male, wired to protect what was his, and now outsiders had invaded his home. It didn't take much of a leap of logic for her to realize that he thought of it as his sanctuary.

Despite the glares he shot Bren when he thought she

wasn't looking, she felt he was conducting himself quite well, considering. And Luca had helped her to position Logan right where she wanted him—on the edge and uncomfortable.

After their tender moment in the kitchen, she felt like they were so very close to a breakthrough, one that would bond them together more tightly. And yet weariness arrowed through her body at all of the maneuvering she was doing to bring him to that edge.

She simply didn't know what else to do, and she wanted him so badly that it made her ache. If she'd had even the faintest sense that he didn't feel the same way, she would have walked away.

But what was between them could be beautiful. It already was.

But it could still be more.

"Thanks for having us, Mistress Scarlett." Luca grinned at her as he leaned forward and placed his elbows on the table. "That title sounds good."

"Feels good, too. Most of the time." She directed the last at Logan, who started, then looked plain old pissed off at her comment.

She felt a twinge of guilt, but swallowed it away. If they were bickering, as they so often did, he wouldn't be focused on feeling like his home had been violated.

"Bren, Mistress Scarlett says that she has dinner ready in the kitchen. You will be serving it to us this evening." Luca didn't look at the other sub as he spoke. Instead his manner was that of someone who knew he would be obeyed.

Scarlett noticed that Bren cast a look in her direction before following Luca's directive, an odd hesitation for a submissive of his discipline.

"I've never seen you choose a male sub before." Scarlett had seen Luca top men in demonstrations at the club, in training, and even when a submissive had expressed a desire to live out a certain fantasy. But she knew Luca well—better than most. And her massive, overly charming Dom of a best friend was all about the ladies. *All* of the ladies.

Luca seemed to consider her comment as he carelessly handed a bottle of wine to Logan. Scarlett felt a quiet glow start in her chest when, though it was obvious that Luca wanted Logan to pour them each a glass, her sub looked to her for permission first.

She nodded, and though Logan scowled at Luca—making her bite the inside of her cheek to keep from laughing—he moved to the sideboard and retrieved glasses.

"I'm not averse to the idea, though you're right. I usually prefer women. But when Bren found out I was coming to visit you, he begged to be allowed the privilege of accompanying me," Luca finally said, holding out a hand for the wine that Logan had poured and brought back.

At Luca's explanation, Logan's hand tightened on the fragile stem of the wineglass, fingers clenching to the point that Scarlett worried it might snap and slice through his palm.

But Luca goaded Logan further, playing him into the hands of a Master.

Instead of sipping at the wine, Luca smirked up at Logan. "Take a sip, sub. I'd like to see how much of the information Alex and Elijah shoved down your throat so many years ago has stuck. If you can identify the type of wine, then you may go sit at your Mistress's feet."

Scarlett had to lift her own glass to her lips quickly to cover the laughter that threatened when she saw the strangled expression cross Logan's face. For a moment she would have put money on Logan dumping the liquid over his friend's head rather than sipping it.

But though he didn't look happy about it, he did as Luca had commanded. Slowly.

"I do believe that this effervescent beverage is a merlot, Sir." His voice dripped with exaggerated politeness, and Scarlett sucked quickly at the wine in her glass to hold back her laugh.

She'd known it would be tough for Logan to play the submissive in the presence of his friend. And he was behaving far better than she'd anticipated.

Which meant he was getting comfortable. Time to switch things up.

When Bren came back into the room, now entirely naked, a platter balanced on each hand, a wicked idea crossed Scarlett's mind.

"Master Luca, I see that you've commanded your sub to strip." Scarlett stretched lazily in her own chair, gesturing Bren to place the serving dishes on the table. "You know, my submissive is a competitive creature. An alpha in every area but the bedroom."

"I can see that." Luca grinned, and Scarlett knew that he was enjoying his friend's discomfort, a true sadist to the bone. "We'd best fix that, then."

Smiling, though her heart was pounding, Scarlett turned to face Logan, who was still standing beside Luca. "Strip."

Logan was already almost naked, that little set of brief black shorts the only thing protecting his modesty. But there was a massive difference between being allowed a few scraps of clothing and none at all, and Scarlett knew that.

Knew it and used it to her advantage.

"I said, strip." A streak of meanness entered her voice. Logan glared at her, his hands fisting at his sides.

"Like hell I will."

She supposed she could consider it an improvement that he was simply refusing, rather than making lewd suggestions about them going somewhere so he could get naked for her privately. But as she watched the struggle pass over his features, she wondered, not for the first time, if Logan was even capable of using his safe word.

It was time to stop thinking things through so much, to go with her gut. So she pushed further.

"You will, or you won't like the consequences." She paused to let the words sink in.

Logan's jaw worked as his entire body tensed. Finally, he shoved his shorts down over his hips, let them fall to the floor. When they reached his ankles, he kicked them in the general direction of Bren, who was still standing quietly by the table.

"That's better." Smiling teasingly, she reached over to take Luca's hand. Linked fingers with him—a joining of equals.

Logan's body quivered, as though he was trying to restrain his rage. He managed to stay still but couldn't quite hold back his frown.

Alpha in so many other aspects of his life, Logan had a hard time accepting anyone else's claim on her, even one as simple as friendship. His response thrilled her to her soul.

But Scarlett cast him a reproving glare. "I will touch whomever I choose, sub. Mind your manners, or I'll gag you."

Though he glared, Logan did as she said, closing his mouth.

"Very nice." Imperiously, Scarlett gestured to him. "Come here."

After stiffly stalking to where she sat, Logan knelt at her side. She saw the emotion and confusion on his face and hoped she wasn't pushing him too far.

They were on the edge—the edge of something. She just wished she could be certain that pushing them to fall was the right thing to do.

At Luca's command, the subs served up two plates of food. Scarlett had prepared a selection of simple finger foods—something that she'd been able to throw together after work that day, ones that could be hand-fed to a sub without becoming too messy. Bren had lined her plate with wedges of toast and soft cheese, crackers and pâté, slices of ripe strawberry and juicy melon, all things that she'd driven twenty minutes into town to purchase at the surprisingly well-stocked little grocery store.

Nibbling on bruschetta and melon, she fed Logan small bites more often than she bothered to take them herself. She had been certain that he would balk at eating his meal from her hand.

But while he still vibrated with tension, glaring at Bren every so often, he seemed content enough so long as her attention was focused on him. And when he brushed a hand over her ankle, a small sign of affection, her stomach pulled tight with a needy tangle of feelings.

"You've behaved very well, sub." The meal finished, Luca reached for Scarlett's hand, unifying them as the Dominants in the room. Tilting Bren's chin up with the toe of his boot, he nodded, his expression pleased. Scarlett tilted her head to one side, observing the pair of them . . . Something was off in their dynamic, just a bit.

"Thank you, Sir." Bren looked up at Luca, but his eyes strayed for a second—just a second—to *her*, and she saw what it was.

She'd never seen Bren anything but utterly focused on his Dominant. But though he had still been far more disciplined tonight than most of the submissives she'd ever come across, his attention was being drawn elsewhere.

To her.

In a rush she saw what was about to happen and swallowed down the words that rushed to her lips.

"I think you deserve a reward, slave." Luca grinned fiendishly over at Scarlett, and her heart sank.

"You're stirring the fucking pot! Stop it!" she hissed to him, but it was too late.

Bren turned his attention to her, inclined his head gracefully. Against her leg, she could feel Logan tense.

"If Sir permits it, I would like to serve Mistress Scarlett. However she will have me." Bren's eyes flashed with desire, and though she tried to control her facial expression, Scarlett felt her lips part with shock.

This—she would never have expected this from mild-mannered Bren. He had expressed interest in her before, yes, but she'd always thought that he was the kind of submissive who simply obtained pleasure from serving his Master or Mistress—whoever that Master or Mistress was.

Frantically trying to phrase a response, Scarlett felt the tension in Logan's body, still leaning against her leg, pulling tighter and tighter. Finally, his self-control seemed to snap, and he jumped like an attack dog on a chain.

"Hell no," Logan whispered, but in the sudden silence of the room, it sounded like a shout. "You don't touch her. You don't ever touch her."

Heat spread throughout Scarlett's midsection as realization washed over her.

This was exactly what she'd been searching for, a man who might let her lead in the bedroom, but who was strong enough to stand up for what he wanted without her.

A man like Logan. No, not even *like* Logan—just him. Only him.

The realization hit her like a sledgehammer—she loved him.

Her heart pounded in her chest, and she struggled to focus. She was trying to accomplish something big with him tonight.

But at that moment, she wanted nothing more than to send Luca and Bren on their way and to lose herself in Logan.

Focus, Scar. Discipline—he needed some, or he was doing them both a disservice.

He wasn't fully submitting to her. And neither of them would be happy—*could* be happy—until he did.

"Sit down," she told him quietly.

He looked at her, eyes narrowed. "You can't be serious."

Shifting in her chair, Scarlett placed one booted foot delicately in his naked lap. She didn't press—she didn't have to.

He flinched, but when he sat tall despite the threat, she was proud.

"You do not accept me as your Mistress, so you do not get a say." She felt a pang as she spoke, but her gut told her that this was the right thing to do.

"The hell I don't." Logan ground out the words, but she saw the flicker in his eyes, the hint of confusion.

It almost killed her to turn away from him, but she did. Luca caught her gaze and nodded slightly, the movement almost imperceptible.

She needed to get control over her hormones, because this was the perfect moment to push Logan further, to break him down.

"Follow me." She didn't look at Logan as she spoke, instead pushing away from the table.

Logan started to climb to his feet, and she froze him in place with one steely-eyed stare.

"On your knees." She licked her tongue out over her suddenly dry lips. "Subs who don't show proper respect don't get to stand tall."

From the corner of her eye, Scarlett saw Luca nod in approval, and her confidence grew. Sauntering across the room with no set plan in mind, she led Logan to the padded bench that Luca had had Bren bring in from his car earlier.

Logan clenched his jaw when she gestured for him to

climb up on the bench, but to her pleasure, he did it without comment.

"Very nice." She spoke quietly as she arranged him on his front, then knelt down in front of him. Starting at midthigh, she slid her hands down his legs to his ankles, her fingers making tiny circles over the solid expanse of his flesh.

"I'm going to secure your ankles to the bench." Scarlett massaged the sensitive skin of his instep lightly. Her heart thudded rapidly, knocking against her rib cage so hard that she thought it just might bruise. "And then I will bind your hands behind your back. What color are we at?"

Securing his ankles in the leather cuffs at the base of the bench with sure fingers, she looked up, waited for him to reply.

Though a muscle in his cheek twitched, he nodded easily. "Green."

"All right." Rising, dusting her hands off on her thighs, Scarlett circled behind Logan, admiring the view of his taut, naked ass as she reached for her toy bag and pulled out a pair of supple leather cuffs with a short length of chain behind them.

After tonight . . . maybe she wouldn't have to reach for her toy bag so often. Maybe she wouldn't have to use the symbols of dominance.

But tonight she did.

Scarlett secured his hands behind his back, ran a finger beneath each loop of leather to ensure that they weren't too tight.

Then, with her pulse accelerating to the point where she thought she might explode, she moved to the center of the room, meeting Luca's gaze.

It was time to push Logan's limits.

"Bren." The other sub, still kneeling at Luca's feet, looked up eagerly when she gestured to him. "I've decided how you may serve me."

"Anything you wish, Mistress." When she gestured for him to come to her, he crawled, though she would have let him walk.

She didn't like his complete and easy submission. She wanted Logan's fire.

Deciding not to make an issue of it, she crouched before him, looked into his face. "Bren, has anything changed on your limits list since the last time I saw it?"

"No, Mistress." A small smile curled the edges of his mouth—he clearly saw where she was going with this.

"Good." With her hands, she turned him to face Logan. "Do you think that my sub is attractive, Bren? Your honest answer, please."

"He cannot hold a candle to Mistress." Bren's lips twitched with amusement. "But he has a certain rugged appeal. If you're into that kind of thing."

Don't laugh. Don't laugh.

Doing her best to keep a straight face, Scarlett nodded, as soberly as she could.

"What about his cock? Do you think you might want to suck it?" The mental picture hit her like a sledgehammer, and she clenched her thighs together against the thought of Bren with his head between Logan's legs.

"No!" Logan's words were full of panic. "I don't want that. I don't want him to touch me."

"In your file at Veritas, I saw no mention of homosexual touching as a hard limit, sub. Has that changed?" Scarlett waited. In truth, there hadn't been much of anything on Logan's limit list.

He would let her push him; of that she was certain. But she would have to keep a close eye on him, to gauge how far was too far for her stubborn sub.

When they'd first met, he'd been proud of the fact that he had never used his safe word. But Scarlett was certain that he'd used his charm and his clever brain to keep all of his Mistresses from delving so deeply into his secrets that he would ever need to.

She was going to take him beyond that point. But she would have to make sure that she didn't take him too far.

Waiting for Logan's response, she watched his body language, the rising tension in that long, lean frame of his.

He didn't care for the idea; that was easy to see. But he wasn't panicking, wasn't showing any signs that this was a hard limit.

As she waited, he pressed his lips together mulishly. Scarlett nudged his ankle with the pointed toe of her shoe.

"Answer me, Logan."

His eyes spat fire, and he shook his head. She knew he wasn't going to use his safe word.

"Green. I'm green." But if looks could kill . . .

What he needs, not what he wants.

"Bren." Scarlett nodded at the sub kneeling at her feet.

"Whatever pleases Mistress." His tone told her that he had hoped she would command him to serve her more intimately, but he did as he was told.

A triumphant glare on his lips, Bren took Logan's cock in one hand. Scarlett swallowed her moan as the submissive fisted the shaft, then stroked up and down, his thumb swirling over the fat head, catching the moisture that beaded under his touch.

"Don't tease him, Bren," she chided gently, though in truth she could have watched him stroke Logan's cock all day. The sight was terribly erotic, all hard muscles and lean planes. But then, she'd always enjoyed watching two men together. "I want him as excited as you can get him, as fast as you can do it."

"Yes, Mistress." Bren looked up at Logan again with a wicked grin; Logan looked at Scarlett with panic.

"Mistress, please. Not like this. I'll behave."

Then Bren swallowed the head of his cock, and Logan let out a low moan, part in protest and part, Scarlett recognized, with pleasure.

He might not have chosen another man to bring him pleasure, but she was confident now that he wasn't as opposed to it as he would have her believe.

Slowly, Scarlett positioned herself behind Bren, so that she could watch what was happening. Placing her hands on Bren's shoulders, she looked at Logan's tortured expression and felt herself weaken.

Then she thought of the way he'd broken down after she'd pulled that first orgasm from him, that very first night they'd met. How he'd opened up once the control was taken away from him.

Steeling herself, she squeezed the hard muscles of Bren's shoulders with her fingers and nodded her approval.

"I'm not looking for you to simply behave, Logan, and if you don't understand that by now, then I've failed somewhere along the way." Below her, Bren slid the entire length of Logan's cock into his mouth, moving up and down, running his tongue over Logan's glistening shaft.

Logan bucked his hips, pushing his pelvis forward into Bren's mouth. Scarlett fought the urge to drop to her knees, to join that tangle of wild male flesh.

Her own needs had to come after those of her sub.

Logan strained against his bonds as Bren worked him with his tongue, his lips, both pressing forward, urging Bren on, and pulling back at times, trying to get away from the on-slaught of stimulation.

"Why are you doing this?" His words were a groan as Bren took his testicles in hand and squeezed gently. God, but the pair of them made quite a sight, all that muscle and sweaty skin and sinew.

"Logan, you know that you can stop this at any time. You have your safe word." But he was a damn stubborn sub, and in this particular instance, she was counting on it rather than cursing it.

Bren's clever mouth was taking Logan to the peak—and knowing that it was happening because Scarlett had commanded it and that there was nothing he could do about it unless he used his safe word...

It was a strong reminder of what she wanted from him.

Everything he had to give.

He would do what she asked, to prove that he was strong. And when he found pleasure at Bren's hands—and mouth—it would break down far more walls inside of him than if Scarlett had been the one to do it.

"Bren, I want you to bring him to the brink of release. Just the brink, but don't you dare let him come, or Luca will use his bullwhip on your ass."

The muscles of Bren's ass clenched at her words, and from behind her, Luca chuckled, the sound full of malicious intent.

Bren kept sucking, focused anew on his task. His cheeks hollowed as he worked Logan's cock, and Scarlett wondered again why it wasn't him, this obedient man, who made her want him so desperately.

But then she was caught up in the barely banked fury, panic, and need that swirled through Logan's eyes, and she knew.

She'd never believed in love at first sight, and furthermore, at certain times in her life—when she'd been fostered with families who seemed to be in it for the paycheck more than anything—she'd wondered if love existed at all.

She knew that it was way too soon to have fallen in love, really in love with Logan, especially since there was the very real possibility that he wasn't going to be able to give her what they both needed—that she wasn't going to be able to pull it out of him.

But she knew that she would fight for it. For him. For the potential future that lay between them.

Logan groaned and closed his eyes, breaking that intimate point of contact, as Bren sucked faster and faster, his head bobbing up and down vigorously. Scarlett watched Logan closely, noted the tightening of the muscles in his legs, the way his fists scrabbled at the padded leather of the bench.

"Stop. Now!" Clasping her fingers in Bren's hair, she pulled him bodily off of Logan, his mouth releasing the cock with a sound of wet suction.

Bren sighed with disappointment, but Logan—Logan's groan was a noise of pure frustrated agony.

"Son of a bitch!" He opened his eyes to glare at Scarlett. His cock was thick and deliciously swollen, the head purple and wet. After nudging Bren out of the way, Scarlett ran a delicate finger up and down the underside of the shaft, and Logan pulled against his restraints.

"You can be as pissed at me as you want." Bending, she pressed her lips to his in a soft kiss, eyes narrowing in warning when he tried to force his tongue past the seam of her lips. "But you need to remember. Your pleasure, or the lack of it, is my decision. My responsibility. If I want you to come with my finger up your ass, you will, no matter how vulnerable it makes you feel, because I have decided it for you. You can come in the mouth of another man and stop fighting the fact that it feels good, because I have told you that it's okay. Don't you see it yet?"

Suddenly frustrated, Scarlett curled her fingers around the base of Logan's shaft and squeezed, just enough to make sure that she had his full attention.

He shook his head, his body beginning to quiver. "I'm trying."

Scarlett squeezed a bit harder, and a flush from pleasure-pain spread over Logan's chest and neck.

"Until you give me control of yourself willingly—*all* of your control—then I will take it by whatever means necessary. Until you tell me to walk away." She gestured to Bren, who was still kneeling at her feet.

"Bren, go in my toy bag, please, and get me the cock harness. The one with the leather straps."

"No." Logan's voice was hoarse.

"No, or red?" Scarlett stroked him up and down, a gentle reminder—*whatever you won't give me, I will take. You don't have to worry about whatever hurts you, because I will take care of it for you.*

Logan remained silent. Scarlett hesitated.

She'd heard of subs who couldn't be trusted to use their safe words when they needed to. But Logan—it wasn't that he was too far gone to use it. More that he was too stubborn for it, that he felt he could continue to hold on to that thin edge of control if he didn't admit defeat.

Tonight she needed to push him to give his troubles into her care.

If it didn't happen tonight, she wasn't sure it ever would.

"The harness, Mistress." Bren returned with it, a sleek fall of wine-red leather that Luca had given her as a gift for passing the submissive portion of her training.

"Thank you, Bren." Scarlett took the leather straps in her hands and began to unbuckle the metal fastenings.

"I don't need that," Logan said quickly, eyeing the leather that would fit around his cock. "I won't come."

"I know you won't," Scarlett said, then, despite his protests, eased forward and wrapped the first of the leather bands around his waist, buckling it into place. "Consider this a symbol. A sign that you can't come until I give you permission."

That I am the one patient enough to break you down. To care for you, to nurture you.

A low moan escaped his throat as Scarlett wound another leather strip through his legs, then cinched the buckle at the base of his spine. Then, her touch exquisitely careful, she secured another loop of the supple leather around the shaft of his cock, another at the base of his testicles, taking extra care to make sure that neither was too tight.

Stepping back, she admired her handiwork.

God, but he was magnificent, bound to the bench, cock jutting magnificently out of the red leather that bound him.

Arousal was a tight knot in Scarlett's belly, but tonight wasn't about sex, apart from its use as a tool to pry Logan open.

Tonight was about emotion. About the power exchange and what it could bring to them both, if Logan would just finally give in.

Logan looked at her, anger and misery twined tightly together in his expression as he watched her back away.

"I'm doing this for you," she reminded him. "What you need, not what you want."

Turning her back on him when the air between them was so charged that she could feel the sparks crackling in the air, Scarlett retrieved a chair from the dining table, pulling it halfway across the room.

Luca caught her eye as she moved. His expression was cautious, watchful, and a pang of apprehension worked through her.

She was going past the point where even her mentor had experience. But then again, she doubted that even Luca had ever encountered a sub as stubborn as hers.

She owed it to Logan to press onward.

Slowly, making a show of it, Scarlett sat down in the chair. Bending over far enough that both Bren and Logan could see down the front of her skintight dress, she extended one leg out in front of her.

"These boots are gorgeous, but they're killing my feet already." Her fingers found the side zipper and inched it down in a mini striptease. "Bren, there's a bottle of massage oil in my bag. Fetch it, please, and then come kneel in front of me."

"I don't want him to touch you." Logan's expression was fierce, but this time he didn't pull at his bonds. "Please, Mistress."

"If you had been a well-behaved sub tonight, I would have let you pull these zippers down with your teeth." Easing her foot out of one boot, Scarlett started on the other. "Just to remind you that you are mine."

If he could have broken out of his bonds, Scarlett knew that Logan would have in that moment. And he even would have done just as she asked, inching the zippers that fastened her boots down with his teeth, bit by bit, just to show Bren that it was *Logan's* privilege to serve his Mistress.

And it would push him further still, make him want even more of a claim on Scarlett, if he had to watch Bren touch her—even if the touch was fairly innocent.

"The oil, Mistress." Bren returned and knelt in front of her, his expression eager.

"Would you like to massage my feet, Bren?" Scarlett forced

herself to look at the sub at her feet rather than at Logan, though her attention was caught by her own man.

"Very much." Bren was beautiful in his submission, but yet it came so easily to him.

What would Logan be like, in the same position? Always testing, always pushing at her.

Always making it that much sweeter when he did finally give in.

Closing her eyes, Scarlett extended one foot to Bren, knowing that he would consider it an honor to serve her. She let out a true sigh of pleasure when firm fingers found the ball of her foot and pressed, hard. If there was a woman alive who didn't enjoy a foot rub after spending a few hours in sky-high heels, she didn't believe it. And more than that, she was grateful for a moment in which to center herself.

Logan was acting as she had expected him to, for the most part. But there was an edge of desperation to his demeanor, and she just didn't know if the evening was going to end as she wanted it to, or if it was going to blow up in everyone's faces.

Finished with her right foot, Bren set it gently onto the floor, then took her left into his hands. Scraping his nail over the pad of her big toe, he worked in circles down the length of her sole, drawing a moan of pleasure from her.

She shifted uncomfortably in her chair when she heard Logan's grunt of frustration. She was as aroused as he was, and it was all directed at Logan. Stretching her arms above her head, Scarlett allowed Bren to work on her feet for a few minutes more, ever aware of Logan just feet away, watching her every shift, her every breath.

When she deemed that she'd gotten him worked up enough, she pushed herself upright and pulled her foot from Bren's grasp.

"Thank you, Bren." Deliberately turning away from Logan as she opened her eyes, Scarlett looked sidelong at her fellow Dominant. "Luca, I do believe that your sub deserves a reward for obedience."

"I agree." Luca rose fluidly and fixed his eyes on his sub, a predator scenting its prey.

At her feet, Bren trembled.

"You reward obedience." Logan's voice was hoarse, rasping against the air, pulling Scarlett's attention from her mentor. "But is that really what you want?"

Turning her head slowly, Scarlett allowed her eyes to wander up and down the length of his body, all of those muscles of his highlighted by the crossing straps of leather.

The head of his cock was beaded with moisture, the shaft stiff and unyielding, and the sight made liquid heat pool between her thighs.

"You know what I want."

"How shall I reward such a good little submissive?" Luca spoke as if Logan hadn't said anything at all, and Scarlett turned back to him, giving Logan time to think about what she'd just said.

Luca opened his own toy bag, studying the contents, rejecting item after item until he found something that appeared to meet his standards. He grinned, then stood, looking down at Bren, who was still kneeling at Scarlett's feet. In his right hand he held a large anal plug; in the other a set of wicked-looking nipple clamps with razor-sharp teeth.

"I'm sure a well-disciplined sub like you can take both of these without bondage or a gag. Am I right?" He glared down at Bren, who looked both rapt and terrified.

"No, Sir. I mean, yes, Sir. I can take them."

"Mistress Scarlett, if you would assist me?" Luca nodded

to his bag, and Scarlett went to retrieve the lubricant that she knew would be there.

She could feel Logan's eyes following the scene, taking in the details, puzzling over why painfully sharp nipple clamps and a butt plug that would force a submissive to orgasm would be a reward. And Scarlett knew that was exactly why Luca was setting this scene.

Logan needed to see that when a sub let a Dom take over, there was peace to be had. Once a sub gave up control—an easy thing for a sub like Bren—that Dom took away the worry, made sure the needs of their sub were met.

Giving up control didn't have to be scary or painful. It could be a reward in itself.

And Scarlett now understood why Luca had let Bren tag along.

"Hands laced behind your head." Luca stood tall over Bren as the sub assumed the position. Luca toyed with the clamps as he stood, sizing up the other man, and the flickering light from the candles made the metal gleam, the points wickedly sharp.

Scarlett knew that this had to be an exercise in restraint for the sadistic Dom. Luca had said that he didn't mind giving pleasure where he could, and Scarlett knew that this was true . . . but she also knew that her friend found the most pleasure when he could administer enough true pain to release an endorphin high in his submissive—and when the person on the other end of his bullwhip craved the wicked burn.

He was here solely for her benefit. Scarlett owed him one. Though when she thought back to the way that Luca had neglected to mention to her that her future employer had been in Veritas that first night—the way he'd referred her in the first place . . .

She wouldn't have been entirely surprised if the control freak billionaire had planned all of this from the start, thinking that she might be able to help his oldest friend heal old wounds when nothing else could.

"Very nice. See how nicely he holds that position, Mistress Scarlett? Such discipline."

Scarlett murmured her assent, but while she did, she snuck a peek at Logan from beneath her lashes.

His stare was fastened on her. Always on her.

Why wasn't that enough for her?

Because neither of us will be happy while we're both fighting for dominance.

Luca knelt down on the floor, in front of Bren. With a wicked look in his eyes, he dipped his head, fastened a mouth that Scarlett knew firsthand was talented on a nipple, just the way that Scarlett had done with Logan in the barn.

Bren groaned, shifting beneath Luca's mouth.

"Be still." Scarlett caught a flash of white teeth, heard Bren's sharp intake of breath, knew that Luca had nipped at the tender flesh.

Then Bren moaned, long and loud, and Scarlett saw the gleam of the silver metal, all of those tiny, razor-sharp teeth biting into his tender flesh.

Luca repeated the action, and Bren's eyes started to glaze over as he embraced the pain, the first sign that he was slipping into the euphoria of sensation.

Scarlett remembered from their scene together how easily Bren was taken to the edge. There was no challenge, no sense of accomplishment. And there were plenty of Mistresses out there who would be thrilled with a sub of his countenance.

She found that she liked the ones with fight in them.

"Now, then." Pulling his toy bag closer , Luca reached for the bottle of lubricant.

"Turn around. Cheek to the ground. And don't you dare make a sound."

His color rising, Bren did as he was bid, lowering himself to hands and knees, then down to his shoulders, and finally to press his cheek against the sleek hardwood of Logan's living room floor.

He sucked in an excited-sounding breath when Luca drizzled lubricant over the lean planes of his ass and again when a buzzing noise announced that the anal plug in the big Dom's hand was a vibrating one.

And then Luca pressed the well-lubricated tip of the plug to Bren's anus, pressing it in far more quickly than Scarlett would have done with Logan. But then, Bren was far more experienced a submissive than her own man.

And while she might have preferred Logan to Bren, she still found it arousing as hell to watch Luca begin to move the plug in and out of Bren's tight flesh, to see the disciplined sub struggle to hold back his moans.

"Don't you dare come yet." Luca began to speed up his movements when Bren's body tightened, his brow dripping sweat to the floor. His eyes were squeezed tightly shut, his skin flushed, and Scarlett knew that he was quickly approaching climax—a release that would happen for no other reason than because Luca had decided that it would.

"Bren, you're about to have an earth-shattering climax. Why is that?" Luca's voice held grim pleasure, the sadist clearly enjoying making his sub wait.

Poor Bren looked like he was having trouble remembering to breathe, let alone pull his wits together enough to answer a question. But his features scrunched in concentration as he seemed to draw on his inner control, after a long moment in which he shuddered and seemed like he was about to come regardless of his Master's orders.

"I'll come because . . . Sir . . . told me to." Bren sank his teeth into his lower lip so hard that he drew blood. "And that . . . is why . . . I'll like it."

"Very good." Luca spanked Bren's ass then, a violent flurry of blows that would heat the skin. "You may come now."

Unable to hold back any longer, Bren came with a shudder and a shout, pulling away from the intensity of the plug, then pushing toward it, writhing as Luca relentlessly held the vibrator in place.

Scarlett kept her peripheral vision on Logan, wanting to absorb every bit of his reaction to the scene that was unfolding before his eyes. His face was a mask of confusion and need as he watched the other man lose all control.

But it was when Luca cupped Bren's jaw in his large, skilled hand that Scarlett saw the change come over Logan.

"Thank you for giving me your pleasure," Luca said quietly, the words meant only for his sub. "Thank you for trusting me with your needs."

In that moment, as the late-evening sky finally darkened into night and the flickering flames of the candles cast tantalizing shadows over Logan's face, Scarlett saw what she'd worried that she never would.

There, mixed with the confusion and that stubbornness that she knew would never leave him completely, was desire . . . but not the physical kind. For the first time since they'd met, in that moment, Scarlett was certain that Logan wanted to submit to her fully—he just truly didn't know how.

Running her tongue over her lips to moisten them, she inhaled deeply to steady herself. Then she moved to stand directly in front of Logan, blocking his view of the other men.

Planting her hands on her hips, she did her best to stand

tall, despite the fact that she was no longer wearing her heels.

"Please, Mistress," Logan rasped.

Scarlett cupped the chin of her sub in her hand, leaning forward to press the most delicate of kisses to his lips.

"Tonight you will be mine."

CHAPTER FIFTEEN

Though Luca and Bren were still in the room, they were absorbed in their own scene, to the extent that it felt like Logan and Scarlett were trapped in their own world.

Logan's eyes flashed when Scarlett pulled out a gag.

"I don't need it. I'll be quiet." He shook his head vehemently.

Scarlett arched an eyebrow at him before pressing the rubber ball that was centered between two leather straps against his lips.

He tried to push the ball away with his tongue.

"Logan, I know that you don't need this to be quiet if I command it." She hoped that he would pick up on the confidence that was trying to bestow on him.

He stopped pushing, and she slid the ball into his mouth, then secured the strap behind his head. His eyes widened as he struggled to shift his breathing solely to his nose, but when she handed him a rubber dog toy, he seemed to calm down.

His eyes held a questioning look.

"If you need to stop, squeak this toy, or drop it. That's all you need to do." Scarlett's heart warmed when she saw Logan clutch the toy in a death grip, where he normally would have scoffed at it.

He knew that something was about to change, as well.

"And the reason that I have gagged you, despite the fact that I trust you not to speak, is purely symbolic. Like the cock ring, I want the extra reminder that your care is in my hands, Logan. Do you understand? Nod or shake your head."

Slowly, Logan nodded it, the golden hair taking on shadows of crimson and umber from the candlelight.

Scarlett pressed a kiss to his forehead, then set about undoing the buckles that held his cock harness in place.

"Whatever demons you have." She started off quietly, her fingers moving efficiently rather than seductively. "You don't have to be plagued by them when you're with me. I will take care of them for you. It is both my purpose and my pleasure."

And while he had no choice but to remain silent, Scarlett knew, he would also turn her words over in his head, working at them with his busy mind like one would attempt to unravel a knot in a length of rope.

Eventually, progress would be made, no matter the initial resistance.

"You have served me well tonight, Logan." Scarlett reached for her own bottle of lubricant, poured a generous amount in the cupped palm of her hand, even as Logan's eyes widened and he began to shake his head. "I want to give you a reward, like Luca did with Bren. I'm going to make you come. If it's too much for you, you *will* use that squeeze toy."

Logan shook his head, and she heard him try to speak, but the words were muffled by the gag.

His resistance, she knew, wasn't to the fact that she was about to give him pleasure. That, the mutual exchange, was something they had both signed up for when first becoming involved. He was scared of losing control, so she would make him climax in a way that ensured he couldn't do anything about it, no matter how desperately he tried to hold on.

"Did you see how Bren reached for that release, Logan, rather than fighting it?" Moving to stand behind him again, she leaned over and bit his neck, savoring the resultant shudder. "I know you, and I know you won't embrace that loss of control easily. But remember that it's me who has you, me who is giving you pleasure."

Checking to make sure that the rubber toy was still held tightly behind his back, Scarlett slid her fingers down the crack of his ass, then slowly but steadily pressed one finger in.

"Mmm!" Logan's exclamation was again muffled by the gag. After a moment in which he pulled against the bonds, he seemed to settle further into her touch, his body opening, allowing her in.

Biting her lip, Scarlett waited for it. Needing to keep him on edge, she'd chosen a lubricant that heated with friction, wanting to awaken that tight bundle of nerves inside of him instantly. She wanted to pull his climax from him so fast and hard that he couldn't think.

The muffled groan and frantic tightening of the muscles around her fingers a moment later told her that the heat was working. Logan's hips bucked frantically, fucking the air like it was her body, and Scarlett felt her blood heat.

"Fast and hard, Logan." Mercilessly, she rubbed in circular motions inside of him, knowing that his body was on fire, nerves sizzling to life every time her hand moved. "Not because you decide to, or because it feels good, but because I want you to."

When an intense shudder racked his body and she heard another moan, she slid her finger out, added another, and moved back in, zeroing in on that same spot.

"Come for me, Logan." The movements of his hips became ever more frantic as he sped toward the climax she'd chosen as his destination. Grunts and moans came from behind the gag, muffled swears trying to escape as his entire body drew taut against the bonds, turning him into a magnificent specimen of virility at the moment of surrender.

His fingers held tight to his squeaky toy as he thrust forward once, twice, three times, jetting liquid heat into the air. Sweat shone on his skin from the pleasure that had racked his body, and Scarlett pressed herself against him from behind, absorbing the shudders as he quieted.

When he was once again still, she pressed a kiss to the nape of his neck, then moved to stand in front of him. Though his eyes were tired, his body was still tense, wary from what she'd just forced it through.

"You please me very much." He averted his eyes, his brow furrowed, as she quickly cleaned him and the floor, then paused by her toy bag, considering. "But I'm not nearly done with you."

Quickly, she unbound the gag, massaged his cheeks, and took away the squeaky toy, giving him back the power of speech. And just that simple gesture had Logan clawing to regain control.

"If I wasn't gagged, I could do better things with my mouth." He was mad, she knew, mad that she'd forced that orgasm from him without any way for him to stop it without resorting to that toy, mad that she was forcing him to confront how he felt.

Well, he was about to get madder yet.

"Watch your mouth or I'll gag you again." To show him what she thought of his smart-assed comment, she inched the short, tight skirt of her dress up to her hips, then hooked her fingers in the elastic at the edges of her red lace thong. Logan's mouth fell open when she tugged the brief garment down, letting him have only the quickest of looks at her bare pussy.

"You fight dirty." It wasn't the first time he'd said that to her. Scarlett smiled wickedly, then tossed her thong into Bren's lap, where he was wrapped in a blanket, leaning against Luca on the couch.

"Thank you, Mistress Scarlett." Bren dangled the thong from one finger, deliberately taunting Logan. Luca halfheartedly cuffed him on the ear as Logan snarled.

"I'll fight dirtier yet," Scarlett said, pulling a long vibrator from her bag.

"No way in hell are you putting that anywhere near my ass," Logan spat out. Where minutes earlier he had seemed on the verge of surrender, he now seemed to have taken a huge step backward.

"Well, it's certainly not going in mine." This time using her regular lubricant, Scarlett ran her hands over Logan's chest, his hips, as she circled the bondage table.

A muffled snort of laughter sounded from the direction of the couch, but Scarlett barely heard it.

Her focus was on Logan—entirely on Logan. It was do or die—time to master him or let him go.

"What do you want from me?" The panic came out heavier now, weighing down Logan's words. "I'm doing the best I can."

"I want more than that." Flicking the switch to turn the vibrator on, Scarlett pressed the tip right where her fingers had just been. "I want all of you."

She wanted him to the point that he could give no more, wanted all of him, and tonight, she thought with a fresh wash of determination, she was going to take him there.

"Scarlett. No! Fuck it. No—oh!" Logan shouted as Scarlett firmly pressed the vibrator forward, working it through the ring of muscle, then pressing it home. He shuddered at the onslaught of sensation, his muscles pulling it in farther still.

"I want to have you inside of me, to possess you in every way." Scarlett's body had grown slick with sweat, her own nerves humming as she moved the vibrator in and out, watching Logan's erection rise anew before her eyes.

Her clit swelled and pulsed, and her blood sizzled in her veins. It likely would never cross Logan's mind that this was torture for her, too—that while she might be forcing pleasure from him, her equal punishment was one of denial.

"Then fucking take me already." Logan's voice rumbled from his throat. "Stop punishing me for not giving something I don't know how to give."

"I'd take you if I believed that that was true. It's killing me, I want you so much." *In, out. In, out.* Scarlett let the vibrator drag slowly when she pulled it out, before making it slide quickly back in, savoring the rasp of his breath, the swell of his cock when he again began to draw near to coming.

"But I believe that you *can* give everything. And you will. You'll give it to me." Securing the vibrator in one hand—she could feel the rapid contractions of his muscles reverberating all the way up her arm—Scarlett slid the other arm to Logan's front, pinching his nipple hard before sliding her hand down, encircling the steel length of him with her fingers.

"You're going to come again for me, Logan." She began to stroke him, moving her hand up and down with firm, sure strokes. His erection jerked heavily against her palm, and it caused her pussy to flood with her own wetness.

"I can't." But his head was thrown back, his Adam's apple bobbing as he rode the pleasure.

"You can. I want you weak, wrecked." Rubbing her thumb over the head, she pulled hard, rough. "Now."

Logan shouted again as he came, and this time his cry was distinctly more animal sounding. His hips again bucked at the air, searching for her, Scarlett knew, but she remained where she was behind him, holding the thick length of the vibrator inside him as he climaxed again.

"No more, Scarlett. I can't."

Scarlett held him as he sagged back against her, checking that he hadn't damaged the skin beneath his bonds. Taking another wet cloth in hand, Scarlett again cleaned the evidence of his pleasure from his skin, letting him take her silence for assent.

But when she knelt in front of him and caught his stare with her own, feeling the jolt of that connection between them, she slowly drew her fingers into the straps of her dress, tugging them down over her shoulders. Her nipples peaked when the cool air hit them, the sensation frigid against the burning heat of her skin.

Logan licked his dry lips, then looked down at her like she was the only woman in the world.

"Please, Scarlett," he begged, shifting restlessly on the bench. "Please. Let me touch you. Let me make you feel good. Let me inside you. I'm begging."

Begging, and yet she thought that he still might try to wrest control from her the second she released his bonds.

Slowly, she shook her head.

"You can give me more." Distant sounds told her that Bren and Luca had set up another scene, but she didn't care—she couldn't.

The world had narrowed until it contained nothing more than her and Logan. She had him on the very edge of capitulation, and she prayed that she had the sheer will to bring him the rest of the way.

That what was growing between them was strong enough.

She swallowed his protest down as she parted her lips and took his cock into her mouth. Above her, Logan gasped, and when she began to slowly stroke her tongue along the length of him, she tasted sweat and sex before she felt him start to stiffen again for an impossible third time.

She knew there were Mistresses—and Masters—who would never dream of kneeling at their subs' feet.

Scarlett had never believed that true power came from the rules alone, though they certainly had their place as ways of breaking a submissive down.

But when a person was truly the Mistress of another . . .

It didn't matter if they stood tall over the other or knelt at their feet. And so she chose to give him this gift, a way to unravel her beautiful submissive further still.

"No." Logan's voice sounded in air that was thick with lust when Scarlett began to suck harder, hollowing her cheeks, pulling until he was again fully erect in her mouth. "I said no!" He snarled at her, his body beginning to recoil; then he pushed forward, his hips pressing his cock deeper into her mouth with every thrust.

Adrenaline poured into Scarlett's veins in a liquid rush as she watched the man above her—the intelligent, amazing, stubborn as all fucking hell man—transform from an intelligent being to one that was more animal than man. His body tensed, writhed, his movements both begging her for more and screaming at her to stop.

Twining her hands around the base of his shaft, she twisted them in alternate directions as she worked him with her mouth. This—*this* was where she'd been trying to get him, the point at which his mind stopped working and what he truly wanted, truly needed took over.

He spoke, a never-ending stream of desperate words that made no coherent sense as a flood of precome released onto Scarlett's tongue, and she felt dizzy, knowing that it was because of desire for her that he had been reduced to this mindless animal.

When he began to buck in earnest, driven past the point of

control, the bench skidded forward, stopped, then moved again. Scarlett gagged as his cock hit the back of her throat, but she continued to press forward, working him with her mouth, knowing how close he was to so much more than mere physical release.

"No!" Logan howled, and Scarlett let her fingers slide to his hips. Digging in firmly with her fingers, she held tight, keeping him in the wet cavern of her mouth as he cried out an ungodly sound and shattered.

Tears stung the backs of her eyes, and her jaw ached as she rode his bucking body. But though he thrust, and thrust again, no liquid flooded her mouth, his climax expressed solely through the shudders of his body.

Making a humming noise, she held tight as he thrust furiously into her mouth, wilted back against the bench, only to be overcome by a series of shudders once again.

When he finally stilled, Scarlett remained frozen in place for a long moment before she leaned back and let his cock fall from her mouth. Her knees ached and her eyes were full of tears, but as she looked up at Logan and saw the uncharacteristic laxity of his facial muscles as he inhaled, she wondered if she had done it. Or if maybe she had gone too far.

"Shh," she whispered as she stood stiffly, securing the top of her dress in place once again. Her own fingers were shaking from the raw intensity of what had just happened and from second-guessing herself as she undid the fastenings that held Logan to the bench. He slumped back, his muscles seeming too weak to even support himself upright.

"You did well," she whispered as she brushed a sweaty lock of hair out of his eyes—eyes that were wide and filled with the wonder of a child. And he had. She could tell he was cruising very close to subspace, that wonderful headspace that came with the rush of endorphins after an intense scene—a place she was fairly certain no Domme had ever been able to take him.

But she'd pushed him there, had taken him to the edge of her own limits, and still he hadn't used his safe word. Hadn't faced the demons in his soul.

She had failed him. She wasn't strong enough for him.

"Scarlett," Logan whispered hoarsely as the last of the bonds fell away. For her own pleasure, and more, to bring herself some calm, Scarlett ran her hands over Logan's chest, the lines of his hip bones, down the length of his cock.

She avoided his eyes.

"Scarlett."

Her heart thudded in her chest when Logan tangled his fingers in her own and brought their entwined hands to rest on his chest. Beneath her palm she felt the quick, steady *thump, thump, thump* of his heart.

Logan lowered his head until their foreheads pressed together. Scarlett felt her pulse skitter in her veins when those blue eyes of his looked directly into hers, the shutters deep within them finally gone.

"Bunker," he whispered hoarsely. "Red."

The rhythmic thumping of Luca's flogger as it struck the skin of Bren's back echoed up the stairs as Scarlett helped Logan to his bedroom.

Earlier this evening he'd been ready to flay his friend alive for coming into his home and treating him like a submissive. But now he saw that he should thank him.

Not that he would. Or else maybe later. Right now his legs were so weak that he was having enough trouble walking.

He was so exhausted it hurt. That was why, he assured

himself, he made no protest when Scarlett led him to the bed, pulled back the worn quilt, and then tucked it back in around his naked body.

"I'm going to take a shower," she said softly, and though her demeanor radiated calm, in the depths of those wide eyes of hers, he could see the same shock that reverberated through him.

Later he would welcome some time alone, to think about what had happened. But for now . . .

For now his body, his soul accepted what his brain would have trouble with later—that he had finally, completely surrendered.

Before panic could set in, Logan followed his impulse and slid from the bed. For a brief moment he thought about trying to join Scarlett in the shower, and he was swayed both by the thought of her naked in the shower, water streaming over her breasts, and by the temptation of getting clean, of rinsing all the frustration and fear and anger down the drain. A baptism, kind of.

A really kinky one.

But in the end, he followed the urge that had pulled him from bed in the first place.

Padding across the hardwood, Logan chose a place at the end of the bed and knelt on the floor. Arranging his hands palm-side up against his thighs, he sat back on his heels and waited.

When Scarlett came out of the bathroom, followed by a cloud of steam, he sensed her pause rather than saw it, because his stare was trained on the ground.

And then her bare feet were in front of him. He could just make out her shapely calves, and the smell of his own soap was teasing at the inside of his nose.

"Logan." Her voice resonated in his gut, and when she

urged him with a press of her fingers along his jaw, Logan looked up, really *looked* at this woman who had crashed into his life like a wrecking ball, tearing down everything he knew to be true.

She was so delicate-looking—the stereotype of the ballerina that she'd once been.

But he'd never met anyone so strong, anyone whom he'd trust to hold him up when his own strength faltered.

It was humbling.

It was terrifying.

It was amazing.

Words failing him, he just let himself look. Her cheeks were flushed with heat from the shower and free of any makeup, hair wet and tangled and dripping on the floor—and she was the most beautiful thing he'd ever seen.

"Come." Holding out her hand, Scarlett waited for Logan to rise from the floor. His instinctual reaction was to do it himself, but then he saw the symbolism behind her extended hand.

He *could* do it by himself, sure. But he didn't have to.

"There. Was that so hard?" A smile in her voice, Scarlett pulled him to her once he was standing, wrapping her arms around his waist. Wanting more contact, and since he would have had to stoop just to rest his chin on her head, Logan let his hands fall to the round curves of her ass, naked beneath the thin cotton of his T-shirt, which she'd pulled on after her shower.

Scarlett squeaked with surprise as he lifted her, then wrapped her legs around his waist.

"Is this okay?" Logan pressed his forehead to hers as he slowly carried her to the bed. He wasn't entirely sure what she expected from him now.

But what he'd intended as simply a show of affection was

rapidly, impossibly heating his blood yet again. From somewhere he found a reserve of energy that kept him going. The
way he held her had the delicious heat between her legs pressing against his cock and causing it to stir back to life, and with
her arms around him, her smell assaulting his senses, he was
overwhelmed with the need to express physically what he was
feeling in his heart.

Scarlett's soft, steady breathing hitched when he slowly
slid her down the length of his body, placing her on her knees
on the bed. Reaching for the hem of her T-shirt—*his* T-shirt—he
waited before pulling it over her head, his eyes searching hers
for permission.

"Go ahead." She smiled and held her arms up to help as he
tugged the cotton up and away, throwing it over his shoulder.
Hesitantly, he traced his fingers over the delicate lines of her
collarbone.

"Is this . . . I mean . . . may I touch you?" Logan had had
plenty of sex in his teens and early twenties, and he had always
been the aggressor. Since returning from overseas, a series of
frustrating, failed encounters in which he felt driven to be
both passive and aggressive had led to Luca taking him to his
first BDSM club, thinking that he might be dominant.

Instead he'd found the most satisfaction playing the submissive to a dominant woman, and he hadn't had a vanilla encounter in more than a decade.

And while he wouldn't label anything that he did with
Scarlett as vanilla, since they both had their established roles,
he was a little uncertain of how to proceed without all of the
props that kink provided.

"Logan." Taking his hand, Scarlett mimicked what he had
done downstairs, linking her fingers in his and pulling his
hand to cover her heart. The steady thump of its beat soothed
him, lured him, like a siren with its steady consistency.

"Just do what feels right. What feels good." Smiling, she bent forward to place a kiss on his chest, the highest point that her lips could reach.

Her next words floored him. "I trust you."

Logan blinked, his mind whirling, searching for the perfect way to respond, to tell her what that meant to him.

Words eventually failing him, he did the next best thing, tangling his hands in the damp tendrils of her hair, tilting her face up, and kissing her.

"Oh." Scarlett sighed against his mouth, and he inhaled the sweet scent of her breath. Her lips parted beneath his, opening for him, and Logan let his tongue slide over the front of her teeth.

The kiss heated in a slow simmer that finally had them both gasping for breath. Logan savored the way that she shuddered when he let his hand close over her breast, his thumb playing over her nipple.

When he sank his teeth delicately into the curve of her shoulder, she cried out, reaching up to fist her hand in his hair, tugging not so gently, urging him to do more.

Logan couldn't quite hold back his grin. Scarlett had the decency to look abashed.

"I like to be in control." She shrugged, let her eyes narrow playfully. "That's nothing new."

"Maybe not." Pulling back, Logan let his eyes wander over her entirely, from the top of her dark head to where her knees pressed into the mattress, and all of the luscious skin in between.

He wanted to explore. He wanted to taste.

He wanted to *learn* her the way she'd learned him.

"No, you being in control is nothing new. But all of this is, for me." Clasping her around the waist, appreciating the soft curve of her belly, Logan lifted her, then laid her back down on the bed.

Eyes locked on hers, he pulled her until her hips rested just over the edge of the bed. He watched her every step of the way, silently asking for permission as he knelt on the floor, hooking first one leg, then the other over his shoulders.

He waited one more moment, giving her a chance to say no.

"Please." Propping herself up on her elbows, Scarlett looked down the length of her body toward where he knelt, his head between her thighs.

"Please what?" He couldn't help the response, grinning as he mimicked the words she'd said to him so many times.

Scarlett mock glowered, drumming her heels on his back.

"Lick me, slave." She growled at him, arching her hips toward where his lips waited. "You've begged for it often enough. Take your chance before I change my mind."

"Whatever Mistress wants." Logan lowered his head, nuzzled his nose into the soft curve of her belly. He could smell her—that spicy hint of arousal that he'd scented every time she'd played with him.

His body tightened with anticipation—he thought he could come, just like this, just being so close to what he'd wanted for what felt like forever.

He heard Scarlett sigh as he parted her thighs, then blew a warm breath over her glistening labia. He wanted to devour her whole, but something inside of him was forcing him to take it slow.

To savor.

"Logan." He could hear how difficult it was for her to hold back the commands, to let him explore, and he appreciated the gift.

But he also wanted to give her every bit as much pleasure as she had given him. So he lowered his head and put his mouth on her, making sure to keep the caress frustratingly light.

She arched when he used his thumbs to hold her open and circled her clit with his tongue, her back curving up off the bed, a gasp escaping from her lips.

"*Logan.*"

He couldn't hold back a smile as he intensified the pressure of his tongue. He knew that this woman would never beg, but hearing the need pulling her voice tight was every bit as satisfying.

Applying himself to his task, he licked, long slow swipes of his tongue, then flattened his tongue and brushed it over her swollen nub with a series of hard, quick flickers.

Scarlett propped herself up on her elbows to watch, her gaze catching his as he slid two fingers inside of her, groaning himself when he felt the snug heat suck at his hand.

He held the eye contact as she began to rock against his hand, surprised that the connection felt almost as good to him as his fingers surely did to her.

Still looking up at her, across that expanse of beautiful creamy skin, Logan intensified the pressure of his tongue and began to slide his fingers in and out. Her lids dropped to half-mast, though she held his stare, and her hips began to rock, pushing her wet heat into his mouth, where he devoured her, his need to possess her rising like a summer storm.

Fuck my mouth, he wanted to say. *Use me.* But he was afraid to break the spell, to disturb this chance he finally had to take her over the edge.

And he understood now why she'd made him wait.

This was the first time he'd used his mouth on a woman

for the sole purpose of pleasing her. He wasn't using climax as a way to take control.

Above him, Scarlett moaned low in the back of her throat, the rocking of her hips increasing in speed. He continued to slide two fingers in and out of her slick heat, continued to slide the flat of his tongue over the swollen nub of her clit, savoring the taste of her arousal on his tongue.

He slid his free hand across her belly, then up to cover one breast. Catching her nipple between thumb and forefinger, he rolled it tightly, enough to give her a bite of pain, a spark of sensation.

"Aah!" Scarlett cried out, shifting restlessly on the bed. This was the closest that Logan had ever seen her come to losing control, and yet he knew that she was in no way submitting.

Even in this, as he played her body with his hands, his mouth, it was because she had said so. And so Logan was free to channel every dirty thought he'd ever had into driving her higher, ever higher, until her pleasure spiked, and her inner walls clamped down on his fingers and tongue, and she cried out as she shuddered beneath his touch.

Scarlett growled when he eased his fingers out of her, propping herself up again to watch him as he wiped the back of his hand over his mouth.

Her stare was so fiercely possessive that Logan felt his pulse stutter before picking up again to beat double time.

"Condom." Fisting both hands in his hair, she tugged until he did as she asked and slid up her body. She parted her lips beneath his, her tongue sweeping out to taste, to claim his mouth. "Now."

He moaned into the kiss, sinking his teeth into her lower lip before pulling away. "I need a minute."

She nipped at his ear, hard enough for a spark of pain to ignite before shoving him away with both hands. "Hurry."

Though it nearly killed him to take his hands off of her, Logan hurried to the closet—he stored the one piece of luggage that he owned in the spare room. The small bag he'd taken to Vegas with him lay on its floor, empty now save for the one thing he always brought with him. Even though a Domme usually supplied them, he always brought a backup.

Condoms.

Pulling the small box from the bag, he turned to find Scarlett watching him with a smirk on her lips.

"Were you just ogling my ass, Mistress?" Grinning, he sauntered back over to her, enjoying the way she could make him feel ten feet tall. Standing beside the bed, he tore into the box, extracted a condom, and ripped open the small foil packet.

"No, I was ogling *my* ass." Pulling the ring of latex from his fingers, Scarlett pinched the tip, then slowly rolled the condom down his length, causing Logan's eyes to roll back in his head. "This ass belongs to me."

The woman had wicked fingers. And when she trailed those fingers lightly through the crease of his behind, then smacked him hard enough to sting on the hip, he felt his cock stiffen to the point of pain.

He wanted to climb onto the bed, to cover her body with his own, to possess her.

He needed her to tell him that she wanted that, too, and so he stood by the bed and waited.

Their gazes met, held, and Logan felt everything inside of him stir, aching with need. And then her beautiful lips curled into a smile, and catching his fingers in her own, she tugged him toward the bed.

"Take me, Logan. However you want to."

However you want to. Downstairs, while she'd been teasing him, torturing him, deliberately stirring all of those forbidden feelings inside of him, he had wanted nothing more than to let his passion explode, to come together with Scarlett hard and fast, a mating explosive in its intensity.

But now he found himself climbing onto the bed, kneeling between her parted thighs. He bent to lay a kiss to her belly, then clasped her hips and pressed the head of his cock to her pussy.

"Oh." Scarlett sighed when he slowly eased forward, rocking back and forth, a little further each time, until he was immersed inside of her, the heavy weight of his balls pressed against the tight curve of her ass.

Beneath him, she shifted restlessly, arching her pelvis up to meet his.

Settling his elbows on either side of her, Logan brushed his lips over hers.

"I just want a moment. Just one moment like this." A moment to savor the way she felt around him, her muscles working to accommodate his cock, her slick heat embracing his erection.

Both the softness of her body and the steel of her will voluntarily yielded to him for this one perfect moment in time.

Catching his face in her hands, Scarlett pulled him down until they were nose to nose. "Mine."

And then her nails were digging into his shoulders, his back, and the bite of pain made it hard for him to breathe. Logan pulled back, pushed forward again, wallowing in the pure pleasure of being inside her delicious heat.

"Yes!" Scarlett was no passive bed partner beneath him, her body arching and bowing and demanding that he service her, demanding *more*. "This. More."

Bracing his weight on his hands, Logan moved inside of

her again and again. He wanted to stay this way forever, to be lost in her.

"You're so beautiful." Though by that point he couldn't have stopped his hips from moving, he slid one hand in her hair, brushing it away from her face. Her cheeks were flushed, her eyes half closed, her lips slightly parted.

No matter what happened between them, the mental picture of her, like this, would be burned into his memory forever.

"Isn't that my line?" Scarlett smiled at him, and the utter trust in her eyes—trust in him now that he'd reciprocated—nearly undid him.

"Mistress." Burying his face in her neck, Logan began to move harder, faster, craving that delicious friction more and more.

He could have called her by her name—he knew in that moment that she would have allowed it.

But here, like this, there was only one true title for her.

Sliding his hand between their bodies, he worked his way down over her belly, through her folds, to find her clit. She cried out when he worked his thumb back and forth, and in turn he heard a roar building at the back of his throat when his climax began to gather in his toes, his testicles, the base of his spine.

"No." He didn't mean to speak out loud, but he couldn't help it. He fought desperately to stave off his release, just long enough for her to come. "You first."

"Together." Then Scarlett wrapped those long dancer's legs around his waist, arching up to meet him, and he felt the shudders begin to work through her body. When she called out his name, he felt everything inside of him drawing tight, felt the erotic pull of her body demanding his release.

He exploded with the intensity of a runaway train, jetting

inside of her so hard that he saw stars. He came, and shuddered, and pulsed again, emptying himself, giving himself to her.

It wasn't until that very moment, his entire being wrapped up in Scarlett, that, despite having returned home from overseas and moving to Montana a decade ago, he finally felt like he had come home.

CHAPTER SIXTEEN

A n incoherent cry woke Scarlett from a deep, delicious sleep, the kind that comes only when both body and mind are exhausted and empty.

Opening her eyes, she blinked into the weak, pale light of dawn, momentarily disoriented.

She was in Logan's room in Montana, not back in Vegas. The events of the previous night flooded back in, and with them came a bone-deep satisfaction.

Her stubborn sub had finally surrendered. She wanted to wallow in the bliss.

But then another cry sounded, and she came fully awake, remembering what had pulled her out of her dreams in the first place.

The mattress rocked beneath her, and hands reached out against her skin. Lurching upright, Scarlett squinted into the dim light, discovered Logan thrashing in agitation on the bed beside her. Sheets were entangled around his legs, binding him in place, and while restraints might have brought him a certain kind of peace while he was awake, they certainly had the opposite effect when he was sound asleep.

"Let me go. Let us out!" His voice was hoarse, raw. He turned toward her, and Scarlett jolted when his wide-open eyes met hers, unseeing, a quick glimpse of him before he rolled away again.

He was asleep, locked in the throes of a nightmare. And

judging by the sweat slicking his skin, the convulsive movements of his body, he wanted out of it, desperately.

"Logan." Scarlett placed a hand on his shoulder, then just
as quickly pulled it back. She'd heard that it was bad to wake
someone while they were sleepwalking or dreaming. But she
couldn't leave him to ride out this dream, not when he was
clearly so miserable.

Helplessness washed over her, and she detested it, rejected
it. Moving on instinct, she lay back down in the bed, shifting
so that her front pressed along the length of his back.

"It's okay. I'm here." Wrapping her arms around his waist,
she held on tight, leaving his arms and legs free to move.
"You're not alone."

She continued to whisper soothing words to him even as
his long, lean frame jerked and shuddered in her arms, ini-
tially resisting the embrace.

When she pressed a kiss between his shoulder blades, he
stiffened. She did it again, and the first hint of tension began
to melt from his body.

"I'm here," she whispered again, holding him close. "Give
all of this to me. I'll take care of it."

It could have been five minutes or it could have been an
hour, but finally, the big, hard body relaxed, melting into hers.
Scarlett could hear her pulse pounding in her ears as the threat
passed and her body started to come down from the adrenaline high.

What the fuck was that?

Slowly, the man in her arms shifted, rolling over to face
her. His lids were open but at half-mast, his eyes sleepy.

"Scarlett?" Though he wasn't fully awake, she still saw the
shame reflected in those pools of deep blue—shame that he
had lost control, even in his sleep.

"Don't." Though she whispered, she made her tone sharp. She didn't elaborate, but saw the shadows in his eyes start to drift away under her command.

She held him until at last his breathing was deep and even, and it was clear that he'd fallen back to sleep.

Scarlett was surprised to find herself shaking a bit as she eased out of the bed, pulling the quilt back up, tucking it in around Logan so he wasn't subject to the early-morning chill.

Knowing she wasn't going to be able to go back to sleep, she padded back to her room and quickly dressed in jeans and a thick woolen sweater. A Saturday, there would still be chores to do, but not as many.

Scraping the mess of her hair back into a bun, she blinked at herself in the mirror, startled by how vivid and alive she looked, even in the early dawn hours.

She'd thought she had a pretty good handle on who she was when she left Vegas—had thought she'd known what she wanted. She'd always had an innate confidence, a belief that she could handle whatever life threw her way.

She'd had to, or she never would have made it through the foster system in one piece.

But as she turned from the mirror, headed down the stairs in search of coffee, Scarlett contemplated the fact that being with Logan was showing her that she might have facets of herself that she didn't know yet at all.

Until now she'd thought she had all the answers, that she could be the rock for him to lean on as he learned how to give up control.

"Christ." Scrubbing her palms over her face, Scarlett entered the kitchen to find a half-empty pot of coffee. Pouring a mugful, she chugged it black, burning her tongue in the process.

But it cleared her mind enough to think.

She hadn't spent a night in Logan's bed before. She hadn't known he suffered from nightmares. And the dream she'd just helped him escape told her that his demons were far darker than anything she'd ever anticipated.

She was a twenty-four-year-old woman. She wasn't sure she had the tools to do the right thing faced with such deep-seated pain.

But she also knew she would do everything within herself to try, to be there for him. Still, the intensity of the scene the night before, his ultimate surrender, and the events of that morning had left her more than a little shaken.

She couldn't handle any more caffeine. Setting her empty mug in the sink, she pulled the kettle out of the cupboard, filled it with water from the tap, and set it on the stove to make some tea.

"You're up early."

Scarlett heard the quiet click of the back door before Luca spoke. She turned with a fresh mug and a packet of chamomile tea in hand, not bothering to smooth out the troubled crinkle that she knew furrowed her brow.

"Let the dogs out into the dog run."

"Thanks." She smiled tiredly at Luca before opening the paper packet, extracting the tea bag, and twining the string around the handle of her cup. After Logan had fallen asleep the night before, she'd tiptoed downstairs to make sure that Luca and Bren had found everything they needed. She hadn't been worried about them making themselves at home—Luca was close enough to both her and Logan that she'd known he would feel comfortable. "Couldn't sleep anymore."

"Do you need to talk about last night?" A Dom to the core, Luca touched others like he had every right to, and while she might have bristled if another Dom tried it with her, when he wrapped his arms around her waist from behind, she simply sighed and settled back into the hug.

"No," she replied honestly, placing her hand over Luca's much larger one where it rested at her waist. "Last night went better than I'd hoped."

He squeezed her waist, and then Luca lifted her onto the counter, turning her as he did so that their eyes were nearly level. "What has you so troubled this morning, then?"

Looking into Luca's dark chocolate eyes, Scarlett was tempted to lean on him, to beg him for help, to let him take away some of her burden. And he would let her—entirely apart from their friendship, the Dom in him wouldn't be happy unless he gave her the support she couldn't give herself.

But she was a Domme, too. And by pushing Logan until he'd surrendered to her, she had said without words that his burdens were hers to share.

Hers, not Luca's. And as the minutes passed, taking her farther away from that awful moment upstairs, when she had seen her long, lean alpha male writhing in agony on the bed, she felt stronger, more able to handle it.

So rather than accepting the implied offer, Scarlett smiled wryly and reached out to cup one of Luca's cheeks in her hand for a quick squeeze. The dark shadow of his stubble tickled her palm.

"You warned me he wouldn't be easy." Pushing Luca away, she slid down off the counter when the kettle began to whistle, wanting to catch it before it shrieked.

"I see." Luca's eyes tracked her around the kitchen as she poured the steaming water into her teacup, adding a squirt of honey. She'd been here in Montana, in this house, for only a few weeks, but it already felt like home.

"I know you do."

Luca would see what she wasn't saying—that she'd discovered that Logan's complexities ran so much deeper than just a stubborn alpha of a submissive. He had history that would be hard to navigate.

But they would do it together.

"Go easy on him, Scarlett." The corners of Luca's eyes crinkled with concern as they regarded her thoughtfully. "I know you must be a little upset that he hasn't told you everything yet. But believe him when he says that he can't."

"I'm not upset with him." The thought hadn't even crossed her mind. Some Dominants demanded a certain level of trust right from the beginning, but Scarlett had always thought of a D/s relationship as a dance, a meeting of two sets of needs and desires trying to entwine in a way that worked for both parties.

She had only just broken him down to his first level of submission. There was plenty more to work through between them before he would trust her with his darkest secrets.

But the fact that he'd done so in his sleep, turning to her to shelter him, to be soothed, warmed her heart.

"All right, then." Running a hand over the stubble that lined his jaw, Luca nodded, accepting her decision that the subject was now closed. "Well, we've got to get going. The meeting at the restaurant is in a few hours, and I need to check into the hotel and clean up first."

"Off the farm, into the boardroom?" Scarlett teased, blowing on her tea to cool it.

"Hardly." Luca's tone told her exactly how excited he was to be conducting business in such a rural location. But he was thorough—he wouldn't have been able to make his billions any other way—and Scarlett knew that he would do what needed to be done, regardless of how long it kept him out of the city.

"Is Bren staying with you?" Though Scarlett now understood that Luca had allowed the submissive to accompany him just as a means to help her work with Logan, she was still a bit curious at the full nature of their relationship.

"No. I'm taking him to the airport before I check into the hotel." Luca's voice was wry, and Scarlett saw that he knew exactly where her mind had strayed. "We enjoyed each other last night, more than I had anticipated. But he came out here just to see you."

"Oh." A pang of guilt took up residence in Scarlett's chest. She knew that she'd never led him on, but she also knew what it felt like to have feelings that weren't returned.

"He'll be fine." Again, there was that hint of something *more* in Luca's eyes, something regarding Bren, but it was gone in a flash, so quickly that Scarlett thought she might have imagined it. "But I do have to get going."

"Thanks for coming." She accepted Luca's hug, inhaling the familiar scent of her mentor. When they drew apart, she hesitated, then blurted out the question that was plaguing her.

"Luca, you know things about Logan that I don't yet. Do you think . . . ? Do you think I'm capable of handling everything? Of being strong enough to support him?"

Luca ran a hand through her hair, a gesture of simple affection. "Do you remember what I said to you that first night you met him?" He waited, patient with her as always.

"You said . . ." Scarlett racked her mind, and when she remembered, she felt relief at her mentor's confidence flood her body.

If anyone can handle him, it's you.

Clutching her tea, she saw Luca to the front door, waved at him and Bren as they drove off. If Bren was upset with her for not returning his feelings, he didn't show it as he grinned out the passenger's side window at her and waved goodbye.

Making her way around the side of the gigantic house

once Luca's sleek, ridiculously expensive SUV had disappeared into the horizon, Scarlett retrieved both Mongo and the new rescue dog, herding them inside for breakfast.

"And you'll let your new friend eat first," she told Mongo sternly. "He needs it more than you."

In response Mongo did a little dance that made the belly in question jiggle, and Scarlett couldn't help but laugh.

Scooping the smaller dog off the ground, she carried him back into the kitchen, hugged him close to her shoulder as she measured out more kibble samples.

"He sure doesn't look like he has anyplace else he wants to be."

Scarlett stiffened, but forced herself to relax before turning around to face Logan as he walked into the room.

Freshly showered, he was dressed for work already—well, half dressed, the button of his jeans still not done up, his plaid shirt open over the solid wall of his chest, his feet bare.

He made her mouth water and her heart stutter all at once. And that feeling, she realized, would help her be whatever he needed her to be.

"What about you?" she asked, stroking her hand idly over the pup's matted fur. "What's on the agenda for today?"

Her eyes searched him anxiously as he made his way across the kitchen, then pressed a kiss to her forehead.

Did he even remember waking her with his nightmare a few hours ago? Did he know that she now had a bit more insight into why he was the way he was?

And then he knelt at her feet, the amber light of the morning sun making him seem lit from within.

He lifted his head to look at her, and though she could tell that some of the apprehension over submitting that he'd had before last night had returned, he seemed to be doing his best to hold it in check.

"We're going to take a day off," he told her, his eyes a clear, bright blue. "To do whatever your heart desires."

After so many years of locking away the trauma deep down inside where even he couldn't have access to it, last night he'd let someone get a step closer to opening him up, something he'd never intended to do. He knew why he was submissive, and it wasn't a deep, dark secret—he just enjoyed sex more when someone else had control.

Part of Logan—the loudest part—wanted to pull away from the bright, beautiful creature living with him for the next year, to hide in the darkest corner and analyze what had happened and why.

But now that Scarlett had gotten her foot wedged in the doorway to his soul, he wondered if maybe, deep down, he'd always hoped to find someone who would force their way past all of the boundaries that he had set, who would see inside him and still care.

It was terrifying. And yet, now that that door had been opened with her, he wasn't entirely sure that he could ever go back.

He had never before had anything—anyone—to cling to when he lost control.

And as he led Boone, the horse he used most often on the trails, out of the stable and he saw Scarlett perched on the edge of a hay bale, swinging her legs and looking like she belonged, his heart did a slow roll in his chest when he realized just how tightly he wanted to cling to her.

"You want to go for a ride?" Logan asked, reaching out a hand to help Scarlett up. She'd told him to put a saddle on only one horse, so he'd assumed she wanted a riding lesson.

"I do." She let him steady her as she shakily climbed onto

the horse herself, but surprised him when, instead of taking the reins from his hands, she looked down at him with amusement on her face as she adjusted her backpack, turning it so that she carried it on the front side of her body, leaving room for a rider behind her.

"Are you coming?"

"I figured you wanted a riding lesson." When they had first spoken on the phone, Scarlett had admitted that while she had been on a horse a few times, she really didn't know how to ride, though she was eager to learn.

"I do want lessons. But not today." Leaning down from the horse, she extended an arm for him to grasp. "This is how I help you get on, too, right?"

Logan laughed; she looked calm and cool, but her fingers were wrapped in a death grip on the reins. He placed his hand in hers, but didn't need to use her for support as he hooked his foot in the stirrup, then swung himself up behind her, reaching around her waist to pry the reins from her hands.

"So Dr. Scarlett Malone is afraid of riding." Logan adjusted himself on the horse. The two of them in the saddle together made for a tight fit that he didn't mind all that much, since it pressed her ass so sweetly against his cock.

Craning her neck to look over her shoulder, she shot him a prim look. "I most certainly am not afraid of riding a horse. I'm afraid of falling off the horse."

His spirits rising, Logan nuzzled his face into the soft clouds of her hair. "Good thing I'm here to hold you on, then."

Whistling to Boone, he started off at a slow walk, letting Scarlett get accustomed to the movement of the animal beneath her. "Where did you plan on us going?"

She shrugged, leaning back into him, seeming content to let the warm morning sunlight shine onto her face. "You told me you liked to ride. So we'll just go ride."

Lazy contentment stole through him. This was so different from the way they had interacted so far.

It won't last. That nasty little voice in his head snuck through the door that Scarlett had opened, making him worry more than he ever had before.

He knew it couldn't last—he saw now that that was part of why he had fought Scarlett so hard. Part of him had sensed that he had met his match, that this was the one woman who could make him care.

He already cared.

And then she would leave, because she was not the kind of woman who would be happy staying out here, confined to an existence in the middle of nowhere.

And he couldn't live anywhere else.

Guilt sliced through his contentment, and Logan shifted guiltily in the saddle. He remembered Scarlett asking what he wanted and telling him that she wanted it all.

He had replied that he wasn't sure he could give her that. And now he wondered what would happen if he did and she couldn't keep it.

"What has you so tense?" Leaning back on his chest, Scarlett craned her neck to peer up into his face.

The word *nothing* was on the tip of his tongue—it would be so easy to just brush the worry aside, to pretend that it didn't even exist.

But that would be a lie, and not only would Scarlett detect that in an instant . . . he found that he didn't want to betray her by giving her anything less than the truth.

"I'm thinking about what's going to happen in the future." He could feel his brow furrowing as he spoke, and he had to hold himself back from smoothing it down with a hand.

He expected Scarlett to zero in on what he *wasn't* saying,

but instead she smiled and reached behind her to smooth those worry lines away herself.

"For today, I just want you to live in the moment." Those gray eyes caught his stare and held. "Okay?"

The sense of relief that filled him was as warm as the sun. "Thank you." Giving in to the impulse, he stroked a hand down her cheek, savoring the way her cashmere-soft skin warmed beneath his fingertips.

His hand came to rest on the backpack that Scarlett was carrying in front of her.

It moved beneath his hand.

"And just what do you have in here?" He grinned when a hint of guilt twisted Scarlett's lips. He noticed the bits of fluffy fur sticking through the mesh front of the bag.

"He cried when I headed for the door," she said, raising her chin in the air. "I might like to use whips on men, but I'm not heartless."

The pup chose that moment to press its nose against the mesh, letting loose a pitiful whine. Logan couldn't help but laugh.

"Hang on to your puppy," he advised. Then, with a light snap of the reins, he urged Boone into a canter, causing Scarlett to shriek with alarm and clutch at his thighs . . . which was not a bad side benefit at all, to his way of thinking.

The day was warm, and Logan didn't think he'd ever enjoyed a ride more than this one, with Scarlett snuggled in between his thighs.

By the time they approached the edge of the small lake on his neighbor's property, about a forty-five-minute ride, Logan felt more at peace than he had in years. He slid off Boone's back, then helped Scarlett off. With a smack of his hand on Boone's butt, he sent the horse off for a drink, and Scarlett turned to him with wide eyes.

"This is going to probably sound dumb, coming from a vet," she started, eyeing the horse that trotted over to the lake's edge. "But shouldn't we be tethering him?"

Logan grinned and reached for the backpack she still wore. His hands skimmed the sides of her breasts, and he savored the sharp inhalation of her breath.

"We're in cougar country. Tying your horse up could mean condemning them to death." Scarlett's hands tightened on her backpack; Logan pried it from her fingers.

"If he wanders off, he knows his way home." Unzipping the backpack, Logan removed the bundle of fluff that had been lulled to sleep by the rocking of the horseback ride. "And I don't think that this little guy is likely to stray too far."

Beneath the pup, he found two slightly squished sandwiches, wrapped in plastic, and two bottles of water. Extracting them, he set out their picnic, and the pup took a few cautious steps, making it to Scarlett's lap before curling back up.

Her fingers ran over him competently, and Logan watched the familiar motions as she checked him over.

"I've been neglecting your internship," he said, grimacing as he reached a hand out to help still the dog when Scarlett probed his belly. "I'm not being a good supervisor."

Scarlett cast him an incredulous look, lifting the puppy to kiss his head. "Are you kidding me? I've learned a ton out here."

Logan scowled down at one of the sandwiches as he unwrapped it, then handed it Scarlett. "It feels like we haven't done much work."

And even when he was working, it was . . . easier. Lighter, because he carried thoughts of her with him throughout the day.

"Excuse me, but I've learned lots of things I never would have in the hospital." Playfully, she poked him in the side, then bit into her sandwich. "I now know how to suction out a horse's nose. You think they teach that in college?"

Logan laughed; she always managed to tease him out of the serious moods, away from the darkness that still stole over him from time to time, no matter how many years passed.

"And we actually have been keeping to a pretty regular schedule," she reminded him, her voice mild. "Taking a Saturday off isn't going to kill you."

He knew that—he even did it himself from time to time. But it was hard to accept that he'd been working as hard as he always had, when it didn't feel like it anymore.

"Work can be fun, you know." Her voice was light, but Logan heard the underlying seriousness. "Some people actually prefer it that way."

Her attention was caught by the pup, who had gotten brave enough to trot a little ways off, and this time, Logan didn't push to tell her the full truth—that he'd lived so long by himself, entrenched in the way he needed to do things, that having lightness in his life just felt wrong.

"Six! That's far enough." Crawling after the dog, Scarlett snagged him, then returned to her cross-legged position by Logan.

"Six?" Logan asked, willingly letting himself be pulled out of his thoughts.

"See if you can figure that one out." Scarlett handed over the squirming bundle.

Eyes narrowing at the challenge, Logan ran his hands over the dog, checking him—and it was a him—over with the same thoroughness that Scarlett had used.

When he came to the left front paw, he paused, then grinned.

"Six toes." The grin and the softness in her eyes when she

looked at Six told Logan that Mongo was going to have a new roommate. At least for as long as Scarlett stayed.

But he had to remember that it wouldn't be for more than a year. She had big plans to open an animal hospital back in Vegas, and he wouldn't be the one to stand in the way of that. Not even inadvertently by consuming time that should be spent training her.

"Starting Monday, we need to make sure to keep all of . . . this . . . outside of work." He started, his heart clutching in his chest when he noted her frown. Reaching over, he stroked his finger down her nose. "For your future, Scarlett. Humor me."

Frowning, she nodded, and he forced himself to smile, even though the thought reverberating around his brain made him wince.

Your future once you've left. Your future without me.

CHAPTER SEVENTEEN

Two weeks had passed, filled with work, sex, and easy companionship—well, easy most of the time.

It was interesting, trying to figure out how they got along when the whips and chains weren't present. But the more that Scarlett got to know her rough-around-the-edges submissive, the more she wanted from him.

It made her a little bit uncomfortable—her life plans hadn't included becoming involved with a man who ferociously avoided cities, towns, even places where lots of people would be under one roof.

He hadn't told her anything about why he lived way out where he did, or why he was so strongly claustrophobic, and until he offered the information freely, she wouldn't ask.

It had to do with his dreams, though; she was sure of it. He didn't have them every night, but about once a week he would stiffen in terror beside her, muttering about letting him out, letting him free.

And while Scarlett still hoped that he would share that secret part of himself with her, she was pretty sure that even sharing wouldn't heal his need for open space.

Could she be happy here? She didn't know. Her anxiety over being able to handle Logan's demons lessened as she waited—and waited—for him to share them with her.

But instead she worried about what would happen if they could make it work.

Was she being ridiculous, thinking so very far ahead? But

still, she had gone ahead and made her demand and wondered how he would react.

I want you to take me on a date.

Even now, as she waited for Logan to respond, she tried to push away that thread of insecurity. It would work or it wouldn't, and if it didn't, she would grieve and try to move on, no matter how much the man in front of her had changed her life.

But she was tainting the time they had now by forever wondering and doubting.

Forcing herself back into the present, she raised her eyebrows and tapped her foot when Logan leaned around the edge of the stall where he was rubbing down Boone to look at her, perplexed.

"What?" he asked, and Scarlett scowled, straightening.

"You heard me just fine," she told him. Reaching for a length of rope that hung on the barn wall, she coiled it around her fist and elbow, watching Logan's eyes darken as his mind strayed to exactly the place she'd intended for it to go.

"If you can't be bothered to listen to what your Mistress says, then maybe we need to have a little reminder lesson on how a good sub behaves." She swung the end of the rope back and forth, saw interest spark on his face.

They had made love at least twice a day since the night that Luca and Bren had visited, and while she didn't use kink props every time, her toy bag was still a big part of their sex life.

But her insides heated at the thought of another meticulously plotted scene, and she could see that Logan felt the same.

She filed that away for future use.

"We're still on the clock here, *Mistress*." Finishing with Boone, Logan stood and wiped his hands down the front of his jeans. When he sauntered to her, sweat highlighting the planes of the chest she had full access to since she'd ordered him to work with no shirt on, she felt her pulse trip pleasantly at the base of her throat.

"So maybe it's you who needs a lesson." He took the rope from her hands, crowded right up into her space. Trailing the frayed ends of the hemp down her cheek, between her breasts, he smirked when she sucked in a breath.

"Insolent submissive." She couldn't help but grin as she pushed him away. "Remember how much you hated spanking me? It would never work."

Logan coiled the rope neatly and hung it back on the wall as he tracked her movements with his eyes. "You're partially right. I could never punish you. I hated every one of those marks that I laid on you, and I won't do it again."

His gaze took on a predatory glint as he started to stalk toward her slowly. Scarlett planted her feet and tilted her chin up, refusing to retreat even an inch.

Pulling her flush against his body, he ran a finger along the length of her collarbone, then slid his hands down her body, and with a light touch, cuffed her hands in front of her, her wrists caught in his long fingers.

"But I might not mind having you in some light restraints. Keep you in place so that I could really explore you. Could find all the places on that luscious body of yours that make you scream."

Scarlett held perfectly still until he released her, then stepped back. Her gut told her that this time he wasn't testing her. This was a fantasy for him.

"Perhaps that's something we'll explore later," she said lightly, leaning forward to sink her teeth into his biceps hard enough to leave a mark. Marking him as hers.

He jumped at the sudden bite of pain, but then she saw heat flash in his eyes. "We could explore it now."

"On the clock, remember?" Teasingly, she slipped out of his reach, running through the barn door before he could catch her. "And you have a date to plan."

"When?" he called after her, sounding somewhat puzzled with the freedom she'd given him. Though the rigidity in their sexual roles had relaxed somewhat since that night when Logan had surrendered so beautifully to her, Scarlett had found that he still was the most relaxed when their out-of-work activities were planned by her.

"Friday." Thinking of the way he'd challenged her moments earlier by binding her wrists with his fingers, she decided it was again time to push him out of his comfort zone a bit. And if he did well, then maybe she'd reward him the way he wanted.

Maybe. Her heart pounded at the very idea of letting someone else take control.

"It's all up to you."

Scarlett enjoyed watching Logan put his mind to the task over the next few days. She would catch him watching her, paying excruciating attention to detail as she selected clothing in the morning, or even just when she chose a flavor of tea.

He could snap at her one moment for disagreeing with him over a potential treatment for a sick dog on a house call, and the next he would be watching her again, even as his blue eyes were darkened by his scowl of irritation.

She imagined that some would say she had become a Domme because she wanted to exert control over her life after the chaos of her early years in the foster system. Perhaps that had played a part in her choices, but Scarlett was more inclined to think that she was just one of those people who needed something that the vanilla world couldn't offer.

Watching Logan, she often found herself puzzling over which camp he fell into—was he a sexual submissive because of whatever haunted him? Or was he the same as she was, just drawn to something a bit left of the norm when it came to sex?

The attention to detail he applied to planning their date told her that in the end, it didn't really matter. And it no longer even seemed strange to her, to have this bossy, domineering man find ultimate pleasure when she took away his choices.

It was just . . . Logan.

Friday night, three weeks after Luca and Bren had visited, Scarlett descended the stairs from her bedroom. Her new pink skirt—something she'd been surprised to find in town—swished around her knees, and the clingy fabric of her black top made her feel very aware of herself as a female, something that was all too easy to forget out here in cowboy territory.

Logan had asked her to wear a skirt for their date. She wondered where they were going. Wondered how he would handle being in any kind of crowd.

"Wow." Logan exited the kitchen just as she stepped off the last stair. His eyes devoured every inch of her—the girly skirt, the length of her legs, elongated in her high-heeled sandals, the way her breasts pressed against the clingy fabric of her top.

A fire began a slow burn inside of her. Even without any of the trappings of kink, she wanted this man.

"You look absolutely edible." He made his way to her slowly, hands shoved in his back pockets in a way that made the denim of his jeans stretch tightly over his impressive package. Though he didn't touch her, he dipped his head and sniffed at her perfume. "*Mmm.* Vanilla."

Scarlett watched, fascinated as his cock began to swell, pressing against the front of those jeans.

"If I'd known that smell gets you hard, I'd have started

baking cupcakes for breakfast every morning, just to get you worked up." She growled a warning when he took her hand, but he pressed it over his growing cock regardless.

"Everything about you gets me worked up," he said simply, and Scarlett's temper was defused. He wasn't trying to take control; he was paying her a compliment.

Her heart melted a little bit, but she swallowed it back. They would both get more out of this evening if they played their roles, his the submissive eager to please, hers the Mistress with her slave.

"Well, I hope you can still feed me if you're worked up." She grinned up at him then, and to please herself, linked her hand in his.

"You'll just have to come and see." Looking awfully pleased with himself, Logan pulled a bandanna from his pocket and held it up for her to see. "May I?"

Scarlett nodded, though she didn't much care for the idea of being blindfolded. She wasn't overly comfortable with anything that spoke of submission.

But this whole exercise was for Logan, so she would suck it up. Plus, somehow over the weeks since she had met him, she had come to trust him with almost anything.

Yes, almost anything, she thought as he led her through the kitchen and into what she knew would be the living room. She rubbed a hand over her heart, the one thing she still tried to hold close to herself, as Logan carefully guided her across the room and helped her to sit on what she discovered was the couch.

"Sorry about the blindfold. I wanted you to see it all at once." His fingers slid between the worn cotton and the back of her head. "And I asked Luca about a few things. I don't think that's cheating," he added in a rush, his voice a growl that dared her to contradict him as he pulled the blindfold away from her eyes.

"Oh!" Her senses were assaulted as she looked around the room, her mouth falling open in shock.

The simple living room had been transformed. White fairy lights twinkled from the mantel, the backs of chairs, the legs of the furniture. Candles illuminated the places that the fairy lights couldn't reach, and the combination of the soft white electric lights and the golden glow of the flames was stunning.

And somehow . . . somehow he had given the impression of people . . . a tall shadow here, a couple chatting there. Squinting through the low light, Scarlett saw that he had brought in various odds and ends from the barn—horseshoes, grooming tools, a saddlebag. He had arranged them behind the pillar candles in clever ways, lending to the impression that they were in a quiet restaurant, somewhere back in Vegas.

"I know you miss the city." Logan let go of Scarlett's hand to gesture to the table. Scarlett was stunned to see that Logan, the man who was most comfortable throwing a steak on the grill or slapping together a sandwich, had set out not just a bowl of pasta and another of salad, but a platter of some kind of hors d'oeuvres and even a martini glass filled with pink liquid, the vessel so new that he'd forgotten to take the price tag off.

More than that, he had laid out on the floor a sheet of plywood painted glossy black, surrounded by yet more lights. Scarlett recognized what it was instantly, and her heart leapt into her throat.

A dance floor. He had made her a dance floor.

At a complete loss for words, she looked at him, her heart in her throat.

"Did I . . . Do you like it?" The man stood tall and had

enough muscles to make Superman feel threatened. And yet when he looked at her like that, Scarlett understood how vulnerable he felt, how much this man who radiated confidence in so many other aspects of his life had put himself on the line.

And it was all for her.

Turning to the stereo that was set along the wall, Logan started some music. Scarlett cocked her head as she heard the first few notes—it was an older song, one that had been big when she was back in junior high, about lightning crashing, old mothers dying.

But she had heard it more recently . . . The memory was tickling at her mind.

"This is what was playing at Veritas the first moment I set eyes on you inside." Logan's words were raw with emotion, and she could see everything that she was feeling reflected back at her in his eyes.

"I can't believe you remember that." When he held out a hand, she went to him quickly, muscles quivering.

This feeling—this was new. She'd had strong feelings for men before, had experienced infatuation, attraction, lust.

This didn't fall neatly into any of those categories.

"Dance with me." Wordlessly, Scarlett reached for the hand that Logan held out for her, let herself be folded into his arms. She was surprised when he placed one hand at the small of her back, folded the other in his, and moved her into a simple but smooth step.

"You know how to dance?" She couldn't help the shock in her voice. She kept thinking she was reaching the core of him, discovering all but that one most hidden facet, and then he would surprise her with something like this.

"This is pretty much the extent of it." Bending, he pressed his lips into her hair. "I had a girlfriend when I was just a kid who dragged me to a dance class. This one thing stuck."

"You liked bossy women even back then, huh?" Scarlett teased him as she savored the romantic moment. Leaning back so that she could see his face, she ran her hand over his cheek, a tender gesture to match the emotions swirling inside her.

"I guess I did." He grinned. "And that actually reminds me." As the song came to an end, he released his hold on her waist and reached into his back pocket

Scarlett was baffled and more than a little amused when he handed her a bright blue leather collar. "For you."

"I think you might have this backward." She arched an eyebrow, reached up to trace her fingers over his neck to make a point.

Huffing out an exasperated sigh, he waved the collar, pressing it into her hand. "It's not for you."

Lips quirking up in a smile, Scarlett examined the strip of metal. Her heart thudded when she came to the tag that was attached to it.

It was likely another sample that companies liked to send to veterinarians. But he had taken the time to scratch the name "Six," as well as Scarlett's cell phone number, into the metal with some kind of engraving tool.

Combined with the dance floor and the meal, now this simple, thoughtful gift . . . Scarlett was done for. And she wasn't about to revel in those feelings alone.

This was in no way just about sex anymore. Whatever he was still holding back, Scarlett was determined to win from him.

This man was a treasure. And no matter his reservations, she intended to keep him.

"I'm very glad you don't cook like that every night." Scarlett groaned as she collapsed on one end of the couch, kicking off her shoes and then tucking her skirt beneath her legs even as she rubbed a hand over her stomach. "I'd get fat. And what would you do then?"

She meant it as a joke. Logan had settled himself on the other end of the couch, taking one of her feet in his hands. She moaned out loud when he began to work at the soles of her feet with his thumbs.

He paused in his movements long enough for her to look up from the hypnotic view of his moving fingers to his face.

"There would just be more of you to delight in serving." His expression was so serious that Scarlett knew he wasn't joking, even though she had been.

He just kept flooring her, this wonderful, amazing man with so many twists and turns that he might as well have been a labyrinth.

"That's why I had to stop dancing." The words fell from her lips before she could stop them, and she winced.

She didn't even like to think about that, herself. She certainly didn't make a habit of telling people.

"What?" Logan frowned, his brow furrowing.

Scarlett's cheeks flushed. Damn it, this was not what tonight was supposed to be about. But she couldn't just leave it hanging.

"I loved to dance." Her voice was quiet. She still did—that simple thrill of bringing her body in tune to the music. "But I was a ballerina. And I didn't have the right shape."

She'd had curves. Breasts and hips, even though her legs and arms had been willowy enough.

It had turned her world upside down to hear that then, and even now, it still pained her to admit it.

She dared a glance at Logan. His eyes flashed with indignation, and her pulse skipped a beat at his next words.

"You are perfect. Just the way you are."

"You said you've never been in a real relationship," she blurted, resulting in his touch on her feet again slowing to a stop. "Why? You're amazing."

"I'm pleased that you think so," he started to answer, then quieted again, his fingers moving in slow strokes while he thought.

"There are women in town," Scarlett persisted. "I know you don't care for crowds, or for closed buildings. But look at you—you're a professional; you're caring; you're fucking hot as hell. Surely there are women who have caught your eye, who don't mind coming out here to see you."

The pressure on her feet tightened just the slightest hint before relaxing again. Logan was silent for almost a full minute, and when he spoke it sounded like it took real effort.

"It's because of what I need." His fingers began to trail from the sole of her foot to the inside of her ankle, tracing the lines of her calf, then up to the soft skin of her inner thigh. "Not every woman enjoys tying up and flogging their men."

There was no censure in his tone; Scarlett knew he would never judge her for needing what she did, not when he had such deep needs of his own.

"No diversions." Scarlett caught his fingers, twisted hard enough to catch his attention. He cursed, then went silent.

"I believe you might keep to yourself because of your need for kink. But that's only part of it, isn't it?" She waited. Logan remained silent. "You were in the army. I think something happened while you served overseas. Am I right?"

More silence.

"Logan." She rubbed her fingers over his hand. "I want to know. I want to learn every part of you. And I could probably find out just by going online. But it means nothing if it hasn't come from you."

He shifted, hesitating. Scarlett held her breath.

"Yes, something happened." Then they expelled deep breaths in tandem, eyeing each other warily. "Something happened to make me need a quiet life, under an open sky. Working with animals helps. Like . . . kind of like therapy." He stopped. Scarlett wanted to push him further.

But something told her that pushing with words wasn't going to do a thing.

Maybe it was time to revert to pushing with her body again. If she had to break down the physical to get to the soul, then that was what she would do.

Nimbly, she slid her leg from his grasp, slid off the couch. He grabbed for her, and she cast him a glare. "Mind your manners, sub."

And with just those words, the air in the room changed. She watched Logan's pupils dilate, saw him become more aware of her, a sub to his Domme.

In response, her spine straightened, and though she was wearing a flirty pink skirt, she felt as powerful as she did in leather and heels.

Casting a warning look his way, she turned to the stereo and switched off the radio station that had played throughout their dinner.

Sifting through his CDs, she grimaced. "Don't you have anything but country?" she called back over her shoulder. Ugh. So not what she had in mind.

Then her fingers found one disc that wasn't adorned with a man in cowboy boots or a woman with big hair.

"Bingo." Sliding it into the stereo, she heard the soft whir of the disc spinning to life. She turned back to Logan as the first notes of a driving rock song pounded out, the music loud enough to have a corresponding beat pounding in her blood.

Slowly, confidently, she made her way back across the

room, making sure to exaggerate the roll of her hips with every step.

He was now sitting straight up on the couch, hands flat on his lap, eyes taking in her every movement.

Straddling his legs, she toyed with the hem of her shirt.

He clasped her around the waist, fingers sliding beneath the silky fabric to find her skin.

Lifting his hand to her lips, she nipped at his fingers in warning.

"You haven't earned that touch yet," she informed him, then swiveled her hips before settling down onto his lap to dance.

His cock was immediately hard, pressing against the silken heat of her panties as she undulated on him. He growled, and she saw his knuckles go white as he fisted them at his sides in an effort to keep his hands to himself as she had ordered.

She suspected it would be like this between them for as long as they were together—him pushing her, never surrendering until she had worked for it. Her reining in the attitude that made him who he was, only to have it come through again, after.

She loved it.

When she slowly peeled her shirt over her head, letting him see her breasts displayed in her simple but pretty black bra, she watched frustration take him over.

"Let me fuck you." His words were arrogant, designed to shock her out of the game she was playing. Shaking her head, she backed up a bit, putting distance between them.

"No." Reaching behind her back, Scarlett slowly released the hooks of her bra. Letting the straps fall, she caught the garment against her breasts before it fell to the floor, and Logan groaned.

"Please let me touch you." Beneath the cockiness, he looked shaken, though whether it was because he'd managed to share something from his past with her, or because she was teasing him, she wasn't sure.

But she wasn't done. Until he was a mindless, aching bundle of need, she wasn't done.

Calling on her years of dance training, she let herself get lost in the music, every sway of her body made all the more sensual because Logan was watching.

She let her bra fall to the floor.

She slid out of her skirt.

She hooked a finger in one side of her panties, cocked a hip, ran her tongue over her lips as she looked Logan in the eye.

He had undone his pants, and his erection rose from his lap, tall and thick and already wet at the tip. Bending until she could just swipe her tongue over it once, she smiled slowly.

"Looks like you have a bit of a situation here." She kicked his feet apart, came to stand between them, knew he could feel the heat radiating from her skin. "What do you want, Logan?"

"I want you to stop being such a cock tease." Goaded past the point of control, he grabbed her waist, ripped her panties right off her body with a ferocity that made liquid surge between her thighs.

Taming this wild beast was the absolute hottest thing she ever would have been able to dream up.

"Let me fuck you, Scarlett." Pulling her close, Logan buried his face in the curve of her belly. The soft scrape of his stubble woke nerves all over Scarlett's skin.

She pushed at his chest until he was forced to lean back into the couch. Grinning as she pulled a condom from his pocket and sheathed him with it, she slowly lowered herself onto his erect cock, gasping as she struggled to work her way down, to take all of him in.

"Haven't you learned yet?" she cried out when she finally managed to take him in to the hilt, when the tight pressure of his testicles rested against the curve of her ass. His hands found her hips, dug in, rocking her in his lap.

"You don't fuck me, Logan Brody." Short of breath, she began to move, taking them both to the edge of release fast. "*I* fuck *you*."

Afterward they lay twined in Logan's bed, naked and with the sweat on their skin cooling in the breeze from the overhead fan. Well, *their* bed—most of Scarlett's belongings had migrated to Logan's room, since by that point she spent most nights in it.

Logan's limbs were clumsy with sleep as he pulled Scarlett close to him. She had ruthlessly stomped all of his misgivings about telling her as much as he had into submission with her striptease, and even though it left him feeling naked, he admired her for it.

As he crept farther toward sleep, he thought that maybe that was why he was finally able to submit to a woman—because he'd found a woman capable of bringing him to his knees.

And when she was with him, the nightmares stayed farther away.

She shifted beside him as he was on the final edge of slumber, swinging her legs over the edge of the bed. His unconscious took over, and he grabbed for her, finding her hand and pulling it tight.

"Don't leave." He flinched even as the words came out of his mouth, and he blinked his way back to full consciousness.

He hadn't intended to say that, especially since she was probably just getting up to use the bathroom.

But rather than freezing up, or running away, or ridiculing him, Scarlett stopped and smoothed a hand over his hair.

"I'm not going anywhere." He felt her eyes on him, contemplative.

Hot with embarrassment, he avoided eye contact as she sat on the edge of the bed, then reached for the wooden jewelry box she'd placed there days earlier. He listened to the sounds of metallic clinks, the slithering of serpentine chains, as she sorted through it, wondering what she was doing.

Craning his neck, he lifted his head in time to see her pull a cuff bracelet from the sparkling depths of the box. Simple and silver, the band was about half an inch thick all the way around, with an interlocking clasp to hold it in place.

His heart stuttered when he realized what she was about to do.

"I would like to give this to you." Scarlett's voice was deceptively light, but Logan understood without the words being said.

She wasn't just offering to let him wear her bracelet as a token of friendship, or even as anything so simple as a promise ring, though it was, in fact, a promise.

This bracelet was the equivalent of a temporary collar in their world—a way for the world to see that she had marked him as hers. Not as serious as an engagement ring or a formal collaring ceremony, she was still offering him a promise.

If he would give himself into her care, then she would take care of him.

"You don't have to." Quickly, Scarlett folded her fingers over the shining silver, hiding it from view. Even in the shadows of the dim room, he could make out the flush on her cheeks. "It was presumptuous of me. I'm sorry. I—"

Logan reached for the bracelet before she could close her hand all the way, catching hold of the metal. It was cool in his palm, a sharp contrast to the heat of Scarlett's skin.

"Will you put it on me?" He shouldn't; he knew he shouldn't. But in that moment, a force of nature couldn't have stopped him from trying to get that circle of metal—that promise—around his wrist.

Silently, her eyes large and luminous in the low light, Scarlett opened the bracelet, which hinged on the side. Placing it around his wrist, she then clipped it closed. Since it was made to be a loose bangle on her, it fit his wrist snugly.

It would be a constant reminder of her throughout his day, and the thought made warm light spread through the dark places inside of him.

Scarlett opened her mouth, then closed it again without speaking. It was rare for Logan to see his Mistress at a loss for words, and that he was the cause of it overwhelmed him.

"Come here." Pulling her into his arms, he laid them both down on the bed. Scarlett twined her legs with his, wrapped her arms around him before moving his arm so that it rested across her hip, where they could both see the bracelet.

Later, he felt the mattress dip when Scarlett again climbed out of bed, presumably to do whatever she'd been heading for before he'd stopped her. But this time, the physical reminder of her promise to care for him kept his demons at bay.

CHAPTER EIGHTEEN

"I t's a mild case of wool block, I think." A week later, Scarlett squatted in the cool, humid air inside the main building of the angora farm that had placed a call to Logan that morning. Returning the animal that looked like a giant cotton ball with a nose back to its cage, she blew an errant wisp of the angora hair off her shirt, turning to the rabbit breeder who watched her nervously.

"That's what I thought, but I wanted to make sure. Shit." Axel Webber was not at all what Scarlett had expected when Logan had sent her on this call—though what she'd expected from an angora breeder, she wasn't sure. But though the delicate way that the massive lumberjack of a man handled the rabbits that lined the spacious crates of what he called their "habitat" might have been incongruous with his appearance, she saw that he was very skilled at what he did. "All the rabbits have a salt lick and I check their water several times a day. And I groom them regularly, all just to prevent wool block. What am I doing wrong?"

"Well, you probably know more about angoras specifically than I do, but it sounds—and looks—like you're taking good care of them." She brushed more angora hair, which was softer than any wool Scarlett had ever felt, off her clothes. "I'll want to do some reading up on it, but from what I can tell, it's not a massive block yet. A papaya or pineapple vitamin supplement dissolved in the rabbit's water will help break down the fur that's been swallowed. Apart from that, just keep doing what you're doing—encourage regular drinking with the salt and the water, make sure that their pellets have plenty of fiber, and give me a call if you notice something off, just like you did." *Give Logan a call,* is what she'd meant. He was wearing her bracelet, yes, but she still couldn't get him to talk about anything too far in the future . . . or in his past.

Reaching down into the open-topped crate into which she'd just placed the rabbit, Scarlett stroked her hand through the amazingly soft hair that made a pale blue cloud around the surprisingly small body.

"That's Deidre." Axel grinned at Scarlett's surprised look. "I name them all. You might have noticed, but it can get lonely on your farm, between visits into town."

Scarlett hadn't noticed—mostly because she and Logan were so wrapped up in each other, and in work, that she hadn't had much time to be alone. But she could see how Axel, who was big and warm and gregarious, might feel that way.

"I kind of like the quiet out here," Scarlett admitted as she packed up her things. This was the first call that Logan had sent her on alone, because he'd had someone coming to the house with their sick cat. Scarlett felt a calm pride that she'd been able to figure out the problem on an unfamiliar animal. "I didn't think I would—I'm from Vegas, and I thought I'd miss the city more. But it kind of feels like home out here."

The admission jolted her down to her toes, as it was something she hadn't fully accepted even in her own head yet. She'd never imagined setting up her hospital anywhere but the outskirts of Vegas. She'd never lived anywhere else. But now . . .

Why *couldn't* she?

With the new thought buzzing through her mind, Scarlett dragged her attention back to Axel, who was watching her absentmindedness patiently.

Great, Scar. Really professional.

"Sorry." She smiled sheepishly, picking up her bag. "Log—Dr. Brody will mail you the invoice in a few days. You can pick up those papaya or pineapple supplements at the health food store in town. Was there anything else you needed me to look at while I'm out here?"

Axel stepped back, waiting for her to walk ahead of him out of the barn, which had specially installed double doors to keep the weather outside from making its way into where the rabbits were housed.

There was deference in his gesture, a way of movement that had recognition going off in Scarlett's head.

"Nothing else I need, no." Axel kept his eyes down as he spoke, though there was a smile on his lips. "But would I be overly forward in asking if Mistress would be interested in staying for a beer and some dinner?"

Scarlett thought she might have squeaked as her mouth fell open. Her lips worked silently as she tried to form a response.

Axel looked up—how had she missed his tendency to keep his eyes lowered, how he urged her to walk first, both signs of a well-trained submissive?

She hadn't been looking for it. Not out here.

"How did you know?" she finally asked. Once she recognized him for what he was, obvious now, she knew there was no use denying it.

"Some people are submissive or Dominant, right down to their core." He nodded, smiling—a gentle giant. "Sometimes you just know."

Yes, sometimes you just knew—like when Scarlett had looked at Logan, felt that spark between them.

No other submissive—no other man—was ever going to be able to make her feel the same way.

"So have I scared you off of that drink now?" Axel teased gently, and Scarlett couldn't help but smile. Here was a man she also had an instinctive feeling about—she sensed he could be a good friend.

But while she was flattered, she was also very much not interested, because her heart was bound elsewhere.

"Maybe some other time." She smiled ruefully, feeling bad for letting him down. But when she thought of Logan's face when she had placed that bracelet on his wrist, her blood sizzled, and she suddenly couldn't wait to get back to Folsom Farms.

"I shouldn't be surprised that you're already taken." Axel didn't ask by whom, and Scarlett certainly wasn't about to tell, even if the answer was obvious, at least to her.

One of the rules of kink—you kept the secrets of other members of the lifestyle.

"I would love to have a beer together some other time." If Scarlett did stay out here—and that thought had her stomach doing a slow roll of anticipation—it would be nice to have a friend with the same inclinations nearby.

"Anything for the Mistress." Axel smiled, and if there was a hint of disappointment in his eyes, Scarlett tried not to feel guilty about it.

Maybe sometime she could invite another Domme from Veritas out to the ranch to play . . . and invite Axel, too.

Waving as she pulled out of Axel's long drive, Scarlett's thoughts turned toward home. And she realized then that was how she had started to think of Folsom Farms—as home.

When was too soon to tell someone that you were serious about them? She'd warned Logan right at the beginning that she wasn't looking for something casual, but those were just words until the reality of true, strong feelings set in.

Preoccupied as she pulled up the drive to the farm, Scarlett noted absently that there was a dark green Volvo parked in front of the house. Mrs. Donovan and Voodoo were still here, then.

Scarlett smiled as she imagined cornering Logan later today in the back room that he used as his exam room. He rarely wore a lab coat, but he had one . . . and she thought that maybe, just maybe, she could convince him to wear it for her.

It happened in slow motion, or so it seemed to her mind. She was halfway to the house when the front door opened and Mrs. Donovan stepped out, cat carrier in hand. Logan was right behind her.

Mrs. Donovan smiled and waved, and Scarlett returned the gesture, which pulled her attention away from the tiny scrap of a dog that, seeing Scarlett's car, sprinted straight in her direction.

Scarlett saw the bundle of gray fur jumping a millisecond before the thud reverberated through the vehicle. She screamed, was halfway out of the car before she'd even managed to jolt the vehicle into park.

"Six!" From across the yard, she heard Logan's shout, Mrs. Donovan's cry of distress, the yowl of the cat in its carrier. And over it all, the pitiful, high-pitched whine of the beloved animal she'd just hit with her car.

Scarlett threw herself down on her knees in the grass. Her instinct was to pick Six up, to hold him close, to make it all go away. Luckily, her training kicked in before she could harm him further. The veterinarian in her knew that moving him could exacerbate his injuries. Though her whole body began to shake when she saw the blood, she tried to wrestle the racking guilt inside of her, to find a professional calm, to do what she had to do.

Six wasn't trapped under the wheel. That was good. But the way two of his tiny little legs were bent awkwardly told her they were likely broken.

When the big brown puppy eyes looked up at her, blurred with confusion and pain, his pitiful whine turned into a howl. Scarlett tried to keep it together—she had always been the strong one. She'd dealt with veterinary emergencies before during the clinic hours needed to get one's degree . . . but she'd never been the one to cause the animal distress.

Her arms were shaking, but still she tried to think of the best way to pick Six up without injuring him further.

"I've got it." Logan landed beside her on the lawn, one of his large arms gesturing Mrs. Donovan and the caterwauling cat back. Running his hands over Six's tiny body, he finally gathered the little dog into his hands, standing at the same time.

I can do this, Scarlett thought as she stood with them. She needed to help, needed to be part of fixing what she had done.

But then she saw the splintered white bone sticking out of Six's tiny little chicken leg and had to slap a hand over her mouth to keep from screaming with hysteria.

"Pull yourself together." Logan made his tone deliberately harsh as he laid Six on the table in his exam room. Blood had matted the fur of his leg, staining the pristine paper sheet beneath his body crimson.

Scarlett was standing just inside the door to the room, looking as though she'd been the one hit by a car. He knew from her references that she'd handled worse than this and with apparent ease.

But she'd never had to perform surgery to fix something that she'd caused, though she couldn't have done anything to prevent it. And she'd never had to do surgery on *her* dog.

And because it was her dog, Logan would do whatever it took to fix him back up. And for that he needed a second set of hands.

"It looks worse than it is, Scarlett." His hands covered with blood, he gestured toward his bag with his head. "Two fractures, bone went through the skin, one other gash. He'll be fine. But we need to give him morphine to knock him out. I need you to draw it up for me."

Scarlett looked back at him, eyes wide and unfocused. She was so pale that he was pretty sure she was going into shock herself.

He knew she was stronger than that. And he needed her.

"Dr. Malone!" His tone came close to shouting, which caused Six to whimper again but caught Scarlett's attention. "Go into my bag. Determine a morphine dose for a seven-pound canine and draw it up."

Scarlett blanched, presumably at the idea that hitting Six with her car had caused him to need morphine.

"So help me God, Scarlett, if you don't snap out of it, I'll whip your ass myself." The statement sounded so strange coming out of his mouth that Scarlett finally seemed to jolt out of her stupor, a flush of pink coming into her cheeks.

"Shit." Hurrying across the room, she opened Logan's medical bag and pulled out the drug and a fresh syringe. Six whined when she approached with the needle.

"I'm so sorry, buddy." Shaving away a patch of hair on the animal's rump, Scarlett slid the needle into his skin and depressed the plunger. A minute later, Six visibly relaxed, the tension in his tiny muscles starting to droop until he looked like he was asleep.

"I'm so sorry," Scarlett whispered as Logan washed up at the sink in the room. But as she spoke, she was getting out the supplies they would need to reset and stabilize two fractured bones and to sew up the gashes.

His strong woman was still with him. So even though he wanted to take care of her first, he gave her instructions, and together they mended and set and stitched, and in one case cleaned up a puddle of doggy vomit.

"All done." Scarlett looked at Logan with eyes that were more than a little wild when he snipped the thread to the last suture. Six was still out, with several bald patches where they'd had to shave his fur, but his breathing was deep and even, aided by the narcotic, and Logan's professional opinion was that he was going to be just fine.

"Come on." Logan set fencing around the table so that Six couldn't fall off if he woke up. "Staying here to stare at him won't do him any good and will only make you more upset."

He watched as two shiny trails of tears spilled over from her eyes. He'd never seen her cry, and it just about sent him to his knees.

"It was my fault," Scarlett said, the guilt stabbing through her like a knife. "I was going too fast."

"Scarlett, you were driving down the road like you've done a hundred times before. Like I've done a thousand times. It was an unfortunate accident. It's not your fault." Logan looked at her, hesitated for a moment, then scooped Scarlett into his arms. She tensed, then let herself melt against him as he carried her into the kitchen and deposited her on a chair.

"His vitals are good. He's young and he'll heal fast. It could have been far worse." Scarlett blanched as Logan turned to wash his hands at the kitchen sink, though she knew he hadn't intended to add to her guilt.

But it *could* have been worse. She could have killed the poor little dog that she thought she'd saved.

"I'm making you some soup and some tea." Logan pulled a pot from one of the cupboards.

"No." Scarlett's stomach rolled at the thought of ingesting anything.

"Remember what I said about the whip?" Logan's voice was mild but underlaid with steel as he found a can of soup and opened it. "You need something so you don't go into shock. You'll eat."

"Remember that you're not the one who gets to hold the whip in this relationship." Scarlett knew she was being nasty, but she couldn't seem to help herself. She felt awful—worse than she remembered feeling anytime in recent memory.

She didn't deserve comfort, so she let her misery spill forth.

Logan was silent as he heated the soup, ladled some into a bowl, and brought it to the table. Scarlett watched, feeling like she was underwater, as he set it down in front of her, then drew a chair close to her.

"I'm well aware that I'm not the one who holds the whip." He spooned up a bite of soup and held it to her lips. Incredulous that he would think to do so when she was being so awful, Scarlett opened her mouth and swallowed.

"But we're in this together because we take care of each other's needs." He spooned up more soup and pressed it to her lips. His words had her furrowing her brow in puzzlement.

She was supposed to be the strong one. She was the one who was supposed to take care of him—giving him the bracelet had been a symbol of that.

But she'd watched as the alpha male in him had taken over during the surgery to repair Six's fractures. And now he was nurturing her the way she'd seen some subs do to their Doms—serving her, pampering her.

It felt good. It felt right.

Did it matter so much if what they had together fell neatly

into a predetermined slot? He was a domineering, alpha male, yet chose to submit during sex, which didn't make a hell of a lot of sense.

So why couldn't she just let him take care of her now, since it felt so right?

With that thought in her head, she let him lead her up the stairs to his bathroom, let him draw her a bath filled with pine-scented bubbles. When he undressed her like she was a doll, then carried her into the tub and sank into the water with her, she felt a little bit of the coldness inside of her begin to thaw.

She borrowed his strength as she leaned back against him, held tight in his large, capable arms. When she'd siphoned enough of his energy, she finally managed to form the question that had been swirling through her mind.

"How do you deal with it? When you lose a patient?" She knew he wouldn't think she was silly for referring to animals as patients, though some would, because he felt the same way. He would understand that every animal who looked up at them with wide, innocent eyes was asking for help the way a human would.

And so—to her, at least—causing an animal pain was akin to causing harm to a child. She didn't think she'd ever forget the image of Six lying crumpled on the ground by her tire.

"I won't give you some song and dance about the circle of life, or any of that bullshit." Logan's arm tightened around her waist, and Scarlett pictured herself pulling strength from the embrace. "It will never be easy, not when you lose a patient, not even when one is hurt."

"Then why do we do it?" Maybe she'd chosen the wrong career path—she'd fallen to pieces down there, when Logan had needed her help.

"We do it because it's the right thing to do, and because somebody has to." Logan pressed a kiss to the top of her head, then gently began to rub her shoulders.

"And sometimes the only way to get through is . . . just to get through."

Scarlett woke in the middle of the night with her heart pounding a wicked rhythm up into her throat. Caught in a blind panic, though it took her a moment to remember why, she frantically searched the room for Logan, tendrils of cold air creeping across her skin when she couldn't find him.

The sheets on his side of the bed were cool. He'd been gone for a while. Sliding from beneath the quilt, Scarlett reached for her robe against the chill of the air and made her way downstairs in the dark to check on Six . . . and on Logan.

"Oh." She stopped short when she stepped into the living room. Logan had built a fire, which had burned down to no more than glowing coals and small flickers of blue flame.

And on the floor in front of the fire was a makeshift bed comprised of pillows, couch cushions, and blankets.

Six was on a cushion of his own, and even from the doorway she could see that his breathing was normal.

And laid out on the floor, looking ridiculously long on the makeshift bed, was Logan. Dr. Logan Brody, her submissive, guarding over the teeny-tiny dog that she cared about.

And looking at that scene, Scarlett fell head over heels. Crazily, truly madly deeply in love.

Her heart full, Scarlett moved quietly toward where they slept—her two boys. Rearranging the quilts so that Logan's feet didn't stick out at the bottom, she then ran her hands over Six gently, reassuring herself that the tiny heartbeat was steady.

Six gave a sleepy, disoriented yip, and Scarlett felt happier in that moment than she had in a long time. She curled up next to Logan on the floor, wrapped her arms around him, squeezed tightly.

And together, they fell asleep.

CHAPTER NINETEEN

"Something smells good."

Scarlett turned, light on her feet despite the early hour, as Logan stumbled through the archway that led from the living room to the kitchen. His golden hair was sticking straight up, and he had creases from his pillow on his cheek.

"Just checked Six. He's still sleeping, and he might for a bit longer. He'll be hungry when he wakes up, though." Wearing just the underwear he'd thrown on after their bath the night before, Logan crossed the kitchen to the coffeepot. It was all so blessedly normal—so much like what she'd yearned for her whole life, when she'd felt like she never quite fit into any of the families she lived with—that the words fell from her lips before she could truly think them through.

"I love you."

And in that moment, in her heart, she really believed that they wouldn't need anything else. She could finish her internship here and then open her animal hospital. It didn't have to be in Vegas. Or maybe she didn't have to open the hospital at all—it seemed so very far away at the moment, anyway. She could work with Logan—partners in a practice. And she would find another way, an even better way, to help local children in need.

Her smile started to fade when she realized that Logan hadn't said anything in response. She anxiously searched his face, but he remained as he was, frozen by the coffeepot.

His face was set in an expressionless stare.

Scarlett's heart thudded unpleasantly against her rib cage. What had happened to the sweet submissive who had taken care of her the night before?

"I know you feel the same." He did. She was sure of it.

But the way he was looking at her—like a man being burned at the stake—had terror clawing up inside her throat.

"I didn't mean for this to happen." He wasn't saying he didn't love her, exactly, but those sure weren't words that any woman wanted to hear after she'd bared her soul to a man.

"For what to happen, exactly?" Turning the burner off, Scarlett set the pan of eggs aside and crossed her arms over her chest.

"I can't give you what you need." She could hear the pain in his voice, as well as the determination. "I didn't think you . . . I didn't . . ."

"Didn't what?" Temper was surfacing with her panic. She gestured at the bracelet on his wrist with a nod. "You didn't mean to accept that? Didn't mean for us to find something so wonderful together?"

"This can't work long-term." Logan crossed his arms over his chest, unconsciously mimicking her stance. His tone held a trace of the belligerence she'd heard in it the first night they'd met.

"Why?" Scarlett demanded. "You know by now that there's nothing you can tell me that will send me running. So tell me why."

His jaw set, Logan met her eyes. The resolution Scarlett saw there told her everything she needed to know.

No matter what she did, no matter how she pushed him to face the reality of the feelings between them, he had already locked a part of himself away so tightly that no one was getting at it.

Not even the most determined of Mistresses.

"All right, then." She didn't even recognize her own voice. Her mind ran through her choices—and she came to the conclusion that she really didn't have even one.

All of the power in this kind of relationship lay with the submissive. She had done all she could to get to his heart— hell, she'd thought she *had*, that he trusted her enough to let her in.

She'd been wrong. And she couldn't flog that last bit of trust into him, couldn't tease it from him with sex.

She'd been willing to give him everything. But before she'd even had a chance to tell him that, he'd shut down, put himself on lockdown.

And from the familiar shutters she could see lowering over his eyes, she wasn't going to get them open again.

"All right," she repeated, trying to get ahold of herself. Her insides felt like they were slowly turning to lead, making her limbs heavy, her brain slow. "I'd like the day off, then, please. To move my things."

"What?" Now it was Logan's turn to sound panicked. "Move them where?"

"I'll finish the internship. I'll meet my obligations." Logan, she knew, had committed himself to a busier workload in the spring, thinking that he would have a second pair of hands, and she wouldn't renege on her word. "But I think it would be best if I got an apartment in town."

Anger licked over his features. "A condition of the internship was that you live here."

"Logan, don't." Suddenly weary despite her pain, Scarlett held up a hand.

"Don't go." Scarlett heard the same panic that she felt in Logan's voice. It made everything worse.

He felt the same way that she did—she knew it. So why the hell couldn't he—*wouldn't he*—take that final step?

"What did you think I would do when this moment came?" And she saw now that he had expected it to come, all along. He knew that in the end he wasn't going to give her that last bit of himself—not because he didn't want to, but because, in his mind at least, he couldn't.

"I . . . Scarlett." Logan stepped toward her, and when the bright morning sunlight glinted off of his bracelet, Scarlett winced. "Please. You know how I feel. I want you for as long as you'll have me. I just . . . can't . . . not like that."

She wouldn't cry. She was too numb for that. But as Scarlett made her way to the stairs, where she planned to go pack up her hopes along with her floggers and her work boots, anger began to melt some of the ice in her veins. She turned, one hand on the doorjamb, and let her eyes shoot daggers at Logan.

"That's bullshit. You could have me forever. We're good together." The anger built and built, and she wanted to scream, to throw things.

Later, when she was alone, she would.

"This secret you have—I think you keep it on purpose. It's your cushion, to keep you from fully submitting, from committing to someone, to letting yourself go that far. You won't risk getting hurt."

Now it was his turn for his eyes to narrow in anger. Like blue ice, they frosted over, and his lips pinched together before he responded. "You don't know anything about it, little girl."

"No, I don't, because you won't tell me." Scarlett sucked in a mouthful of air. "I would have stayed, you know. The reason I was so distracted in the car yesterday was because I realized that I felt more at home out here, on the farm, than I ever had back in Vegas. I wanted to stay. But I won't settle. And I won't let you settle, either."

A choked sound escaped Logan. "Scarlett . . ."

"No." She held up her hand again. It was too late. She needed his feelings without the safety net he wrapped around himself.

"We both deserve it all. And unless you'll give me that last piece of you, I'd rather have nothing at all."

Logan wallowed in his misery for two full days. He snapped at people on the phone, shouted at his surroundings, and muttered until even the horses looked at him like he was crazy.

"Just you wait," he told Loki when the horse rolled his eyes after Logan had forgotten to bring him an apple yet again. "Some mare is going to get you tied up in knots, and then she's going to disappear, even though she said she'd stay."

The bracelet winked on his wrist, mocking him. He hadn't been able to take it off, though he had hidden it under long sleeves when Scarlett had come to the house to do the chores that would fulfill the terms of her internship.

He might have been able to deal with it better if she had shown anger or sadness. But no. She hid everything she was feeling—and he damn well knew she was feeling something—behind that impenetrable Domme control.

He'd fucked things up but good. And he had no idea how to make it right . . . or if it was broken for good.

As he stalked back into the house after his evening chores, Mongo nipped at his heels, whimpering. Logan wasn't the only one suffering—Mongo missed Scarlett, and they both missed Six, whom Scarlett had taken with her.

A few calls had told Logan that she was staying at the

motel in town. But even knowing that she was safe and apparently going on with life just fine couldn't soothe him.

"That's what you wanted, dumbass." Logan thought about dinner, then dismissed it, knowing he wouldn't be able to eat. "You wanted her to be happy, and you knew she wouldn't be, stuck out here with you."

But the look on her face when he hadn't returned her words of love had told him that he'd made a grave miscalculation somewhere along the way.

His phone rang, vibrating in his pocket just as he contemplated punching the wall. The call display told him that it was Luca.

He knew what Luca was going to want to talk about. And Logan had just enough of a masochistic streak in him to answer anyway.

"You're a stupid motherfucker, Brody." As always, Luca went straight to the point. "The best chance you've ever had at happiness, and you throw it away. You son of a bitch."

"I won't subject her to this. To life out here with me. You of all people know why." Pushed by someone who wasn't his own Domme, Logan clammed up.

"Then you shouldn't have started anything in the first place." Luca's words were a blow that hit home. He knew he shouldn't have. Hadn't he fought it?

But Scarlett was like a force of nature, and he'd been too selfish to hold up against the hurricane.

"Didn't she teach you anything?" Luca's voice was heavy with disgust, and each word hit Logan like a new blow. "Ultimately, the choice lies with the submissive. I'm sure she told you that. But this decision isn't yours to make."

Logan had no words for that. Scarlett had stunned him when she'd said she wanted to stay. He couldn't let her do that, couldn't let her throw away her dreams, and he had said so.

"You're a fucking idiot," Luca told him, and by now Logan had had enough.

"Stop with the insults," he snapped. "You're not in my shoes. You don't know what you would do."

"Did you bother asking her what she wanted?" Luca asked. "Or did you bend things the way you thought they should go?"

Logan opened his mouth to tell his friend to fuck off, but then he stopped abruptly.

There was a moment of silence.

"That's right, dumbass. And that's the biggest topping-from-the-bottom move I've ever seen." On the other end of the line, Luca heaved a big sigh, and Logan felt his anger fade, replaced by all of the feelings he'd been trying to stem over the last two days.

Without his Mistress, he felt as though one of his limbs had been torn away.

He didn't know if they could make it work long-term. But he'd been wrong, so wrong, in not at least giving it a try when they had something so good going between them.

"Figure it out, man. She's leaving. She got another internship," Luca warned, and Logan felt his hackles rise again. Best friend or not, if Luca had been here in person, he might have taken a swing at him, just to get some aggression out. "I love you both, but if you don't fix this, I'll beat you with every whip, paddle, and flogger that I own."

And then Luca was gone, leaving Logan with nothing but the sounds of a small farm in early evening, and his own thoughts, whirling around his head.

He had to make this right. He had to give Scarlett the one thing that would convince her to give him another chance.

If he wasn't already too late.

CHAPTER TWENTY

Scarlett,

I was wrong. So wrong. I tried to be noble, to push you away so that you didn't waste yourself on me.

But I'm not that strong. If you'll have me, I will give myself to you. Entirely to you.

Because that's what you do when you love someone.

I will wait for you on the far perimeter of the farm.

I'm staying there until you come.

I need to make this right.

I need *you*.

Logan

Scarlett almost missed the note as she passed through the kitchen on the way to the barn to do her chores. And she had trouble comprehending the words, written in his now familiar scrawl.

Her last round of chores at Logan's farm. She'd checked out of the motel, and her things were packed in the car. She wasn't going far—just to the guest house on Axel's property, where she would be living for the next few months while she became an expert on angora rabbits and local wildlife.

What Logan's actions had cleared up for her was that she did actually want to stay here, in rural Montana. Somehow, despite her love for the city she was from, she felt at home here in a way that she had never known before.

She didn't need Logan to stay.

Though she really wished he'd given her the choice.

She wavered when she saw the note. This would be a good time to leave a note herself, to slip away without a fuss.

But she'd never been the type to just slip quietly away. And part of her—okay, *most* of her—really wanted to hear what he had to say.

Did he really mean what he said? Was he ready to give himself to her entirely?

Could he . . . love her?

Shaking her head at herself, Scarlett made her way to the barn. Her lips quirked when she saw that Logan had left Boone waiting for her, saddled and ready to go.

Loki was missing from his stall, so that meant Logan had ridden him out to the edge of the property—which showed the state of mind he was in. But it also gave her determination, made her feel competitive.

If Logan could ride a demon horse just so that she, the nervous rider, could have the calmer one, then she supposed she was obligated to listen to what he had to say.

"Easy now." She shakily mimicked what she had seen Logan do so many times, placing her left foot in the stirrup and swinging herself over. She knocked the breath from her lungs when she landed, but felt a sense of accomplishment regardless.

She managed to get herself squared away in the saddle and even got Boone moving out of the stable. The horse seemed disgruntled, and she couldn't blame him.

"You miss your master. I know." She soothed him as she tried to get the hang of steering—was it called steering on a horse? "I miss him, too."

As though Boone had been waiting for her to say just that, he picked up his pace, beginning to trot.

Scarlett's heart was lodged firmly in her throat by the time the back fence of the property was within view. And it threatened to choke her as she squinted and made out the figure of Logan, standing by a fence pole.

Boone trotted her closer. And when they got close enough, Scarlett saw that Logan wasn't *leaning* against the fence post.

He was naked and chained to it.

"What the *hell* are you doing?" Sliding off Boone with far less grace than she'd hoped for, Scarlett let her anger overtake her as she stormed the remaining steps across the field to stand in front of Logan. "You idiot. How did you figure you were going to get loose?"

"You came," he said simply. "I figured you would free me at some point."

"What if I hadn't?" She was seething, all the anger from the last few days boiling up and out of her. "What if a cougar had come? A pack of coyotes? What then?"

"I timed it for just before you would arrive." His voice was infuriatingly calm. "And I knew you would come. I trust you."

"Jesus, Logan." His words were an arrow through her heart. Scarlett staggered back a step, running a hand through the strands of hair that the wind had snarled on the way over.

She opened her mouth—to say what, she wasn't sure— but Logan cut her off when he gestured to the backpack lying at his feet in the grass.

"Could you open this for me, please?" There was an expression in his eyes that Scarlett had never seen there before and couldn't quite identify.

"Logan—" She'd come here hoping he had something to say, not to play games.

"Mistress. Please." The way he looked at her told her that it was important—vitally so.

Slowly, she knelt beside the bag and undid the zipper.

Inside was a whip—a long, beautiful thing, made of polished brown leather, coiled neatly.

Picking up the coil, she looked up at Logan. "What are you doing?"

"I need to tell you everything. I don't want to keep anything back from you." A jolt of adrenaline shot straight to Scarlett's heart.

"Why the whip?" She ran it through her fingers. Luca had shown her how to use a similar one, but it had never been her flogger of choice.

"I need help to get the words out." Though on the surface he seemed perfectly calm, like the surface of a lake on a day with no breeze, Scarlett's practiced eye saw that he was too settled. Too still.

In that moment she saw just how deep this trauma ran, and she wondered if she had pushed him too far—if some things were never meant to be shared.

"You don't—"

"I do." Logan had left just enough slack in the chains to turn himself around. Leaning against the fence, he arched his back, offering up the target of his smooth skin for Scarlett's hand. "Please. Now."

He wasn't trying to top from the bottom, she understood. He needed something to help him release the pain—pain that ran through him, on the surface, pain underneath.

She studied him for a long moment—that tall, perfectly muscled frame. The golden hair that dusted his forearms, his calves. The skin that was darkened by the sun in the places that weren't habitually covered by a T-shirt and the skin that was pale as snow in the places that were.

Though it cost her something, a bit of her soul perhaps, to do this, she did as he asked. Raising her arm, she let the tail of the whip fly.

Logan grunted when it struck his right buttock. The angry red mark left in its wake highlighted the muscles that stood out in high relief.

"Bosnia. We were in Bosnia." He shouted the words, then fell silent again.

Scarlett trembled. She didn't want to do this.

But this was what Logan needed. And the bracelet that he still wore showed her promise to fulfill those needs.

She flicked the whip again, and this time, it struck over his shoulder blade.

"I was close with two men in my unit. We had been to-gether since training, had worked our way up to Specialist rank together." Again, his voice lapsed into silence, but this time Scarlett asked a question.

"One of them was Luca?" When Logan didn't answer, she landed another blow.

"Yes! Luca. Luca and Dieter." He shuddered as the pain washed through him, and Scarlett saw that he was beginning to sink into subspace, where the endorphins would take him under.

He wasn't coasting on pleasure, though. No, when his eyes went hazy, they were focused on a memory.

She let the whip fly again.

"Dieter and I were out on patrol." Stop.

Snap.

"There were two children in the road." Stop.

Snap.

"They asked for help. We stopped." At this point Logan started to shake, and Scarlett threw the whip aside.

"No more." She approached the fence, ran her hands gently over Logan's back.

He whipped his head to stare at her with pleading eyes.

"Yes. Please. I . . . I need to get this out." His voice was raw, as though she'd been flogging his throat.

"All right." She felt sick—she didn't want to hear this any more than Logan wanted to tell it.

But she needed to. For him. So he could excise this pain, share it with someone, and try to move on.

"Again," he commanded her. Scarlett pressed her lips together, debating, but ultimately gave in.

This time the blow striped across his entire upper back, and he cried out.

"They were siblings. Brothers. And their older brother had given them an explosive." Logan's voice broke, hitched, and Scarlett felt her heart crack in two when he heaved a sob of anguish.

She raised the whip again, but he continued without it.

"They used it once we were in a building. I . . . I watched one of the boys get blown to bits by this senseless explosion."

Tears started to pool in Scarlett's eyes now, too, scalding her skin when they spilled over.

"The other . . . died while we were trapped. About half an hour later, calling for his brother." The raw agony she heard make Scarlett shake. She longed to touch, to soothe, but she held back.

He needed to get this poison out.

"Dieter . . . he died three days later. Fighting had broken out around us, so no one came. I was trapped with his body, no water, no food, just death and the sounds of war. And I was trained. I was a soldier, and I couldn't get us out."

Logan's voice rose to a shout. Scarlett trembled with the force of her own tears.

"Finally, someone came. I was treated for dehydration and shock." Though his crying was quieter now, his voice still shook with the force of his words. "Dieter was dead. He had a wife and a baby at home. I think Luca still sends them money."

Turning as far as he could in the chains that held him, Logan looked at Scarlett with anguish written all over his face.

"I told Luca back then when we were stationed together. I haven't told anyone since. Haven't thought about it except in nightmares. Haven't been able to." His face was wet, his eyes red, his skin flushed from the pain of her flogging. But the bravery he showed her in that moment told Scarlett that he was a bigger, braver man than he believed. "But since being trapped like that . . . That's why I can't live anywhere else. Cities, enclosed spaces, even windowless rooms. They take me right back there."

Unable to keep away from him any longer, Scarlett threw the whip aside and crossed with long strides to where he stood. Wrapping her arms around him, she squeezed him tight, let him sag into her embrace.

"I thought I wouldn't be able to find peace anywhere at all. Then I found Montana . . . and I found that I could survive here." His words were spoken into her hair. "But the peace . . . I didn't find that until I met you."

"Then why?" She hated to push him further, but she had to know. "Why would you push me away when you felt the same way?"

Logan huffed out a breath into her hair. "Since Bosnia . . . I think I felt like I didn't deserve more than basic survival. I'm not a shrink, so that's just a guess." Pulling back, he pinned her with that brilliant blue stare. "It was locked up so tight, I really didn't think I'd ever be able to get it out. Not even for you. And I didn't want you to give up your life for me. Not when I'm so broken."

Scarlett narrowed her eyes. "And what have you learned from that assumption?"

His lips curled into a wan, tired smile. "That it's not my choice to make. That if you want to spend your life with an old claustrophobic veterinarian, I shouldn't stop you."

"Close." Untangling herself from their embrace, Scarlett looked him up and down, felt a grim sense of satisfaction when his cock began to rise under her gaze.

"You are old. Thirty-five is just about ancient. I'm surprised you can even get it up." She stepped back neatly as he grabbed for her, a low rumble echoing in his throat.

"I'll show you old."

"Maybe in a minute." She smiled when he pulled at his chains. "I planned to stay, you know."

"I know. You told me." Logan stopped pulling at his restraints, and Scarlett saw his remorse.

"No. I mean after that." Picking up the whip again, she swished it back and forth, running the cool leather over Logan's hardening shaft.

He groaned, clearly trying to focus. "What do you mean?"

"The decision to stay in Montana wasn't because I wanted to stay with you. For the first time in my life, I feel like I've found the place where I belong. So I set up a new internship with Axel. You know Axel? The angora breeder?"

Logan's eyes narrowed, and that sexy alpha male that she loved came out to play. "The hell you'll do an internship with him. He's a submissive."

"*Mmm*, yes, he is. And a very well-behaved one." Scarlett smiled beatifically when Logan snarled. "However, it seems that I have a bit of a masochistic streak myself, since I get off on stubborn subs."

Curling the tail of the whip around Logan's shaft, she

tugged on it with her fingers until he hissed. "Turn around. Hands on the fence post."

"If you have a masochistic streak, maybe I should use that on you." Logan growled again, but he did what she told him to, spreading his legs so that his feet were planted shoulder width apart, his palms braced flat on the fence post. "I love you."

His sudden declaration had Scarlett's admiration of his fine backside halting in its tracks.

Happiness like she had never known flooded through her. As well as the desire to do whatever she wanted with what was hers.

She brought her hand down on the flat of Logan's ass. He jolted, clearly not expecting it, then hummed low in his throat.

"This is for putting me through hell." Scarlett rained a series of spanks over Logan's gorgeous behind, alternating cheeks with light blows that landed right over his sac, blows that made him arch into her touch and groan.

She continued past the point where she would normally have stopped. She wanted his nerves to be wide awake, for the pain to take him under. She also wanted him to ache the next day every time he sat down. This was a punishment as well as playtime.

"God, Scarlett." One last flurry of small taps on the crease that divided his ass from his legs and Scarlett stepped back, wiping the back of her arm over her forehead.

"Turn around." He did, and the Domme in her appreciated the wariness in his eyes. "Sit down. Legs straight out in front of you. Start jerking your cock, and do not stop."

She watched, satisfied, proprietary, as Logan's long fingers closed over his shaft. He began to slowly pump as she fisted her hands in the hem of her T-shirt.

When she pulled it up and off, then let her hands stray to the button of her jeans, he groaned, and the movement of his hand slowed.

"Keep going until I tell you otherwise, or I'll get myself off rather than let you touch me."

His eyes flashed at the challenge, but his hand resumed movement.

Scarlett's mouth went dry at the sight as she kicked off her boots and shimmied out of her jeans and panties.

"I should make you finish yourself, for thinking that I cared more about Frappuccinos and city lights than I did about you." Standing over him, she let her hand slide between her own thighs and saw by the flaring of Logan's nostrils that he could smell her arousal.

"What can I do to make it up to you?" His muscles quivered, and she knew that he was doing his best not to pull against the restraints . . . and not to come.

"Stop." She waited until he was panting, and she knew that was just about to come.

"Christ." His face was a mottled red, but he stopped when she told him to, his voice a strangled groan.

Locking stares with him, Scarlett slowly lowered herself until she straddled him. Rising onto both knees, she hovered just above his cock, her hand skimming the wetness that had gathered at the tip.

"I love you," she said, and though she knew his answer would be different this time, her heart still clutched a bit in her chest as she strained to hear it in return.

"And I love you." Slowly, tentatively, he tilted his face down, pausing before their lips brushed, asking permission.

She lifted her head in response. When he kissed her, she pressed the tip of his cock to her waiting heat, working him into her as he parted her lips with his tongue.

"Scarlett." Logan pulled back for a moment, his face etched in concern. "Condom. We don't have one."

"I know." She held her breath for a long moment. This was a big step. But she knew from the records at Veritas that they were both clean. She was on the pill.

"I trust you." And then she sank down the rest of his length, gravity helping her take all of him in.

Throwing his head back against the fence post, Logan rocked his hips upward, dragging his cock over that spot inside of her that always felt so damn good.

With his neck exposed, Scarlett couldn't resist leaning in and closing her teeth over the cord in his neck, hard enough to leave a mark. He hissed at the pain, but liked it, too; she could tell from the surge of his cock inside of her.

"I want all of you," she told him, trying to go slow, but wanting to possess him too much to keep her pace measured. Her hips began to slam up and down, working him until they were both shuddering every time his shaft filled her to the hilt, to the point of pain. "I want the mountains, and I want Mongo. I want the horse shit. I want the angora bunnies."

Beneath her Logan stilled, and Scarlett buried her face in his neck to keep from laughing, even as her breath began to come in pants.

"No angora bunnies." His voice was that of someone who knew he would be obeyed. "You'll come back here. We'll work together again. And once you feel ready, we'll look into building your hospital."

Scarlett's heart skipped a beat at that. "You would help me with it?"

"Of course." Logan's words were a bit harder to understand than usual, and Scarlett could tell that he was rapidly approaching the edge. "Having a solitary practice isn't what makes me happy. You make me happy."

Love and possession, along with a fierceness that Scarlett had never felt before, washed over her. Pressing one palm flat to his chest, she pushed him back to lean against the fence post, then wrapped her hand gently around his neck.

His eyes went unfocused when she did, a quiet moan of acquiescence accompanying it.

"Mine," she said, squeezing just a bit.

The look in his eyes made her heart sing. Those deep blue orbs that had caught her attention so thoroughly the first night they met were full of love, of adoration, of gratitude—and more than that, in that sea of blue, she saw everything that she'd longed for over the course of her unstable life.

A family. Animals. A house. Someone to love.

A life to call her own.

Releasing his throat, she leaned back and rested her hands on his thighs. Letting her thighs do the work, she lifted almost all the way off of him, then slid back down, fascinated by the sight of him disappearing inside of her.

"Watch. Watch us come together." She did it again and again, felt her own climax rising.

"Come with me." When the pleasure coiled tightly, then snapped free, she slid off of him, fisting his cock. It jerked in her hand, then spilled warm liquid that smelled of salt onto the soft curve of her belly.

She smiled as she felt the heat on her skin. "Mark me, just like I marked you. Claim me."

Logan pulled at his bonds then, and Scarlett crushed herself to him, pressing his still rearing cock between their bellies, feeling the warmth of his release, which prompted another shudder, another aftershock from her.

Then she wrapped her arms around his neck, her legs around his waist, rested her cheek on his shoulder. They were quiet together as the sun sank into the horizon, painting the sky with wide swaths of tangerine.

As night fell and they simply listened to the music of each other breathing, Logan nuzzled his lips against her ear. He rubbed the metal of his bracelet over her hip, a cool reminder of their promises.

And then he spoke the words, the ultimate surrender.

"I'm yours."

Lauren Jameson is a writer, yoga newbie, knitting aficionado, and animal lover who lives in the shadows of the great Rocky Mountains of Alberta, Canada. She's older than she looks—really—and younger than she feels—most of the time. She has published with Avon and Harlequin as Lauren Hawkeye and writes contemporary erotic romance for New American Library.

CONNECT ONLINE

laurenjameson.com
laurenhawkeye.com
twitter.com/laurenhjameson

Now that you've enjoyed Scarlett and Logan's
passionate romance, don't miss out on
Elijah and Samantha in

BREATHE

Available from Signet Eclipse.

Keep reading for a special preview. . . .

The sculpture stood on a small marble table in the center of the spacious resort lobby. A perfect, slender column of emerald green glass rose in a straight line nearly three feet high before overflowing into streams of glass that sparkled like crystals. Some were as thin as a pinkie finger, looking delicate enough to snap off at the slightest breath, and some of the tendrils were as thick as a pillar candle. All varied in tones from the merest whisper of mint to the green of a dense forest.

This piece had been the manifestation of a desire that had been haunting Samantha Collins's dreams lately. Dreams that she wasn't entirely sure what to do with.

It had been a long time since she'd had sex, true enough, and her stress levels had been through the roof lately. But these needs that had been tugging at her had been growing stronger . . .

She'd half hoped that putting these urges into her sculpture would exorcise them.

It hadn't.

"Wine, señorita?" An impeccably dressed waiter in a black suit made an appearance at Samantha's elbow. On his hand he balanced a tray of crimson wine in sparkling glasses.

"Thanks." Gratefully she accepted a glass. The flavors hit her tongue as she sipped eagerly, and she recognized it was much finer than any of the wines she was accustomed to drinking.

"Quilceda Creek Cabernet, 2005." The waiter beamed as if he had produced the wine himself.

Samantha pasted a smile onto her face and nodded enthusiastically. "Yes. Very nice."

Samantha liked wine, but the ones she tended to purchase came in a box or, if she was feeling fancy, in a bottle with a screw cap. She'd never heard of Quilceda Creek, though it tasted nice enough.

"Ten-dollar bottle, hundred-dollar bottle, the end result's the same," she spoke quietly to herself before lifting her glass in a silent toast. As she sipped, she looked down at her sculpture, still hit by a sense of disbelief that it had been chosen for exhibition.

Indulgencia was a luxurious resort located in the tourist-saturated town of Cabo San Lucas. It was infamous both for its wealthy patrons and for Devorar, the small BDSM club that catered to the varied sexual predilections of its clientele.

Once a year Indulgencia held an art exhibit with an erotic theme. The owner of the resort, some wealthy tycoon from the States, flew in artwork from around the world to showcase for the event, and when Samantha had submitted her piece, she hadn't been hopeful about her chances.

Though the twists of glass had been created with one of her most erotic dreams in mind, the result was a million miles away from the human-sized copper penis, which was the next sculpture over in the exhibit.

Samantha hadn't been sure that the wealthy mogul, who'd organized the show and selected all of the pieces himself, would see what she did, even though it was the most erotic sculpture she'd ever produced. She had put all the sexual frustration she had been feeling in the last few months into the work.

Being at this show wasn't helping that frustration. Not at all.

"Lovely piece, isn't it?" The voice came from just behind her shoulder, startling her. Samantha whirled around to face the speaker, her wine sloshing in her glass.

When she saw him, she nearly swallowed her tongue.

The man was tall, at least six feet, and though he wore expensive-looking black slacks and a dress shirt, she could see enough of his physique to appreciate the muscular body beneath the clothing. Combined with his dark blue eyes, flaxen hair, and sexy-as-hell smile, his sudden appearance made it seem as if all of Samantha's heated dreams had just come to life.

That sexy dream man cocked an eyebrow at her, and she belatedly realized that he'd asked her a question.

"Do you like this particular sculpture?" he repeated helpfully.

"It's . . . Oh, yes, it's very nice." She wasn't about to tell anyone here that she was the artist. She wasn't ready for anyone to ask what had inspired it, especially this man, who discomforted her with his focused attention.

Deliberately she shrugged, and tried to catch one thin strap of her sundress as it slid down her shoulder. She tugged it back up and caught the man's eyes following the movement. "It's such a pretty color."

She almost bit her tongue as she said it. She knew, of course, the painstaking effort that had gone into creating the gradation of hues in the sculpture, the hours she had spent gathering the molten material on her blowpipe, rolling it into finely ground glass of different shades, then setting the colors in by sweating over the smaller of her two glass furnaces—but she wanted to take care not to tip her hand that she was more than a casual admirer of the artwork.

She assumed the man would simply nod in agreement. Instead, he reached out and ran one slender finger over a curling tendril of glass, much as she had done. The care and attention of his touch over the smooth surface made Samantha think of those dreams she'd been having lately, the ones that had produced a constant ache.

In fact, last night's had featured a man running his hands over her body exactly the same way this man was doing to the sculpture. The memory made her shiver.

"Would you like to know what I see?" His blue eyes pinned her with their intensity, and Samantha lifted her glass to her lips to give herself something to do with her hands.

"Yes, I'm curious." She nodded, her breath catching in her throat as his fingers closed around hers where they rested on the stem of her wineglass.

The man captured the glass from her fingers and handed it off to a passing waiter. He secured a fresh one and had it in her hand without ever once taking his eyes from her.

"I see a meeting of male and female." She felt herself getting lost in the deep, husky tones of his voice as he continued. "But more than that, I see a balance of two opposites, each feeding a need in the other."

Samantha's lips parted in surprise, and her heart began to pound.

That was exactly what she'd intended. How on earth had he known? No one else ever saw what she'd intended in her art.

"That's what I— I mean, yes. Yes, I see that as well." She worried her lower lip with her teeth as she spoke, afraid he would ask her about what she had started to say.

With her heart still beating double time against her rib cage, she turned from the sculpture to look up into the man's face. He looked vaguely familiar, as if she'd met him once a long time ago.

More than the familiarity, though, there was a sense of

connection. He'd understood the meaning behind her art, and with that came a tug on an invisible rope that seemed to stretch between them, pulling them ever closer.

And God, he was sexy. There was something in his demeanor that attracted her, made her want something she couldn't quite articulate.

Liquid heat pooled between her legs and she held herself back from reaching out to touch him.

"What are you thinking?" The man's voice was low, but Samantha could hear him as if he were the only other person in the crowded room. His sharp gaze made her feel like the only woman in the world, and she had the insane urge to spill all her secrets to him.

If she did, would he understand that—more than anything—she yearned for a man who would be strong enough to take control for her?

Samantha started to speak, then shut her mouth tight as the rational part of her brain took over. She couldn't even admit these desires out loud to herself. . . . She certainly wasn't about to tell them to a stranger.

No matter that the stranger was the most gorgeous man she'd ever seen.

"I'm Samantha." Swallowing back everything she wanted to say, she gave him the big smile that she used on the rare occasions when she poked her head outside her studio. Her name seemed to break the heavy tension between them, but the slight cock of his eyebrow hinted that he knew there was something else she wanted to say.

Then he took her hand in his, encasing her fingers in the heat of his palm, and she forgot all about trying to keep her thoughts to herself. The simple touch, the way he rubbed his thumb over the curves of her own palm, sent sizzles shooting through her arm.

If he wanted her, he could have her. It wouldn't even occur to her to say no. *Wait—where did that come from?*

"Elijah Masterson," he said, continuing to stroke his fingers over her hand, his eyes telling her that he wanted exactly the same thing she did. Overwhelmed by his sensual touch, she didn't register the name right away. After a beat, the light went on in her mind.

Elijah Masterson. His gorgeous face, with that devil-may-care grin, had been on the front page of the local paper several weeks earlier, for an interview about the erotic-art show he'd been putting together for his resort.

His resort. Indulgencia.

Good Lord, this man owned the entire place.

"Oh, ah, I mean . . ." Samantha tried to tug her hand free. She should escape this encounter while she could. But she felt she should thank Elijah for accepting her piece into his show, although that would mean admitting it was hers.

"What brought you here tonight, Samantha?" Elijah gave her fingers a firm squeeze that spread through her body before he let her tug her hand away. Those bright blue eyes stayed focused on her as if she were the most interesting woman he'd ever come across.

"I . . . I don't know." The lie left her feeling uneasy. The sculpture had just been the first piece to the puzzle. Once her work had been accepted into the resort's exhibit, she'd longed to know more about the erotic-art scene. From there she had made some subtle inquiries, asking around to see if anyone knew what exactly went on at Devorar, the club inside the upscale hotel. She'd looked online to educate herself, entering every search term imaginable, since she wasn't entirely certain what it was she was looking for.

Yes, she'd been curious to see what her sculpture looked like on display, wanted to see if its sensuality still shone when surrounded by the more overtly sexual pieces that made up this showing. But more than that, she'd thought she might get a glimpse into the lifestyle that had started to fascinate her so much.

Apart from the wildly suggestive art, however, there was nothing there that suggested anything other than opulence and luxury. She wasn't sure what she'd been hoping for—waiters in leather chaps? some whips and chains?—but none of Devorar's secrets were revealed in the posh lobby of Indulgencia.

"Don't lie." Elijah's tone was stern. Startled, Samantha looked up into his eyes. He didn't appear angry, but the look on his face made her feel guiltier than if he had been. "Tell me why you're here."

Samantha couldn't quite work up the courage to speak. She began to tremble with nerves, thinking about what to say, and was exasperated with herself for the anxiety.

With it came an unbidden memory, a face from her past. The man in her mind's eye was old enough to be her grandfather, with salt-and-pepper hair and cold, dark eyes. But he too had been rich, and commanding.

She was her own woman, and wanted to think she was strong enough to live her life the way she wanted, without painful memories overshadowing things. But the truth was, she just didn't know if she'd wind up hating herself for what she wanted.

"You won't find any judgment from me, kitten."

Samantha gaped for a moment. *Kitten?* He'd called her *kitten?* She'd just been insulted. She should have felt insulted.

She didn't.

"I . . . I'm curious," she finally admitted, feeling her cheeks flush the same color as the wine she was drinking. "I've heard about Devorar and I . . . I thought someone here might have some answers for me."

"Answers to what questions, Samantha?" As he'd promised, there was no censure in Elijah's tone. Instead there was heat—enough that Samantha felt herself start to burn as the flush spread from her cheeks through the rest of her body.

But she froze as thoughts of her mother came wending their way into her mind. Another reason she had held herself back from going after what she wanted.

Her mother's . . . vices . . . had nearly ruined her daughters' lives. If Samantha weakened, gave up control, was she any better?

"I . . . I think I'd better go." Closing her eyes against Elijah's penetrating stare, Samantha pressed her hands to her temples and turned away. It was tempting, so tempting, to give in to what she was quite certain she wanted.

But the memory of her mother's mistakes was a reminder that giving in to temptation could lead to disastrous results. No matter how much she felt this need, deep in her very core, she shouldn't have come here.

"Samantha." Elijah's voice was firm as Samantha began to walk away. She turned back halfway, not enough to see the gorgeous man again, but enough that she was confronted with her own work of art.

The sensual visual overwhelmed her senses and made her ache.

"Come back anytime." There was a note of concern in Elijah's voice that made Samantha hesitate. Not all men were like the ones who'd flitted in and out of her mother's life. Rationally she knew that.

But this man was gorgeous, wealthy as sin, and likely into some very kinky things, given that he had opened a BDSM club in his resort. That was enough danger to send Samantha running, even as she nodded, acknowledging his offer.

Even though, rather than walk away, she found herself

wanting to tangle her fingers in that messy golden hair. Wanting to tilt her head up to receive his kiss.

She said nothing, though she felt his penetrating stare on her back as he watched her. It caused heat to simmer low in her belly, a sensation she'd never felt before.

The sensation didn't abate, not even as she exited the resort and walked to her car, a ramshackle bucket of bolts she'd purchased two years earlier, when she'd first moved to Mexico. She sighed as she slid into the driver's seat, the image of Elijah's sexy-as-sin face and his interest in her warring in her mind with the memories of that other man.

Samantha twisted her lips together as she put the key into the ignition and turned.

It was going to be a long night.